River of Angels

by
Abbe Rolnick

For information about permission to reproduce selections from this book or to order copies, write to Sedro Publishing, 21993 Grip Road, Sedro-Woolley, WA 98284.
AbbeRolnick.com

Cover Photos taken by Jim Wiggins
Design & Prepress by Kate Weisel, www.weiselcreative.com

Printed by Applied Digital Imaging, Bellingham, WA

Rolnick, Abbe
River of Angels / Abbe Rolnick—1st edition
ISBN: 978-0-9845119-07

Front cover photo: Rio Camuy Caves: karstic cave entrance within a 200-foot sinkhole, leading down 170 feet to one of the largest underground river systems in the world.

Back cover photo: 400-year-old *ceiba* tree, Vieques Island.

*"From somewhere in the Universe
A connection has been made."*

jrw

Dedication

To my family:

Morton J. Rolnick, a father with a heart
and a sense of humor that reached everyone.

Selma J. Rolnick, a mother
who continues to grow and give.

Harriet Rolnick, a sister
who stands by me with love and encouragement.

Mara, Will, & Elly, my children
who teach me to love and give more.

Jim Wiggins, my husband and partner in life,
who convinced me to move forward to that next level.

Acknowledgements

This book is a work that came from my various life experiences. I want to thank all of the people in Aguadilla, Puerto Rico for the rich life I lived there and teaching me to see beauty in another culture and to feel the pulse of passion. Garred Giles, you are not only a good friend but a great source of information.

I wrote this in the wee hours of the morning and night as I raised my children far from the island and 20 years removed. The Deming Library was invaluable in my search for information. Frances Barbagallo, my friend and Library Director, you have been a constant source of inspiration. My writing group, JoAnn Chavre, Barbara Defreytas, Iris Jones, and Mary Stone, thank you for reading all my works and being critical.

Jim Wiggins, I met you when this book was finished. Your push to read and re-read the manuscript and to return to Puerto Rico with me for photos of the caves and *ceiba* tree, gave me the impetus to follow my dream.

Contents

Abbe Rolnick

PROTEST

THE DANK, SWEATY DARKNESS inside the bar contrasted with the cheering light of the sun-kissed tropical day. It was a contrast accepted by the patrons who came from the sugarcane fields and financial offices. The bright warmth of the sun was almost blinding and its heat a reminder of the emptiness of their hearts. Monica presented herself as a shining star, amongst a black sky. She chose her clothes well, a majestic blue silk dress cut low at the neck and tight around the hips. The red leaf flowers of the *pascua* plant appeared haphazardly interwoven into the silk with one red flame close to the heart and another along the hip. For Monica the flowers alluded to Christmas, happy times, when the plants were all abloom. Stateside they added color to the drab months of winter. Here on the island they were perpetually vibrant, but no less beautiful. Although Monica did not consider herself beautiful, she had a voluptuous body which promised physical gratification, delight in its softness. She was all things for those who fantasized in sexual exploits, offering strength for the abusive, and warmth for those seeking mothering.

Monica wove her way amongst the small round tables. Aisles were non-existent, a design that was purposeful and pushed her patrons in the way of her body. Slight touches, a pat, a pinch, a glance, all created an intimacy, a sense of familiarity cloaked in the forgiving darkness.

Senor Modesto, the owner of Banco De La Gente, left with one of Monica's younger helpers, heading up the backstairs for a private rendezvous. Monica noted his puppy dog behavior as did the other patrons in the bar.

One called out, "There goes Modesto. He is paying for his pleasure with my house payment."

For the most part everyone tolerated his self-indulgent behavior. A good tipper, and not too demanding, he'd be down for another drink in less than half an hour. Monica knew the bank's coffers would suffer accordingly. She speculated on who here would be the lucky recipient of a loan after his latest foray upstairs.

Of more concern to Monica were the two *borrachos* sitting in the corner. Payday brought in the men from the field, and the two she watched escalated their boasts the more they drank. Their insults became bolder, with the ultimate swearing words of *Como tu madre,* Monica sidled in closer. To talk of another's mother begged for a fight. Smoothly Monica slid her body between the two *jibaros* and signaled for the music to be turned up. She danced the salsa, undulating her body to the rhythm of the music, first facing one, then the other. When two, young, pretty dancers tapped the men on the shoulders, she made her exit. Monica could almost predict the future absence of one of these men. Based on years of hosting she knew that sooner or later the drinking and boasting would lead to irreconcilable differences over a bet, a woman, but most usually money. The outcome would be settled forcefully, with intimidating words, pressure from families or eventually brute force, but ultimately someone would be missing. Monica preferred to give them a chance with the natural rhythms of music and the warmth of a woman. She offered a sense of security, which she knew didn't exist outside her doors.

As Monica surveyed the room her eyes fell upon a young man seated in the farthest corner. Blond hair and light skin spoke of *gringo*, but the gestures of the hands and the rapid movement of the lips marked him as a Latino. He was an infrequent, but consistent customer at the bar. Today Carlos was all business. Two men she didn't recognize sat with him. She watched as they shook hands and patted each other on the back. Clearly, a deal had just been sealed, but the men still appeared ill at ease. As they searched the room, only half listening to their companion, their gaudy suits and ties formally announced their stature as foreigners. Their roving eyes announced their impatience.

Normally the bar was where her customers dropped their pretenses, acted less formal and revealed themselves. She sensed something amiss and for this reason, Monica listened to their comments: "We can start on the condominium project as soon as you get the release papers signed, and then we can get access to the land."

Carlos nodded. "Not a problem, I'll have everything in order by the end of the week."

The two men barely acknowledged Carlos' assurances. After their handshake, they carefully scanned the entire bar again. Monica noted a short pause, their eyes transfixed on one of her ladies, Carmen, dancing. Carmen's steps faltered, missing slightly the *salsa* beat. Her face paled, becoming ashen and stricken with fear. Nervously she turned her partner looking for an escape, fixing her gaze on Jesus. Monica felt something awry, but Carlos seemed content, as his business associates made a hurried exit. Within minutes an old friend sat down at the table with him. By the looks of them, they were ending a day of work the easy way; drinking away bad decisions and delaying the return to their home life. At this point her services would not be needed. Their laughter and easy talk was enough to carry them through the night.

From the other side of the room came a familiar call, "Listen my sweetness. Come here."

Monica turned slowly and smiled. "*Mi amor,* take it easy. *No hay prisa.* No, she wasn't in any hurry to go to Jesus. All the girls called Jesus *el bruto* because his idea

of loving could kill. One was never sure when his rough-
ness would turn to ugliness, or if he would be able to
control his anger. Without the liquor, Jesus was a decent
man. Based on the constant flow of girl friends that
continued to encircle him, Monica suspected that his
macho act was more a performance and behind his rough
presence, he was a caring person. This wasn't the first
time she had spotted Carmen, her newest worker eyeing
him. All she really knew about him was that he worked
on the *fincas de coco,* scaling the coconut trees and drop-
ping the fruit.

"Jesus, *que pasa*? How goes the coconut business?"

"*Mal, mi hija, mal*. Come with me and help me forget
it all."

"Why do you worry so, Jesus? You are the keeper of
the land, if one season is bad, there is always another."

"You, my honorable Monica, know lots about men, but
nothing about coconuts. Coconuts grow on sandy soil.
Without sand there are no coconuts. Everybody wants
cement, but you can't eat cement."

"The rumors are true? They sold the farm?

"Monica, come help me forget."

Monica came up to Jesus and whispered in Spanish,
"Look I can't, but Carmen wants to be with you. I tell you
the truth. She has been trying to get your attention all
night." Bending over just enough to reveal her breasts,
she gently kissed Jesus on the top of the head. Content,
Jesus smiled appreciatively and patted her buttocks.

Making her way towards the counter, Monica perused
her potential customers. She couldn't afford to turn
down any more clients. This was a business to her and
she had her reputation to maintain. The men remembered refusals and gossiped. Gossip or as they called it
here, *chismas*, was a way of life. Once a rumor spread,
it was not easy to dispel. Looking for some amusement
and enlightened fun, she sat down at her usual stool at

the counter, close to the table with the blond-haired man. Here she still retained a good view of the entrance to the bar, the stairs leading up to the secluded rooms, but she could relax out of the main fray. She noted Carmen's exit with Jesus. Arms entwined at the elbow, they walked out like brother and sister. Nursing a glass of water on the rocks, she remained attentive to her patrons, but hoped for some intellectual stimulus. Time crawled after the initial rush of early business and after a half hour or so she found her mind wandering. Careful not to appear as an eavesdropper, she listened to Carlos' conversation.

Their laughter had dissipated and their faces were more somber. Monica heard the man who had joined Carlos after the other two had left say, "Carlos, don't worry so much. She will return. She thinks too much about your business."

Studying his drink, Carlos slowly answered, *"Este es la problema.* She says I think more about making money than making love. Pedro, it is what I do."

For Monica, this was both a moment of opportunity and one of sadness. She could score with Carlos, but another woman was losing out on love. Being in the business had hardened her, yes, but deep down Monica was a romantic. Listening further, she realized with some surprise that Carlos and Pedro had switched to English. Perhaps they thought no one could understand them.

"My thoughts are consumed with work and when she asks me what I'm thinking I tell her, "Nothing." It is as if she is too smart. When I share my thoughts, she wants to discuss a business transaction as if it were not already a fact. Pedro, she has even questioned this last deal with the farm." Shaking his head, Carlos stared out looking both baffled and hurt.

"It is true, Carlos, she is a difficult woman. Buy her something with the money you make from the sale."

How silly these men were. Whoever this woman was,

she wanted to be treated like a person who counted. She was asking to be real. Monica became impatient. Abruptly she got up from the counter, appeared to slip and dumped her drink on Carlos' lap. "*Pardoname.* Excuse me for my clumsiness. Let me dry your pants." Briskly massaging his wet leg with a napkin, Monica looked up. She hadn't expected his eyes to be so blue, or that he would be surprised. Caught off guard, she started talking in English, "I am really sorry. I don't know what got into me. Can I get you something dry to wear?"

Before Carlos could answer, the doors to the bar burst open. The light from outdoors was blinding, but not so much as to block the horror that walked in. Carmen, Monica's friend, covered with blood, fell forward, knocking down a stool, and falling across Carlos' lap. Bending over her, Monica felt the silence of the bar, saw the slow movements to the door as patrons tried to leave. She noted with anger that Jesus' table was empty. From the looks of Carmen, Jesus had been gone long enough to savagely attack her friend. It was her fault, she knew, for not taking on Jesus herself instead and suggesting that Carmen wanted to be with him. In despair, Monica lifted Carmen's head and whispered, "Carmencita, I love you. I am guilty for this, I will make you better."

Carmen only moaned in response. Monica cringed at the sound. It was bad enough Carmen had been attacked, but even worse, they could not take her to the police or the hospital. They lived outside the law. It didn't exist for them. The officials of the town begged for her services but they refused to soil their hands with the immigrant women they favored or dirty their lives at home.

Cradling Carmen's head, Monica shook her own head in disgust. "Cowards, all of you. You are so afraid of showing compassion. Run back to your safe lives."

From the silence came a whisper, "I might be a coward, but I'm in no position to run, as your friend is bleeding on my lap. It is none of my business, I don't know you, but you need help. I have a woman who might be persuaded to come to your aid."

Monica looked up. It was Carlos. "Who is it?"

Answering in English, Carlos raised his eyes and firmly stated, "My wife, she is different, a healer of sorts."

"She won't turn us into the police? Carmen is here without paperwork. She is my responsibility and I can't afford to let her or the other women down."

"You will be able to trust my wife."

"*Vamonous,* I have no time to question your motives. Please hurry."

Carlos and Pedro carefully wrapped Carmen in a tablecloth and carried her outside into the back alley, where Carlos's truck was parked.

Pedro hissed, "What are you doing? *Estas loco.* You haven't seen your wife in weeks and you are bringing her this? She is a great healer, but how can you be so sure that she'll do this for you?"

Carlos ignored the questions as he helped Monica into the back with Carmen. He swallowed hard, almost gulping the air around him. He was as breathless as if his own life were being squeezed out of him. For some reason the blood of a woman made him sick. Once Monica and Carmen were settled, he turned and whispered to Pedro, "This is beyond my experience. Women should be at home, not on the streets, not getting hurt. Rosie will know what to do."

The truck crept along the slow and bumpy roads. It was clear that where they were going was *en los campos,* up in the hills where they say the roads were made following the cows' paths. Monica felt each twist of the road, and every one of the ruts. Still breathing, Carmen had only opened her eyes once. The blood around her mouth was dry and Monica used her own skirt to soak up the blood oozing from below her dress. Whatever possessed her to come with Carlos, or for that matter for Carlos to come to their rescue, was beyond her. She listened to the song of the *coquis*. It was already evening and the tiny, heard-but-not-seen, frogs' gentle chorus, *co qui co qui,* echoed through the hills. The answering calls calmed her by their resonating sound. Please let us arrive soon, she prayed.

Within minutes they rounded a steep hill and Carlos abruptly stopped the truck. Looking out, Monica saw a small cabin perched on the hillside. Even in the darkness the freshness of the cool breeze, the smell of banana trees, and the lone light from the cabin encouraged her. Carlos quickly ran to the door. Hesitating for a moment, he knocked, opened the door, quickly slipped in, and disappeared.

Rosie stood small behind the kitchen counter; a tea kettle steaming in the background, guava skin and fibers piled up alongside a pitcher of juice. Turning her head towards the front door, she called out, "Carlos, I'm in the kitchen making one of my healing potions. I expected you earlier."

Already Carlos felt his heart accelerate, his face get red. It infuriated him how she knew things. He had had no intention of visiting Rosie tonight. To talk with Rosie he'd rather be on neutral territory, some place where they both would be comfortable. He wasn't sure that place existed anymore. He closed his eyes and rubbed his temples trying to obliterate a vision of Rosie tinkering with her medicinal herbs and juices, Rosie seeing the invisible and just knowing. Despite his resolve to be calm, Carlos headed as an accuser for the kitchen. "Rosie, you couldn't have expected me. If you know so much, why am I here?"

Wiping her hands on a dish towel, Rosie turned to

face Carlos. She studied the fierceness in his eyes, his tight jaw, and his hunched shoulders. Ignoring his question she softly asked, "Who is hurt?"

"A woman from the bar. Your friend Jesus attacked her. I told you he was dangerous. Now look what he has done."

Keeping her eyes fixed on Carlos, she repeated her question. "How bad is she hurt?"

"She is moaning and bleeding. She couldn't talk. I told her friend that you could help."

Rosie walked towards Carlos and took his arm. "Come with me to make a bed ready. Tell me the names of the woman and her friend."

Carlos had to follow Rosie, as he was lost in her cabin. He was only an occasional visitor, displaced by Rosie's hobbies. They walked silently through a hallway into a small room off the back of the cabin. Rosie handed him a pillow and blankets. As she tucked the sheets into a mat, she gently prodded. "Did you hear my question Carlos? Do you know their names?"

Carlos thought for a moment, "Wait, I'm trying to remember. I know that Monica is her friend. She is the hostess at the bar, and I think the other ones name is Carina or Carmen, but I'm not sure. Her name doesn't matter. You'll still help her even without a name, won't you?"

"Everything matters Carlos, even a grain of sand. Can't you see that? Bring them in. You know that I will always help someone who is hurt. You never wanted my help or advice, but I am always here to help. You can count on me at least for that."

"You should stick to being a wife. I know about business and what is good for the island. I know that you should trust me about Jesus."

Rosie saw the stubborn wall surrounding Carlos. No matter how she tried she couldn't get past his blindness.

"Carlos, you never could see the deeper values. With all your education you have lost something precious. Never mind. They must be anxious, waiting outside. We can talk later."

As Monica waited, she could feel Carmen stir and begin to moan. The wait seemed to stretch on and with it, so did Monica's apprehension.

Monica called out, "Pedro, what is taking so long? Is this going to work out or did your friend misjudge his wife?"

In answer Pedro walked to the back of the truck, peered in and said, "Carlos may have misjudged you, but not his wife."

The door to the cabin opened again. This time it swung out wider revealing to Monica the silhouette of a small woman. The silhouette spoke with command, "Pedro, help Carlos lift the woman and bring her inside. We have made a bed ready. Monica, please come quickly, I am going to need your help."

Surprised at having her name called out, Monica felt something shift. An energy force surrounded this small woman. From its center kindness, warmth, and strength floated towards her. Used to being in command, she was out of her element here. Somehow this aura penetrated her shield; her normal armor of toughness, and left her without protection. She obeyed. Quickly jumping down from the truck, she followed Carlos and Pedro into the house. They took Carmen into a small room, empty except for a thick mat, which had been hastily made into a bed. It lay on the floor and beside it was a figurine in the shape of an old man. It held a lit candle, which created shadows on the wall. Elongated and whimsical, the shadows resembled the tall, thin *caballero*, Don Quixote. Orchids hung from baskets and formed a canopy over the mat. Catching her own reflection, she jumped. Inside a greenhouse, glass walls surrounded the room, mirroring back her image and encasing them in a jungle of plants.

Without a word, Carlos and Pedro gently placed Carmen on the bed. Carlos turned and said, "Monica, *este es mi esposa*, Rosie. She understands and will help you."

Before Monica could say anything, Rosie stepped forward. Arms outstretched she took Monica's hand and held it between her own hands. Turning her head to look at Carlos, she held his gaze and said, "Carlos, do you understand?"

Expecting the jealous wife to finally explode, Monica held her breath waiting for the fall out. Instead she heard Rosie whisper, "*La tierra*, the earth, is more than your precious cement, your important business deals. Everything has its place. You tell me that Jesus has raped this woman. I have my doubts, but I know that your planned projects are raping his world. Go, Carlos; go to your business. Think about tonight. If Monica and I need anything we'll let you know." Letting go of Monica's hands, Rosie held out her arms and hugged a stiff Carlos. There were tears in her eyes as she turned back to face Monica.

"Well, Monica, welcome. Let's get to work on helping your friend to heal. I am not a doctor or nurse, but between us I think we can manage. I have some clean cloths and disinfectants by the side of the mat."

The two worked quietly. Monica washed Carmen's face, cleaning the blood and applying ice to bruised, swollen cheeks. Rosie cut away Carmen's dress, exposing minor knife wounds on her forearms and chest, where she had held up her arms as protection. These wounds had already begun to close, yet centered near the vagina, a mass of blood clots continued to ooze. Rosie looked up and asked, "Monica, could your friend have been pregnant? I think after her beating she miscarried."

"If she was, I didn't know about it. We talked, but not about the present. Carmen always told me stories of her homeland. She loved the place. I'm not sure, but I think they forced her to leave. I never knew why." Monica shook her head, regretting the significant conversations she had missed with her companion. Fearing the answer, she asked, "Do you think she'll survive?"

Rosie flashed a smile at Monica, "Don't be so frightened. Carmen is young and healthy like you. The wounds aren't too deep and the blood is already clotting. We'll bring her some tea mixed with guava juice to keep her from dehydrating. With some rest and care we'll get her strength up. Please go into the kitchen. The tea and juice are on the table."

When Monica returned, she stood quietly at the door just watching Rosie. Her first impression of Rosie had been that of a centered, impenetrable woman. Rosie was short. Probably not measuring five feet, but her height was deceptive. Emanating strength, Rosie seemed twice her size. With an olive complexion, her face narrowed from high cheekbones to a somewhat pointed chin. Thick, shiny black hair cascaded down to Rosie's shoulders. Her real power, however, came from the eyes. Large, dark, expressive eyebrows moved to punctuate Rosie's thoughts.

Rosie sat by Carmen's head, with her legs straddling Carmen. Placing her hands under Carmen's shoulder blades, Rosie rearranged Carmen's body. Monica heard Rosie whispering to Carmen, but could not make out what she said. She listened to Carmen's breathing, at first quick, short gasps, but gradually the rhythm smoothed out. As Rosie progressed, softly touching the shoulders, arms, hips, legs, and finally the feet, Carmen's body dropped all tension and her breath came in full and strong. Monica had never seen a body transform almost magically into calmness.

Tentatively Monica walked in with the drinks. She felt confused. She couldn't explain the intimacy between Rosie and Carmen. She'd never witnessed anything like it before. This intimacy was different from the one she experienced with her sexual partners, different from anything she shared with her family. Rosie's eyes and hands seemed to sense people from the inside. Monica's experience had taught her never to get that close, not even with herself. She both longed to be Carmen, receiving the magical touches, and envied Rosie her gift. Yet, to succumb so totally, threatened her independence. Monica feared letting go, losing control, but she feared most of all that she would never experience this soulful, unselfish intimacy.

As she approached, Rosie looked up. "*Gracias*, Monica. Carmen seems to be doing... What's wrong? Your face looks like you have seen a ghost! Does what I am doing scare you? Because I am different, because I take the time to see who you and your friend are? Do I scare you because you are afraid to see yourself and the world?"

Sighing, Rosie shook her head and laughed a deep guttural laugh. "I should fear you, blood-stained lady of the streets! Set the drinks down and go into my bedroom. I have some clothes somewhere in my closet that might fit you. Take a shower and change. We'll leave Carmen to rest and I'll fix us something to eat."

Abbe Rolnick

LA FINCA

CARLOS DROVE SLOWLY, DEEP IN THOUGHT, as he left Rosie's place, her hideout away from him. Her parting words had stung, stung deeper than she could imagine. Why did his wife, his woman, have to be so critical? With the price of coconuts falling, he had to find a way to make a decent living. Developing their land made sense. Rosie had no idea about economics. In the form of cement, sand gained value. Merely looking out at beautiful sandy beaches, or sandy farmland with failed crops, didn't pay the bills.

"Carlos, what are you mumbling about? You got what you wanted. Rosie will help the prostitutes. Put tonight behind you."

Carlos narrowed his eyelids and shot Pedro an incredulous look. His thoughts remained on the land, land they had bought years ago when Rosie was a professor at the University and they were newly wed. At one time they had thought about building a home in the center of the one hundred acres of palms. Rosie could continue her studies in agriculture and they would have a home to raise their children. But that had all changed. Their physical separation only emphasized their chasm, and continued to draw them psychologically further apart. Angry, he gunned the gas pedal.

The truck lurched forward. *"Mi pana*, slow down. It is not like you to be so angry and jumpy. What has gotten into you these last few weeks? Is there something else happening besides your breakup with Rosie? Rosie and you have been together a long time. She is my friend as well. What did she mean by your precious cement? Tell me, Carlos, you need to talk."

"Talking won't do any good. Tonight when we took those ladies up to Rosie, she already knew that I was coming, which is impossible, since there are no phones to her cabin. She must be spying on me. Why else would I feel that I was handing over my life? That some horrible darkness was lurking around the corner, a shadow waiting to grab me."

Pedro stared hard at Carlos. His foot began to pump up and down. Beads of sweat collected above his lip. He fiddled with the radio knobs until a familiar *salsa* played. "Carlos, you sound like me. I didn't know you believed in Voodoo."

"I don't. It is just that Rosie and I have always been close, but since I have become involved more with politics and city development, it is as if we are spinning in different orbits. Rosie's orbit is out of sync. I can't control her anymore. I need her by my side, listening to me without her opinions getting in the way. *Contra*, Rosie seems to listen to everyone else's problems, but ignores mine."

Carlos shrugged his shoulders, rolled his head from side to side, and loosened his grip on the steering wheel. "I forgot to check on our last shipment of coconuts. I have to pass by the coconut farm on the way home, do you want to come or should I drop you off?"

"You still haven't answered me about the cement. Are you selling the sand on the farm? I thought you were only selling a few acres of the farm to build homes?"

"Everything depends on Rosie. She and I signed for the land adjacent to my family's property with both of our names. Now our funds are co-mingled. I don't want her to know anything else until I am sure about an agreement. I have to convince her stubborn pride. Talking to you will only make matters worse."

"That does change things. I thought you were being a gentleman, trying to include her. You really can't sell anything until she agrees. I had no idea of her importance in the deal."

Pedro could see that Carlos had lost interest in the conversation. His body was moving to the music and his eyes were fixed on the road ahead. "Never mind the questions. I'll go with you, but I have some errands to attend to before I head home."

Smiling, Carlos joked, "Are you seeing someone? Since when do you have errands to do after work? Your government job ends at 5:00 PM sharp. It's close to 9:00 PM."

Calmed somewhat by joking with Pedro, Carlos drove more sensibly. Even though he had been traveling these roads since a child, the multitude of twists and sharpness of the turns demanded his full attention. Fallen stalks of sugarcane littered the one lane road. During the harvest cycle, trucks overburdened with sugarcane windrows used the cool of the night and the absence of traffic to travel. Farmers burned their entire fields in order to quicken the harvest of stubble left behind the initial cutting. As testimony to this phenomenon, he smelled the pungent odor of burnt *cana,* mixed with that of salt water as they neared *la playa.* His and Rosie's land rose gradually, situated on a high cliff above an isolated cove. The highest point was sixty feet above sea level, but gently tapered down to meet the beach. A grove of coconut trees stood along the flattened area. The trees had been there since before he was born.

As a child he had tried climbing the trees, but soon gave up when his parents objected. Carlos believed their objections stemmed from fear for his safety, but equally from the fear that someone from his class should not be seen mingling with the workers. Coconut scaling was an art that was fast disappearing. Jesus was one of a handful left who retained the skill.

Reminded of Jesus, Carlos thought back on the evening. He remembered seeing Jesus at the bar *bor-*

racho, but certainly not so drunk as to beat that woman. Rosie had such a high opinion of Jesus. She might be right. Perhaps Jesus was more upset that he knew. Carlos had talked to Jesus just last month about some of his plans, but nothing had been definite then.

Two New York Ricans, Puerto Ricans born in New York who had moved back to the island, had approached him. They met at a trade meeting in the capital. One was a lawyer, Tomas Garcia, and the other was a businessman named Roberto Gonzalez. They wanted to develop the island and promote tourism. Carlos had listened to their ideas about condominiums and time sharing with interest. Over drinks they had discussed it further. If Carlos could come up with $100,000, he could be one of the investors. Carlos contemplated selling some of their land to do this, and utilizing part of the sand for the cement that would be needed for the building.

The only people he had mentioned this plan to were Rosie, Pedro, and Jesus.

Rosie's reaction had been extreme. She was possessed by the land, and would not hear of its sale. Even though they had separated, she came out daily to work on her projects, or to swim. Pedro had thought the idea was a good business move and Jesus had only shrugged him off, saying he would help him in *cualquiera* way.

And Carlos had taken that to mean that Jesus would support him in his decision, and as in the past, do whatever work there was. Jesus' father had worked for Carlos's father *bregando*, fighting the sugarcane, and Jesus had also worked in the pineapple fields.

"Pedro, I am trying to make sense of what Jesus did to that woman. I know he has a temper and a bad reputation, but I've always known him as more a worker than a womanizer. His family has worked for us for years."

Pedro took his to time to answer, choosing his words carefully. "Perhaps Jesus has grown greedy. Maybe he is tired of just working for someone else, watching everyone else succeed."

"I'm not so sure about that. He didn't seem that drunk tonight, just sad. He knew I was in the bar, and if he were angry he could have fought with me. Fighting with a helpless woman doesn't make sense. *Contra*, that Rosie, she knows something. Jesus must have confided in her."

Pedro cleared his throat and shrugged his shoulder. "You let Rosie have private talks with another man? Maybe that is your problem. I wouldn't let my woman around another man. He is probably turning her mind and her heart."

They were almost at the farm. Just before Carlos made the turn off towards the beach, he swerved his truck to avoid piles of sugarcane littering the road. "Pedro, look, to your right. There is a truck full of sugarcane lying on its side." Carlos pulled his truck off to the side of the road and jumped out to investigate.

Pedro followed right behind. Shaking his head, Pedro muttered, *"Esta cabron.* This is the worst sugarcane spill I've seen. Look at the angle of the truck, it's not normal. Can you see the driver?"

Carlos was at the front of the truck, which was tilted so that half of the tires were in the air. The door to the driver's side was opened. "No, *no hay nadie.* There is no one here. He must have gone for help. I think the truck belongs to Sanchez. We can call him in the morning. Let's get out of here and go to the farm."

Hopping back into the truck, both men were silent. Pedro finally said, "This night feels bad. First the scene in the bar, Rosie's stubbornness and sadness, and now this accident. I hope all is well at the farm." In answer, Carlos only groaned. He backed up the truck and continued on.

They arrived at the farm moments later, welcomed by the sounds of waves thrashing against the sand.

Although they had never built their dream house, Carlos and Rosie had put in a good road and various out buildings. Their favorite spot was up on a hill where a pair of *ceiba* trees grew, overlooking the coconut farm. The trees had huge canopies and trunks shaped like the knees of elephants. It was to these trees that Carlos always headed; a habit both Rosie and he had acquired over the years. They came for the tranquility and also to take in the vastness of their property. Even at dusk, the scenes from above had an order, familiar shapes and shadows created a composite of the day's activities. Intuitively they could sense if all was well. At the top of the hill Carlos stopped the truck. The frantic barking of a dog obliterated the sounds of the ocean. Carlos looked out into the dark and saw only the shadows of palm leaves swaying slightly in the breeze. He called out *"Nada, que pasa? Nada, soy yo, Carlos."* The barking ascended into a series of excited of yelps.

"Pedro, get me the flashlight under the seat. You were right. *Este noche esta muy mala.* Something is wrong. Nada knows my truck and usually comes. Let's go see what she is so upset about."

They didn't have to go far before they were assaulted with the stench of alcohol and the sound of more barking. Nada stood by the *ceiba's* massive roots, scratching at the ground, barking, and running around the perimeter. Carlos knelt down next to her and tried soothing her by patting and whispering in her ear. Nada repeatedly jumped up in the air and barked louder. Moving the flashlight up and down the tree, Carlos and Pedro spotted the reason for Nada's distress. The root system of the *ceiba* tree extended upward to five feet. The massive gnarls of roots branched into sections of the elephant-like trunk. Scrunched inside the crook of the elephant's knee was a body. It was Jesus, still holding a bottle of rum in one hand, motionless. Carlos checked to see if he was asleep, but the cold body and empty eyes stared back at him. Checking for a pulse, Carlos felt nothing.

A chill ran up Carlos's back. He could feel the grip of death surrounding him. Trying to clear the heaviness of the air, Carlos waved his arms and shook his body. The reflection of metal caught his eye. Off to the side of Jesus lay a machete and a birdcage.

The full darkness of the night sky set over the scene. Carlos closed his eyes, wishing for the disappearance of this nightmare. Street fights, bar brawls, domestic squabbles, all populated island existence. But never had violence entered his farm, never before had it touched him. Moving closer with the flashlight in hand, Carlos saw blood stains on the machete's blade and handle. The birdcage was open and empty. In a whisper, Carlos called out to Pedro, "Jesus' machete has blood on it. Check to see if he was wounded before he died."

Pedro whispered back, "No, no there is no wound, but there is blood on his right hand."

Thinking out loud, Carlos muttered, "If there is no wound how did Jesus die, and whose blood is on his hand and the machete? I'm afraid we can't avoid calling the police in now. But let's not mention what happened earlier tonight. The less we are involved the better."

"What good will telling the police do? It would be better to give them money not to investigate. You don't want them here on your property, asking questions."

Pedro nervously paced. He wanted to leave. He refused to look at Carlos directly, eyeing the road, looking for a way out. Not one to disagree with Carlos he attempted to appease his friend. "Should we both go, or should one of us stay with Jesus? Whatever you need, my friend, you know I will help."

It struck Carlos that Pedro saw this as his problem alone as if Pedro hadn't discovered the body at the same time. But Pedro was right; someone should stay here with Jesus' body. "Pedro, you can take my truck. Go. Say as little as you can and hurry back. I'll stay with Nada; she'll protect me from the bad spirits." Throwing Pedro the keys, he said, "*Vaya con Dios.*"

Carlos watched as Pedro turned the truck around and left the way that they had come. Only one main road divided the farm. Carlos had wanted two separate roads, one for normal traffic and one for the large trucks that transported the crates of coconuts out to be distributed around the world. But no, Rosie had insisted on preserving as much of the land as possible. For someone not born on the island, she was infuriatingly protective.

In the past that quality had ingratiated Rosie to him, but more recently she had become hostile. Her love of the island, her passion for life and her devotion, fueled him. Now these passions seemed misplaced, no longer centered on him or his dreams. It was almost as if she didn't trust him anymore. She questioned all of his actions. Over the years he had sacrificed passing time on the land and with her, trying to develop markets for coconuts and for the honey Rosie produced from her beehives. As the markets failed, he had looked elsewhere, traveling to other islands and to the states. Now he sought other sources of income. He still thought the condominium deal looked promising.

Nada nuzzled against his leg and Carlos remembered why he was standing on the knoll. He had come here to contemplate and view the operations of the farm. Now he was here protecting the dead body of his long trusted friend, Jesus. Friend wasn't exactly the word for Jesus. He and Jesus had never gone out socially. They were from different economic backgrounds, and Jesus had never finished grade school. Carlos remembered there had been some scandal surrounding the death of Jesus' parents, and he had gone to live with Abuelita.

Abuelita was not Jesus' real grandmother, but a

good friend of the family. She was really too young to be anyone's grandmother, only fifteen years Jesus' senior, but she was single with no kids, and available to take Jesus in. Her real name was Donna Teresa, and over the years she had become everyone's grandmother. Jesus left school to support himself, and began to work for Carlos' father on the coconut plantation. Carlos had lost track of Jesus when he had entered private Catholic school, at the request of his parents. After Carlos graduated, he went to the States to a university.

When he got back to the island years later, Jesus was still working on *la finca*. The years of demanding physical labor had hardened Jesus. His body was compact, with muscular arms and legs hardened from scaling the trees. His skin was the color of rich coffee mixed with a touch of cream, and lined with creases baked in by the sun. He had become a hard laborer who after hours would drink rum when he was in the money, and *canita*, illegal white rum made from sugar cane, when finances were tighter. More recently, Carlos had noticed Jesus had switched to drinking *cerveza*, and had grown a belly to show for it. Jesus had never married but had sired three children by different women. From the rumors, all three women still loved Jesus, but could not take his mood swings. A man plagued with a temper, he paid his obligations to society, sent money to his children when needed, and went to church every Sunday to absolve himself of his sins.

There would be no church for Jesus on this coming Sunday, no more absolution for his latest sins. Carlos wondered if the blood on the machete had been that of the woman he had left with Rosie. The farm was too far from the bar for her to have returned on foot. Where had Jesus attacked her, if not at the farm? On the way up, he hadn't noticed Jesus' truck or any other vehicle. Just three hours earlier Jesus had been alive passing a typical evening at the bar, just as he had been doing. He felt himself being drawn into Jesus' sins as if they were his own. Jesus' dead body weighed on him. With no bodily sign of harm, the harm permeated the air, making the hours feel like days, aging and scaring him into paying attention. Whatever sin Jesus had committed, he had paid for it with his life. Carlos wanted to remain living.

Breathing deeply, Carlos tried to think of who he should inform of Jesus' death. Jesus still had a room at Abuelita's house, although he didn't actually live there. Carlos knew that Jesus felt indebted to Abuelita for all her love and caring for him throughout his childhood. The two of them shared a love of pigeons. The empty birdcage next to Jesus' body must have had pigeons in it. Abuelita had no phone at her house, and to save travel time, often they would send each other messages via carrier pigeons. It was an ingenious solution to an economic problem. When Pedro returned he would go up to Abuelita's. Abuelita lived near Rosie, so he could check in on how the muddled affairs of the night were faring and also return the birdcage and deliver the sad news.

ABUELITA – DOÑA TERESSA

"CUKKOO KAROO, CUKKOO KAROO."

Monica woke up and tried to decipher the sounds around her. Panicking she sat up and listened. Again she heard "Cukkoo karoo." Smiling, she realized it was roosters welcoming in the day with their morning song. For no reason in particular she felt hopeful. Dinner last night with Rosie had been a lighthearted affair. Carmen had drifted in and out of sleep while they feasted on *tostones*, plantains sliced, fried, smashed and fried again. Rosie created a fresh salad that included leaf lettuce, not the imported iceberg variety, small cucumbers and firm tomatoes. Monica couldn't remember the last real salad she had eaten on the island. It was as if the entire island were allergic to fresh garden vegetables. Chuckling to herself, Monica said to the empty room, "Simple, crisp, and fresh. That's Rosie, just like her meal."

As she listened, the morning song had changed, with the roosters quieting down and the sounds of human voices filling the air. Monica quickly roused herself, throwing on what must have been Carlos' work clothes. They fit her ample physique, and made her feel both worthy and ready for a different type of physical work. Pleased that there were no mirrors in the room, she felt content at not having to verify her well being by her own looks.

By the time she had made her way to the kitchen some of the previous night's qualms had begun to return, and she entered tentatively. An elderly woman sat at the table. She looked as if she had sat in that same chair many times before. Monica stared, fascinated by the woman's face. It might have been physically beautiful years before, but had aged in such a way that only life's hardship remained imprinted. The skin had a hardened texture from having been baked by the sun, but the permanent smile lines fanning out from the eyes and lips softened it. Her nose was a snub mark on her face and as she talked her nostrils flared in excitement. This woman was a ball of fire animated by life itself. As she talked with Rosie, her hands moved from her chest and up to her hair. Her long, curly black hair held back by elegant tortoise combs made Monica realize that this woman was far younger than her wrinkled skin portrayed. The hands were signing a story of their own, contrasting the elegance of the combs with the raggedness of knobbed knuckles and leathered palms. Hair to chest, head to heart, the hands carried her words from mind to spirit.

Fascinated by the pantomiming hands, Monica kept quiet and stood back from the doorway, eavesdropping on their conversation. Rosie was chuckling nervously.

"I'm glad we can rest now. I can't get Carmen's raging out of my mind. Treating her physical wounds was minor compared to dealing with her frantic lashing out. I wouldn't have bothered to get you if I thought I could handle her. She clawed at me with such vengeance. I can't imagine where she got the energy. You saved me once again Abuelita."

"I'm not sure I've saved anyone. But at least we can rest now. Carmen will sleep for at least a few hours. With the loss of so much blood, her bodily needs will take over the mind for awhile."

"I don't want Monica to worry too much about her friend. She feels so guilty as it is. She doesn't need to know all that happened."

Abuelita nodded in agreement. "Does it bother you that Carmen and Monica are prostitutes?"

"How could you think such a thing, Abuelita? Remember what the *pueblo* thought of you years ago. Everyone was afraid of your beauty and youth. The only one you could get to build your house was Don Tuto. All the other men were forbidden by their wives."

"It seems like centuries ago. Some things never change, though. When I look at Carmen and Monica, I think of my mother, her problems with men, and her attempt to save me. Don Tuto and Maria are what truly saved me. His love for his wife, and her open heart gave me a purpose, a way to funnel my fear and anger into something more meaningful and productive. I still miss Maria after all these years since her death."

"She is still alive for you and Don Tuto. Maria made sure of that. Her wishes were more powerful than her death. I think of my father in that way."

Abuelita smiled slowly with her eyes glistening with joyful tears. "Your father's work in the jungles saved my life. I wonder what he would say now if he could see all the experiments you have tried on his vines."

"Hopefully he would be proud. You knew him better than I did in a way. Remember he died when I was young. I didn't even get to meet Maria. She died before I arrived on the island."

"Maria wanted me to find peace and not have to run from my past. More important she knew that other woman suffered so many injustices. Physically she couldn't go on, so she left this world. Her spirit is everywhere in the caves."

"Sometimes while I dry the *liana* vines, I sense my father's presence. He paces back and forth, hovering over my shoulder, peace eluding him. I felt him last night as Carmen lunged toward me. Maria's spirit was there in the shadows."

"Rosie, we can't linger too much in the past. Right now we have to decide on how to help Carmen and Monica."

"I agree. The present is complicated enough. Abuelita let me make some fresh espresso. Hopefully by then Monica will be awake."

Monica took her cue. She poked her head inside the doorway just as Rosie was pouring the coffee. Rosie turned to face her. "Good morning, Monica. Welcome. I was just talking with my good friend and neighbor, Abuelita. Sit yourself down and join us."

Monica nodded a hello in both directions and sat down at the small round table next to Abuelita. "I am sorry if I slept late. The roosters woke me; or else I might have remained asleep for weeks. I didn't know I was so tired."

"You must be hungry, too. There are sliced guavas, bananas, and oranges, and of course, coffee. While you eat, I'll fill you in on Carmen's health. After you went to bed last night, Carmen began to fret in her sleep. She was having a nightmare and kept calling out for Jesus to be careful. Carmen's sense of alarm and fear for Jesus doesn't make sense if he is the one who harmed her. I finally woke Carmen up because her fever was rising with her fear level. She was like a different person from earlier in the evening when I nursed her wounds and helped her relax. Her body trembled and she wrung her hands and rocked back and forth, winding herself up like a spring. When I asked her if Jesus had hurt her she shook her head "no," but refused to tell me who had beat her and why. I sent for Abuelita because Carmen abruptly stopped trembling and just started staring out, as though she had suddenly left her body. This was beyond my skill. Abuelita has aided me at various times, so I sent for her in the middle of the night. She understands the unexplainable parts of life."

Monica held her *taza* of coffee with both hands. Listening to Rosie's description of Carmen's tortured night, she found the banana and guava slices stuck in her throat. With a swallow of the strong espresso, a few of her questions broke loose. "I didn't hear a car last night, or Carmen's cries. I'm a light sleeper. How did Rosie send for you?"

Placing both hands on the table, Abuelita pushed herself upright. Her torso was slightly twisted at the spine, but the shoulders were smooth with no rounding. She approached Monica with her head held high, as if she were adjusting for her crookedness by lifting herself off the ground. Her arms opened wide and as she encircled Monica, she whispered, "My child, it is true that I came in the middle of the night. Rosie sent for me the only way she could. There is no phone here, and she couldn't leave Carmen, so she let one of my homing pigeons go. I came by foot. My home is over the hillside. Tell me Monica, what you know of Carmen, for there is something terribly wrong here. She is afraid for her life and she is keeping many secrets."

Confusion replaced her earlier sense of hope, and Monica once again felt the sense of things going out of control. Where was her confidence of yesterday, when she was at the bar? If only she could turn the clock back. Feeling fallible, she swallowed a few times before looking directly at Abuelita. "You have reason to say Carmen has secrets, but I don't know what they are. She is originally from Costa Rica. As I have told Rosie, I don't know why, but I suspect her family has abandoned her. Or it could be that she is afraid someone will hurt her family as a vendetta if she doesn't work off a debt. Carmen isn't really cut out for this business, and I know she came against her will."

"Monica, is Carmen here illegally?"

"Rosie, I apologize. I thought you knew that when you let us come here. One of the reasons I didn't want to go to the police was that Carmen told me that she didn't have paperwork to be in the country. The police would have turned her in or expected us to service them for free. Are you mad at me?"

"I would have helped you either way. The paperwork is meaningless to me. I just wondered how long you have known Carmen and if you can trust her story?"

"About eight months ago, one of my girls found her walking the streets, vomiting on the side of the road. They were annoyed that she was in their territory, making a bad impression. I took her in mainly because she looked so pathetic, tired, hungry and weak. Most of the girls working as prostitutes are running from something. I never really asked her why. For me it's an adventure, one that pays a lot. I can leave at any time, no debts, no strings, and no commitment.

Abuelita slowly exhaled her breath; a breath that seem to come from deep inside her very soul and lingered in the air. "It takes an incredible amount of strength and centeredness to maintain secrets and not have them control your life. Carmen lives in the shadows of her past, and her present life is dark because of them. I sense that Jesus is part of her present life, but what happened to her, is from the past. As much as I fear for Carmen at this moment, my true concern is for Jesus. Before I left my home to come here, another of my homing pigeons returned. This pigeon was with Jesus. He must have let it go earlier. I thought he was joking with me because the only message I could find was yesterday's lottery ticket. *Bolita*—you know, not the official lottery. Jesus has always played with the hope of sometime winning it big so he could buy some land of his own. I have the ticket in my pocket."

Rummaging in her skirt pocket, Abuelita's fingers fumbled as she came upon a crinkled ticket. She brought the ticket in close to her face, studying one side and then the other. As she turned it over her eyes hardened and her body stiffened. A shadow seemed to obscure her face, darkening the room, and at the same time draining all color from her face.

Rosie ran to her side, supported her at the shoulders, and took the ticket from her hands. Staring at it, Rosie said, "What do you see Abuelita? Tell me."

Abuelita closed her eyes and inhaled, drawing strength again from her own breath. She continued breathing deeply for a few moments, and the color finally returned to her face. Slowly regaining her composure, Abuelita whispered, "Look carefully on the margin. At first I thought it was just a doodle, Jesus drawing the tropical vines and plants he sees all the time. But it's a picture of the *liana* vine spun into a web. Jesus was intentionally warning us. The web looks more like dots of time connecting, almost as if it is a pictorial map connecting the past and present. Rosie, I think my worst fears from the past are upon us. Somehow I sense that Carmen's past and future is tied to this vine. I must find Jesus before it is too late."

Monica felt a cold current of air across her chest. She searched the screened windows and plants for any sign of an opening or movement. Again the cold current traveled along her arms and down her spine. She started shaking and tears fell involuntarily along her cheeks. She had never felt such inexplicable alarm and confusion. Nothing made sense. She felt fear for herself, but didn't know why; more importantly, something told her that Carmen's behavior was a warning. Instinctively she turned her head towards Carmen's room and felt the source of the chilled air. The hair on her arms rose. With her fists clenched by her side and her teeth bound just as tightly, she implored, "What are we going to do to help Carmen? What is going on here? I have had enough of all this weirdness. You must have done something to Carmen. I saw you touching her last night. All I wanted was for you to take care of her wounds. I want nothing to do with your touchy feely powers or your *liana* vines."

"There is no weirdness, my child. What you are witnessing is the unraveling of a web of lies and secrets that up until now cocooned many lives. I haven't the time for explanations if we are to salvage these lives. First we must get Carmen to safety, and I must find Jesus and warn him."

Still wary and not fully comprehending or believing what Abuelita had said, Monica retorted, "And where is this safety of yours?"

"Come, I'll tell you as we make Carmen ready." Abuelita rose. As she walked towards Carmen's room she nodded at Rosie and commanded, "Let one of Don Tuto's pigeons go. We'll need his help."

Rosie nodded and stood-up only to sit abruptly down. Her legs had collapsed under her. After a quick massage along her inner legs she stood-up again. Rosie took a tentative step, as though unsure of her footing, her face strained in concentration, every movement clearly an effort. Monica couldn't tell if she was tired or defeated. Was this the same woman of last night who had miraculously helped Carmen? Rosie felt Monica's gaze; she turned and flashed a reassuring smile. Their eyes locked and then strangely, Rosie winked as if nothing was wrong. As Rosie shuffled out, Monica numbly followed behind Abuelita.

PIGEON COOP

THE WELL WORN PATH LEADING TO THE PIGEON COOP lay behind the cabin and wound around the back, where it was swallowed by a dense forest floor covered with lush ferns. Rosie loved the peace she always felt as the tropical forest enveloped her. Normally she would take time to study the vegetation, looking at the forest floor for its richness and among the dripping rocks for scalloped ferns and other hidden prizes. Today there was no time and her feet felt heavy. She was moving quickly but felt like she was dragging leaden boots. Every step demanded her attention, yet she felt her mind wandering. Last night's emergency with Carmen and her friend Monica, her distant interaction with Carlos, and Abuelita's discovery crowded her brain. Overtired, her mind flipped from the present and zoomed back to her childhood. Images of her father kept surfacing. She had not thought of his death in many years, although daily she spoke to him as she worked. He was with her in spirit and kept her focused. Today she could see the headlines that were on every newspaper twenty-five years ago. DR. NAZARIO TAKES WIFE WITH HIM IN DEATH.

Rosie was ten when both her parents were killed. She could read, and she couldn't understand why her daddy would take her mother and leave her behind. Rosie remembered on this particular occasion, that the doctor was angry with her for playing with his specimens. Whenever he returned from the jungle, he brought back funny plants. Rosie had explained to him that she was studying, not playing, and had showed him the books she was referencing. He had lifted her up in his arms and

41

hugged her and planted a kiss on her forehead. She could still hear his chuckling, "My little scientist, whatever I don't discover, I am sure you will."

Rosie tried to erase the rest of the memory, closing her eyes tight, but the image of her mother tumbled forth. Thrilled to have her husband back in the United States, her mother was all dressed up in what she called her "Sunday Best." Heels, earrings, the beautiful pearl necklace her father had given her last Christmas, and a pastel dress covered with spring flowers. It was one of the few times that her parents appeared happy. They took off on a vacation, celebrating a great success in her father's research. During the last few weeks, her father had worked under great stress at his laboratory. His studies centered on a special drug he had brought over to the States when he emigrated from Costa Rica. Rosie's father would disappear for months at a time, returning to his homeland to search for a special vine found only in the jungle. Her mother would fret the entire time he was gone. She worried about his health to no avail, for it was his health that pushed him to do research. Once when Rosie had come home with bruises on her knees and dragging her feet, her father had shaken his head and sadly declared, "Heredity has played an awful trick on us."

During his last visit to his homeland, he had secured a steady supply of vines. Hailed as a breakthrough as important as that of penicillin, his discovery pushed him to work harder. Her mother had hoped that this would mean he'd remain in the States and not travel. Before their decision to go on a needed vacation, Rosie heard them discussing the jungle. Her mother had suggested they go as a family, but her father had refused, saying it was too dangerous, and he didn't want to put his family at risk.

Trying to stay in the present moment, Rosie shook

her legs. She envisioned lightness, ease of movement, but all of her visualizations couldn't fool heredity. Her legs refused to comply with her mental commands, her muscles weighed down by failed nerves. Even her memories blocked her way, blurring images of her father's immobility. On that fateful night, her mother was handing her father a walking stick. Rosie watched her father get annoyed and throw the stick in the back seat of their car. He stumbled getting into the car, but he smiled as they drove off to celebrate his success. That was the last time Rosie saw her parents. The car they were in crashed on a mountain road, not far from their house. No other car was involved. The police investigation stated only that the driver failed to brake as he negotiated a sharp turn. The brakes, when tested, functioned flawlessly. The newspapers alluded to suicide and a large monetary debt.

Frantic squawking from the pigeon coop pierced Rosie's painful reminiscences and brought her abruptly back to the present day. As she moved closer to the clamoring cries of the pigeons, the racket intensified. Camouflaged among the dense understory of the forest, the noise from the pigeon coop floated in the air. Tilting her head upward, Rosie cast her eyes among the lush green canopy and fixed her sight on a small loft. Built on stilts and a large platform, the pigeon coop housed a series of compartments separated by a wire mesh. On top lay a metal roof and a string of cupolas fitted with swinging metal traps. A pigeon returning home after flight would easily spot the cupola, circle a few times checking for danger, and then land on a perch and enter the door that only flapped inward. Once inside, the pigeon would find the security of home, entrapped until its next flight.

Hastily, Rosie mounted the narrow ladder that led to the coop. Her hands fumbled trying to open the latch.

She was all thumbs, seeing her hands move, but not feeling their actions. A sense of dread settled in. She became extremely conscious of her limbs, sensing their weight. Her hands and feet were playing tricks, alternating between freezing numbness and inner burning. In the last few years this had happened before. Each spell at first had lasted only a few minutes, but recently they occurred with more frequency, and endured sometimes for weeks at time.

Instinctively Rosie began to inhale and exhale in an even rhythm. The breath was her first line of defense. Controlling her emotions, calming her fears, and relaxing all her muscles allowed her to focus. It was her father's ruse. She used to watch him late at night when his back hunched over and his brows furled in concentration. He would shake his hands and legs trying to rouse them from their inactivity. When this failed he performed a series of movements that stretched his arms, legs, and even his chest. Afterwards he'd lie prone on the office floor. Appearing like a corpse, he'd rest, and the only clue that he was alive was the gentle rise and fall of his chest.

Her fingers went through the motions of unlocking the latch, but there was no catch, no contact, only hands moving something abstract. Rosie knew she was alive, she felt her own breath, and thoughts of the last few days swam inside her head. Dead people no longer breathe and lack the ability to analyze. For her, the course of events had turned somewhat sinister since Carlos had arrived the previous evening with his wounded bird Carmen and her naive friend.

Rosie habitually came to Carlos's rescue and for that matter any needy soul's rescue. It was a practice that was almost an addiction, and Rosie guessed that it was connected to her own rescue twenty-five years before by her father's sister and her mother's sister. Without them Rosie would still be adrift. Each woman had contributed to her upbringing. Her father's sister, Tia Maria, lived alone amongst the wealthy enclave of Costa Ricans that had fled their country. She spoke little English and depended on Rosie to bring her the news and gossip of the world. Tia Maria was fiercely political and placed much value on the opinions of society. Rosie's mother's sister Aunt Shirley, on the other hand, worked as a receptionist at an agency that connected services for those of lower income. Bounced between the two homes, the aunts treated Rosie as an adult and encouraged her independent streak. In keeping with the Latino tradition, her Tia Maria insisted she become a respectful lady. Her Aunt Shirley, knowing the value of an education, pushed her to study and follow in her father's footsteps. Grateful for her own salvation, Rosie blended their philosophies while stubbornly maintaining her own pride as she strove to repay her debt.

Finally her uncooperative fingers forced the latch to the pigeon coop open. Shrieking cries of a hen in pain and the smell of blood assaulted Rosie. Accustoming her eyes to the change in lighting, Rosie rushed over to the nesting boxes. A young mother hen clearly panicked, greeted her with flapping wings, feathers, and blood. Rosie scooped the hen up. The hen was only four months old, a mere squab herself. The poor thing was too young to be birthing. Holding the alarmed hen firmly in her left hand and close to her chest, Rosie slowly cooed, matching her voice to the labored pulse of the hen. With her right hand Rosie probed and discovered an egg caught halfway inside the expectant mother. The mother hen's bottom was ripping. The laceration was severe and the blood loss excessive.

Tears filled Rosie's eyes. The squab was too young. Too young to bear the burden of delivery. Too young to die. Sadly, Rosie looked over at the squab's mate. The cock strutted back and forth in front of the nest. One other egg lay inside. Pigeons are extremely faithful. Monogamous by nature, they adhere to their partner for life.

Placing the mother hen on the workbench, Rosie made her decision quickly. She removed a small vial from her hip pocket and with her teeth extracted its plug. Taking care not to touch the vial's contents, Rosie dipped a fine needle inside. With a swift motion Rosie inserted the needle into the pigeon's neck. Seconds later the young mother hen's body ceased its trembling and relaxed into death. Silence filled the coop. A hush lingered in the air, heavy with truth. The cock busied himself incubating his one lone egg.

Physically spent and emotionally drained, the strain of the last twenty-four hours caught up with Rosie. Images of Carmen's blood danced in front of her. For Monica's sake, Rosie had made light of Carmen's miscarriage. She had winked at Monica to hide her own frazzled nerves, knowing the devastation of the emotional loss. Carmen's body would heal, but her soul and heart were another matter. She knew from experience. It had been nearly a year since she had had that same loss. Carlos had been at another of his political dinners, and had come home late, toward the early morning. He found her doubled over on their bed surrounded by a pool of blood. Gripping her stomach, Rosie experienced the pains once more.

The physical cramps were a mere unpleasantness, vanishing with time. The true pain came from the vacant look of Carlos's eyes. Rosie heard his words echoing in her head. "What have you done, Rosie? Why do you insist on working, helping others, when you can't even take care so that we can have a family? Don't you know what this means?" Yes, Rosie knew what her miscarriage meant. It meant that Carlos's idea of a perfect family and wife surrounding him in his ascent into politics would not be. She had failed him in a way that neither had anticipated.

Rosie let her salty tears run down her face. As a child

she always stretched her tongue out to meet the drops. Her Aunt Shirley taught her to catch them and swallow them. Teardrops of sadness were meant to be swallowed so that the oceans would fill with only happy tears. Just as she had done that night, Rosie swallowed her sorrow and concentrated on the essentials of the moment. She turned her back on the cock and went to the cages that contained Don Tuto's pigeons.

Surveying the lot, Rosie chose one of the Racing Homers, numbered 22dt. Bred for flying, Number 22dt was not particularly handsome. He was a sleek bird with strong muscular wings, a deep chest, resilient flight feathers and a long tail. Quickly Rosie wrote out a message, *"Dos Hojas Perdidos."* Using a play on words that combined both Spanish and English meanings, anyone finding the pigeon would read the message as two lost leaves. Don Tuto would interpret the note to mean two must leave and be lost. Using an open band, Rosie taped the message inside and wrapped the band around the Homer's leg. With a quick flick of her hand, Rosie sent the brave pigeon out the coop's window and on its mission of liberation.

Wanting nothing more than to rest, Rosie reluctantly began tidying up the coop, sweeping out the bloodstained straw and laying out fresh cane. It had been days since she had tended her crops at the farm. She was sure that Jesus had kept up on her experiments, but it was time she came out of isolation. The last time she had chatted with Jesus he had seemed perturbed about goings on at the farm, but he had been unwilling to discuss any of the particulars.

The two of them had grown close over the last ten years—closeness that Carlos and most people of the town could not understand. To most, Jesus was a lowly loser not worthy of her friendship. She hoped Abuelita's fears were unfounded and that Jesus was not in any danger.

When Rosie finished cleaning the coop, she would take the wasted squab's body and bury it by her favorite *ceiba* tree on the farm.

DON TUTO'S INNER SPACE

DON TUTO WAS ALMOST AT THE RIVER'S MOUTH when he heard the echoes of voices. Surrounded by the black cover of darkness, the delayed noise made him smile. Time moved forward and backward in the caves. The past and future coexisted in the present. With only the echoes as his guide, Tuto anticipated what lay ahead, and knew without seeing what was happening behind him. This ability gave him an advantage. People saw him as a powerful, mysterious man.

He followed the sound of voices. Glancing up at the drifting cave walls, he called out into the darkness, "*Oye*, Miguel, you make too much noise chasing me down. You are getting sloppy. I heard you coming from the last bend in the river."

Tuto stood with his arms folded impatiently across his chest, his feet planted firmly inside the dinghy. From the darkness a package suddenly hurtled toward him. Tuto reached out and grabbed it. "What's this, another of your statues?"

A long silence answered him. Tuto cocked his head upward as if to catch a sound wave, and then he inhaled through his nose. Within seconds Miguel stood by Tuto's side. The boat continued gliding, ignoring the added weight. "I need to ride to the cave's mouth. I've got things to attend to up above. You will hardly notice me," said his sudden passenger.

Tuto smiled again. He knew better than to ask questions. Whatever Miguel was up to, he trusted him. "I notice only that you smell like the bats that live here. It is hard for an old man like me to distinguish the difference."

Miguel took up a paddle and the two propelled the dinghy along the underground river. The gentle swoosh of their strokes barely audible as a familiar stillness accompanied them.

Tuto had been coming to these caves since he was a small boy, wandering with the lust of insatiable curiosity. At first it was his refuge where he could explore the unknown and let his mind escape from the routines of hard physical labor. Later the caves became his teacher, where he learned to study darkness and life in a perpetual nocturnal existence.

It was in these caves that he saw the mighty power of an underground river. Slowly, with the patience of a lover, the river and jungle rains did their work. The tropical rains combined with the soil and atmosphere. Becoming acidic, they gradually seeped through minute cracks in the bedrock from the hills overhead. With time the cracks widened, creating vast passageways and chambers, leaving behind galleries filled with sculpted artwork in the form of hanging stalagmites. Ultimately the rains found their final destination in the underground river.

Tuto was patient, waiting till they had tied up the dinghy and hidden it behind a crevice in the cave wall, before he ventured a question in Miguel's direction. The two were unlikely friends. Tuto was at least twenty years Miguel's senior. His own world was confined to his farm and the caves below. A self-described loner, he had dropped out of school at the age of twelve. Miguel, on the other hand, was a brainchild, finishing not only secondary schooling, but also the University. What held them together was their deep love for their homeland.

"Miguel, it might not be safe for you to come out just yet. The last time you paid the town a visit, the Governor paid a visit to your brother's *colmado*. He can only tell so many half-truths before he tells a lie, and you know how many eyes watch his store." Tuto rubbed his hand along his unshaven chin and shook his head as if to shed unwanted thoughts. Just above a whisper he commented, "Forget I said anything. It is your affair, not mine. I'm sure you have your reasons."

Working in the dark caves, it was hard to distinguish between day and night. The only interruption to the blackness was the occasional lantern that would flicker on and off at varying intervals. Miguel busied himself with hauling out the boat's contents, unaffected by the presence or absence of light. He lifted out three sacks and the package he had thrown to Tuto. "Don't worry, we can stagger our exits. I won't let your neighbors suspect anything. I walk almost as lightly and as quietly as you do. I promise I will be back before dark, unseen and without stirring-up too much excitement."

Tuto smiled appreciatively at Miguel's answer. "I know I have trained you well, your skills are almost as good as mine. Maria would be proud of you. I think of all the years I worked down here alone. We aren't alone anymore, thanks to Maria's vision."

"You still miss her, don't you?"

"No, not really. Even in death she clings to the cave walls. It was so hard for her to come here originally. She was reluctant to travel from our farm due to her blindness. I can still remember walking to and from the caves with a bandana wrapped around my eyes. Maria thought I was crazy when I forced myself to see without eyes, using the cues of smell, hearing, and touching to guide me. I had to prove to her it could be done."

The way out of the caves demanded skill and concentration. The climb was a sheer wall of tiny slippery crevices that extended upward for hundreds of feet. Tuto had years ago solved the problem of ascending and descending. Today he performed the complicated ascent intuitively. From the base of the cave wall, Tuto removed two sets of vine rope from a hidden crevice. Aiming upward, he threw the vines onto a ledge to an anchored hook. He heard the thud of contact on his count of five, and as the rope held taut he made his way up to a small ledge. From there he felt with his hands for a hidden cord. Pulling the cord at an angle released a series of cable ladders.

Ascending the cave walls like spiders, Tuto and Miguel formed a rhythmic pattern. After each step they would listen, move their feet along the cable ladders, and swing their parcels up to next ledge. Hands reached, pulled, and leveraged bodies, all in silence, all in darkness. Ahead of Tuto, Miguel almost flew up the wall. When Tuto finally met up with him on a wider ledge, he was out of breath. They both rested a moment or two, searching the walls for activity.

For the most part the public didn't know about or use this entrance to the caves, but both Tuto and Miguel were cautious. It was important for their work to remain a secret. Only a few trusted workers and guards came to this entrance, bringing up or exchanging handmade baskets. Tuto counted the woven baskets, smelling the dank air. If the order or amount of baskets varied, it signaled either a change in plans or served as a warning. Tuto whispered, "Nothing is out of place."

Miguel was almost on his way when he put his arm out towards Tuto. "I never tire of hearing you talk of her. In a way I think she has given me her abilities to detect danger. I can smell the danger in the air, feel it in the echoes not yet here. Be safe until my return."

Tuto gave Miguel a quick but tight hug, waving him on with a shrug of his shoulders. As Miguel bore to the right, Tuto continued his ascent toward the left. He was still thinking of Maria and danger. The waters had talked to Maria, as did the cave's breath. She could sense the slightest change in the air currents by the temperature and moisture. In some chambers the level of oxygen would be dangerously low, and Maria would detect this by smell alone. Tuto would light a candle, which would immediately go out for lack of oxygen. They had worked together inside the caves for a little over five years. Many of the chambers in the cave still held remnants of Maria's handiwork.

As Tuto stepped along a series of staggered steps, encircling the main chamber; he lit one of the lanterns that were nestled along a thin shelf. He admired all the hammocks, baskets and ladders that were stored as cave supplies and items for resale outside of the caves. Using the giant *liana* vines that lined and sheltered the cave entrance, Maria had spent hours weaving. Her fingers where nibble and more than made up for her blindness. Tuto smiled, thinking of her hands, how they had always seen beauty. She used to whisper to him as she ran her fingers across his face, how handsome he was.

Tuto had always answered her whispers with a wide grin, laughter, and a gentle passion that acted as a mirror. Their marriage had been based on love and trust.

Blinded as a young child from the scourge of a sugar-cane fire that got out of control, Maria had carried herself with confidence few women her age could boast. Beautiful except for the scars on her face, she had relied on her wits and attentiveness to hear thoughts below the surface of normal conversation. She and Tuto had been well suited. Shy and ill at ease with the rigors of school, Tuto skirted the public eye, keeping his opinions to himself, yet always willing to aid a neighbor in need.

His chosen form of education required reading the signs of bats, insects, rain, sun, and plants. Where he lacked the social graces of the literate world—and the confidence to speak-out—Maria bolstered his views, acting as his sounding board. His devotion to her hadn't been out of pity, but because he too lived in a world of darkness—a darkness teeming with life's complexities, needing to be expressed and understood.

Alone now, without his precious Maria, his life still had purpose. His thoughts flashed forward as he pictured Miguel above ground. Tuto intentionally traveled slowly, allowing time and distance to grow between their exits. If, in fact, Miguel was right about sensing danger, he needed to be even more cautious. It had been Maria's vision to use the caves as a safe haven. Before that he had only used the caves selfishly for his own enjoyment. His tendency to dwell below the earth created a mystique that awed his *amigos*, but actually frightened acquaintances. Not many in the area had explored the caves, and most believed them to be haunted with spirits.

Generous to a fault, Tuto would bestow gifts of mammoth crayfish caught in the mighty pools of the cave. Those who ate the crayfish felt blessed and remained healthy, while those around them fell ill with the *Mafunga*, a flu transmitted by mosquitoes. His home above the caves boasted the best bananas, oranges, and guavas in the area. Neighbors had spotted Tuto sprinkling guano from the caves around the plants and attributed their sweetness to mystical powers derived from the cave.

Tuto still felt somewhat hypocritical with his new use of the caves. As Maria lay dying, she had urged him to use his knowledge of the darkness to bring light and a better life to others. Once a place of natural cycles, Tuto had brought the complications and the politics he so much despised to his haven. He wondered if their goal and the accompanying secrets would ultimately prove too much for the caves and himself?

Now as he climbed, Tuto could feel the strain of the day. Already he had made four trips. His weekly trips down to the caves consisted of carrying supplies back and forth. The need for refuge had grown steadily over the years. He was thankful that he did not have to continue this project alone. After Maria had died, Doña Teresa and a chosen few also helped him.

Pangs of guilt occasionally surfaced as he passed from the cave back up to the outside world. He could feel the lingering effects of remorse tighten the muscles in his throat. Tuto swallowed hard and made small guttural sounds, trying in vain to erase the memory of Maria's death. It had been partially his fault. The two of them had become true cave dwellers, sometimes so engrossed in their work, exploring or studying the animal life of the caves that they would pass days without coming up. After five years of intense study, Maria had fallen ill. She had complained of a constant sore throat and a persistent cough, and her body had trembled with fever.

Climbing steadily upward, Tuto paused, resting his feet securely on the cable ladders, and dropped the extra rope he carried on a small shelf that protruded from the moist walls of the cave. From this vantage point the show of light was a promise of hope, and Tuto smiled as he felt the brilliant Caribbean rays filter through the lush jungle growth overhead to light his way.

At the top of his ascent Tuto hoisted his body up and out of the cave's mouth. He brushed himself off and looked around to make sure no one had seen his exit and that he had not left anything behind. While all the people of the area knew of his fascination with the cave, they didn't know of this entrance, and he wanted to keep it that way. He was tired. It was about a four-hundred-foot drop from the mouth, and he had traveled another mile or so by foot until the river was deep enough to carry his boat. This was his last trip of the day through the chambers of the cave. Most of the activity was in the furthest chamber, the Hall of the White Maidens, where the latest group of women gathered. Satisfied that there was nothing left undone and that all was secure, he exited.

Blinded by the full sunlight, Tuto allowed his eyes to

adjust from the darkness. Over the years he had developed his night vision to such an extent that his irises were actually enlarged, allowing more light to enter. He had taken to always wearing sunglasses to relieve some of the pain the sun inflicted. As he fixed the glasses snugly over the bridge of his nose, he carefully scanned the skies. Circling above his house one of his pigeons was getting ready to land. He hurried, knowing that when he arrived there would be a message waiting for him.

The route he took back to his *casita* was invisible to others, as it was covered with bamboo stalks, tree ferns, huge elephant ear plants, *lianas*, and the jumbo leaves of the *yagrumo* tree. Tuto moved quickly out of habit. Although he was now considered *un viejo,* his fifty-five years had been tricked by the patterns of his life, preserving an agility way beyond his years. His body moved with a will of its own, instinctively knowing the way like one of his homing pigeons returning home.

Tuto listened to the birds around him, felt the gentle caress of the wind on his face. Lifting his arm out to his side, a long-tailed pigeon landed on his wrist. Carefully he wrapped his hand around its body and slipped the message band off. Whispering to the wind he read, *"Dos Hojas Perdidas.* Yes, Maria, there is another message." He hastened up the hill to meet Abuelita and the "two leaves."

DISAPPEARANCES

PACING BACK AND FORTH, CARLOS CURSED under his breath, "*Conjo Puneta*, What is taking Pedro so long? It's been hours since he left." During his wait Carlos' eyes had become heavy. He had closed them for what seemed like only a minute. Despite his discomfort watching a dead man, he had somehow drifted off taking a very long *siesta*. After Pedro's departure, he had moved away from the elephant tree, settling off to the side under the canopy of coconut palms. The wind had played with his mind as did the shadows. Fidgeting with each movement of palm fronds, jumping at the drop of a coconut, Carlos forced himself to keep a lookout. He worried that Jesus' murderers would return. His vigilance settled into boredom when he realized he was totally alone. The stillness of the night felt creepier than the eerie sounds of the wind. Sleep overpowered his determination to keep watch. But now he was wide-awake, short tempered, and annoyed at his own folly.

It was no longer night. The sun was already rising in the sky. Nada slept contentedly by his feet. His own body felt stiff. All the muscles ached, not from physical labor, but from the stress of holding onto Jesus' spirit. He felt guilty for giving into sleep. Island traditions mandated the watching over the dead until the spirit was safely carried off to heaven. He had failed to keep his bargain as spirit keeper.

A morning breeze came off the water onto the shore, awakening palm fronds and rustling him into action. He sensed a presence drifting by, formless and more eerie than the previous night's machinations. Walking over to the *ceiba's* elephant roots, he felt his own spirit slipping away. Where Jesus lay dead the previous evening, a void remained. Trembling, his face blanched to a color less than white. Jesus was gone. Death he could accept and with it the soul traveling to whatever the after-life ordained, but he could make no sense of what his eyes portrayed. His failure to watch over the spirit paled to having lost the body of a dead person.

Carlos had a healthy respect for the island ways which combined religion with the traditions of voodoo. He, however, was not superstitious, and figured that most things could be explained. Disappearances fell into that category. Carlos surveyed the area. No footsteps, no body, no machete, no birdcage. It made no sense, but nothing in the last twenty-four hours had. These sudden disappearances tugged at his collar, tightening around his beliefs. He shook his head to clear his thoughts and perhaps see the situation more clearly. Carlos wanted to believe that this was normal but the tightening sensation forced him to remember other unexplained disappearances.

He had a vague memory of his parents once searching for some of their workers that had failed to show up at the farm after years of faithful service. When his father had gone to their shack to inquire if they were ill, the place had been boarded up. Carlos remembered another neighbor who had protested to the Mayor about his drinking water tasting funny. One of their children had died and the others had turned weak and feverish. But nothing ever came of it accept that the neighbor got drunk one night and never returned to his property. Carlos' own parents annexed the land to theirs many years later. People, really did disappear all the time, but one had the sense not to mention the absence. *No hay una problema,* there wasn't a problem if you closed your eyes.

Awake now with his eyes wide open, Carlos suddenly sensed the meaning of one of Rosie's disturbing thoughts. She claimed they were just visitors living on this earth...

that life was transitory and it never stopped. The idea of impermanence had bothered him, and he had always tried to make his mark. He wanted a legacy to be remembered by, a large family and, yes, success.

"Try looking into the void." This was one of Rosie's many irritating quotes. To Rosie the void was spiritually linked to infinity, like the name of their dog, Nada. *Nada* meant nothing; but in Rosie's mind, nothing was as close to infinity as you could get. She saw hope in all the possibilities. All he ever saw was darkness and emptiness, morbid thoughts. He had to get out of here. He couldn't protect a void. He couldn't even protect the dead body of Jesus.

Since Pedro had his truck, Carlos took off on foot. Nada followed by his side as they made their way down the hillside. The magnificent scene that spread before his eyes always made his chest swell with pride. Scores of coconut trees silhouetted against the back drop of the sparkling ocean. The thought that the land was more valuable without the trees puzzled him. Why not share this view with others. A few condominiums, a little less sand, what harm could this really do? He would talk with Roberto and Tomas again. They were anxious to purchase coastline property, and Carlos felt ready to approach Rosie with his deal.

Nada started sniffing at the ground and running in circles. Carlos laughed, watching her chase the scent of a mongoose. Mongooses became problematic for the island after they were brought over from Jamaica in the 1800s, and since that time had multiplied to over a million. Even Rosie, with her love of all living things, had enough of their pestering. Once they had destroyed an experimental crop of rice that she had nurtured for nearly six months. Rosie wouldn't mind Nada's mongoose hunt.

As Nada took off for the chase, Carlos looked out toward the ocean. The sun's glare distorted his vision, but he thought he could see a barge hanging close to the shore. He could only make out part of the name. *The Berma*, originating from New York. Odd place to see a barge, he thought. They usually dock in ports, not just anywhere along the coast. Carlos recalled one of his conversations at the trade meeting. A group of environmental engineers had been talking of a barge that had come in carrying heating oil from New York. There had been an accident, and over a million gallons of oil had spilled onto prime hotel beach land. Officials, fearing a loss of revenue from tourism had quickly moved visitors to different beaches and assured everyone that the pollution was minimal. Carlos knew from other sources that clean up crews were busy for months, and that much of the coral reef had been severely damaged. Local papers covered the story, but according to their version, the barge had been nearly empty and the clean up had been immediate. The sun's glare tired his eyes, but Carlos thought he saw a small skiff next to the barge. This barge was too high on the water to be carrying fuel. He imagined other cargo; drug trade or traffic in people. Neither of which comforted him.

When he turned back, Nada was long gone. Carlos continued down the hill walking along the road, head bent with the weight of too much thought. The ground was dry from a lack of rain. His feet stirred up dust, causing him to choke and cover his nose. Pausing after his choking attack, he raised his head to check on the loading docks where the trucks loaded the coconuts for distribution. It was Sunday and the loading area was quiet. All his workers took this day to attend to their faith, filling the Catholic churches with pious devotion. Just outside the line of his direct vision, Carlos noticed another cloud of dust.

Alongside the road, a narrow set of tire tracks imprinted the sand. He assumed that they belonged to

Rosie, riding her bike. Wouldn't she have stopped to talk to him?

The tugging, tight feeling came back and Carlos' vision seemed to split in half. One scene contained Jesus' limp body inside the roots of a *ceiba* tree and the menacing barge. The other view held the cloud of dust covering the tracks of a friend or foe and the mysterious disappearance of Jesus. Somewhere in the middle his mind tried to merge images. Each scenario contaminated his pristine world of logic and order, leaving him vaguely suspicious. He would have liked to close his eyes and erase the visions, make it all disappear. Instead he quickened his pace. He had to get back into town.

By the time Carlos reached the main road, he was sweating from the exertion. Looking down at himself, he realized that he was out of shape; too much wining and dining, and not enough physical labor. Talking, negotiating, and brainstorming new ideas constituted his exercise regime. He had always taken pride in his diplomatic capabilities, but made a mental note to get outside more and at least walk his land. Mopping his face with a handkerchief, he used his fingers to comb his blond hair off his face. Rearranging his disheveled clothes, he made himself ready to face his world.

Just by standing at the road's edge he was assured a ride into town. A *publico*, the local means of transportation, would pass by and if the battered car had space he'd get in and be taken to the town's center. Individually owned, all *publicos* ran on random schedules, making the timing of rides erratic, but plentiful with negotiable fares. Carlos approved of the drivers' first steps towards being entrepreneurs, showing island ingenuity.

Within minutes Carlos had flagged down a rust-clad station wagon filled with passengers. Climbing in the back seat, he squeezed himself in between two buxom *Doñas* dressed in their Sunday best and their *maridos*.

Carlos nodded his greetings and sat back to listen to the latest *chismas*. Usually these trips substituted for the local newspapers, neighbors and townspeople sharing snip-bits of information gathered throughout the community. No one mentioned the incident at the bar from the previous evening or seemed to have noticed the absence of Jesus at church. But the *publico* was abuzz with talk about Sanchez's accident last night. Carlos remembered the sight of the overturned sugarcane truck and had wondered at the cause.

From what he could gather from the hubbub, Sanchez had been forced off the road by a car, one not from here. It was a rental car and had two men in it. They hadn't even stopped to see if Sanchez was all right. Carlos listened to one of the men in the *publico* discuss the incident.

"They were strangers, coming to do bad business. Strangers always leave destruction behind. My friend, Ernesto, helped Sanchez home. He claims there was a rental car on the side of the road. Even though it was dinner time, they were not going to or coming from dinner. The rental car was parked and one of the men was wounded on his side. Ernesto was sure because he had given them the courtesy of stopping and offered to help. The strangers shooed him away, but not before he saw the blood."

Listening to the banter and the sympathies for Sanchez, Carlos closed his eyes and saw the blood stained machete lying next to Jesus. Well, this at least explained one mystery. Jesus had put up a fight. But who was he fighting? Carlos, lost in his own thoughts, suddenly realized that the *publico* had gone silent. The passengers stared, waiting for him to answer their question. Smiling sheepishly, Carlos muttered, "*Como*? Forgive me, my mind has wondered. What juicy question am I to answer?" They laughed as if he had made a good joke.

Carlos vaguely recognized the woman seated to his

left as one of Rosie's customers for herbs. She smelled of the garden; a pungent odor of mint mixed with the sweetness of orange blossoms. Dressed in a red, baggy shift, her hips and chest appeared as pillows, cushioning her body, taking up space for two. Carlos now fully attentive, focused on her question,

"Your *esposa*, Rosie, how is she doing?

"She is fine, keeping busy."

Across from Carlos, her husband, clean shaven and lean, sat on the edge of his seat. Sucking on a chunk of cane, he continued on with the conversation.

"Do you think this will be a good year for coconuts?"

They were only asking polite questions. But Carlos sensed a slight twist to the last question, hinting at his lack of children. They were goofing with him, or as Rosie always said, *"un goofao,"* but he felt shame at his lack. He chose to answer the question as if they were asking about the coconut harvest.

"Yes the coconut trees are full this year, and if the hurricanes are kind, the yield will be too."

How many people already knew of the imminent sale of one of his groves? He suspected everyone of butting into his business, wanting a piece of his success or judging his actions. Yet the only person really affected was Jesus and his problems were not theirs.

Carlos held his head up and looked directly into his comrades' eyes and did not see suspicion or guilt reflected back. What he saw was friendliness born of years of living in a small community. Their eyes reflected trust and concern. He realized the guilt and suspicion were his alone. It was unusual for Carlos to take a *publico* into town, and in doing so he made his private life open to discussion. No one was prying. They were sharing a sense of belonging.

The rust-laden auto kept crawling down the narrow lanes that passed for roads. Honking its presence and scattering pedestrians, chickens, dogs and whatever else was in its way, the car pulled up at the center of town.

Every *pueblo* had the same basic design. All the houses nestled in close to the mountainside. Narrow roads meandered down to the town's center where a large church took center stage. Surrounding the church, the open plaza hosted the locals who visited, played dominoes, and held celebrations. The stores formed a square on each side of the church and faced the plaza.

Carlos paid *una peseta* for his ride, said his *adios'*, and headed for the local *colmado* where Jesus had to have bought his ticket for the illegal lottery game *bolita*. Jesus, just like everyone and his brother, wanted to make it "big". Money, legal or illegal, seemed to be the answer. Carlos was not so naive to believe he was better than the rest, he too played *bolita,* but Jesus had been obsessed.

Not knowing where to find his friend Pedro and not looking forward to talking to the police, Carlos decided to find some answers to Jesus' disappearance on his own. His eyes were wide open, yet he felt like he was groping in the dark. He shouldn't be bothering with all this nonsense, but a sixth sense told him the darkness would surround him if he didn't pay attention. Fear, more than his concern for Jesus and his sense of obligation to the community, propelled him on.

EL COLMADO

As far back as he could remember, Carlos had been a patron of Don Rafael's *colmado*. He remembered coming to the market with his father, eyes transfixed on the shelves of *dulces*. He knew that the sweets, if he behaved, would most likely find a place in one of his father's sacks. Back then Carlos believed Don Rafael's store had everything a human could possible want. The place was full of people and talk, and money freely exchanged hands.

This morning Carlos made the same evaluation, but with a more mature awareness of what made Don Rafael's place special. As he walked in the door, the aromas of *salchichas* (sausages), *morcillas* (the more pungent blood sausage), and the yeasty smell of *pan de agua* (French-style water bread), all intermingled, drawing out his hunger. Even at 7:30 AM, a few customers, mostly older folks, mingled in the corner, sipping dark coffee; enjoying the intimacy of years of friendship.

Poor lighting made the bruises on the guavas, bananas, avocados, *pina*, and other fruit less evident. Canned goods, *cerveza*, and dry goods lined the store walls. A thick layer of dust and grime covered most of the products except for the beer, which sold so rapidly that the dust never settled. A stale smell of cigarette smoke hung in the air, but those present found this familiar and comforting. Carlos noted the lack of the younger crowd. Their alliance to the old ways held little weight when confronted with the newer *supermercados* located further out of town.

Don Rafael sat on a stool in the far corner of the store. He was dressed for work in his crisp white *guayabara*. Most likely his wife had embroidered the light cotton shirt, and pressed it earlier this morning for Don Rafael to wear. Dapper with his straw hat settled at the back of his balding head, Don Rafael without a glance upward called out, *"M'hijo, hacia tiempo.* My son it has been awhile, what can I get for you?"

Carlos knew it was important to pass the time with pleasantries. He asked about his sons, daughters, and grandchildren. Gingerly he fingered one of the wooden Saint figurines that Don Rafael's once-sane brother Miguel had carved. Found in most religious households, the wooden *santos* sold from Don Rafael's *colmado* gained notoriety. Considered a fanatic, Miguel created meticulously detailed works of art, but ones not religiously accurate. His *santos* represented events that had occurred in the island's history and often depicted recent affairs, sometimes verging on the political.

As the brother of a respected businessman, no one challenged him for his views, but after a series of *santos* scenes appeared showing the island in bondage and the people starving, Don Rafael's brother disappeared. Gossip varied as to where Miguel was—most stating he had finally "gone over the edge", and was in an asylum. Don Rafael was closed mouthed about the subject, but periodically a new series of *santos* would appear in the store. The one in Carlos' hand now was of a woman giving birth, eyes filled with joy, and surrounded by a cluster of young ladies, with bats encircling. Despite the heat, an eerie chill crept up Carlos' spine. Replacing the *santo* on the shelf, he phrased his question carefully, "My friend Jesus, has he been doing business here lately?"

Don Rafael's eyes darkened and became hard as stone. The smile left his face and he became serious. "Your friend Jesus is very popular these days. Two other so-called friends were in yesterday. They were strangers to me, but they were kind enough to pay Jesus' large bill. Are you the same kind of friend?"

Carlos' mind froze on the word strangers. Strangers

meant outsiders. If a person was from the States or another part of the world, he would be considered a *touristo* or *amigo*, but calling someone a stranger implied a separation, and signaled a feeling of distrust. Why would Don Rafael accept money from strangers? Carlos shook his head; "No Jesus can pay his own debts. I was just looking for him to do some more work."

They were both holding back the truth. Don Rafael was really asking Carlos why he was here so early in the morning, on a Sunday, looking for a friend, who should be at church or at home resting. He was acting as if he couldn't be trusted, as if this were the big city where a market owner wouldn't know a patron's ways. Trust was what made a small town thrive.

The bigger cities had lost this intimacy, and many of the *jibaros*, forced off the sugar cane fields, coffee plantations, and coconut farms, arrived in the city vulnerable. Anxious and in need of money, they left themselves wide open. Having no skills appropriate for city life, they got caught in a maze of drinking and trafficking in drugs and women. Gradually straying from who they were, they vanished into the anonymity of the jail system or the larger city of New York.

Carlos was here probing Don Rafael about Jesus' involvement with strangers in his hometown. Carlos questioned Jesus' love and relationship to his home town.

Carlos could feel his reflection burning in the store window. He was no floundering *jibaro*. He'd been to college, mastered the large cities of the States, and had come back to his home. He thrived on the din of the city, on his astute business sense. At home in the hills and by the ocean he equally enjoyed the peaceful pace of the countryside. What about himself reflected back distrust to Don Rafael? Feeling uncomfortable, Carlos sensed Don Rafael waiting for some statement or action to prove he could be trusted. He racked his brain for what in years past would have been instinctive. Sensing defeat in a battle undeclared, Carlos made a start for the door.

Don Rafael called after him, "Carlos you give up too easily. A true friend would not make up lies, when one is seeking answers. I know there is no work on your coconut farm, as Jesus has spoken to me in confidence about your plans. He has been desperate to purchase his own land. The more desperate he became, the more he played *boleta*. Unfortunately for him, the odds did not play in his favor. I was not worried about payment, as over time Jesus has done me many favors. I only took the money from these two men because Pedro was here with them, and advised that I should."

Carlos walked back to the counter, anger reddening his face. Both the town and Don Rafael talked of two strangers. And now Pedro had been linked with them. "Don Rafael, describe these men to me and tell me when Pedro was with them."

"Hold your temper Carlos. I'll tell you what you ask, not because you push me with your hot words, but because you are my *friend*. As of late you have lost your sense of perspective. I am too old to confront the hidden evils of others. I don't care about motives. Honesty must come of all this. Promise me this, Carlos."

Impatient, Carlos was tired of the duplicity that plagued his island. Everyone worked with different sets of rules. Whichever set worked at the time was correct. Greasing the palm with a favor, knowing the right people in the right political climate, all of this was considered fair. Don Rafael seemed to be implying something beyond this. He was asking him to draw the line. Frustrated at the implication that he had somehow crossed the acceptable boundary of honesty, Carlos feared Don Rafael knew something sinister about his past behavior. His words sounded frighteningly like that of Rosie's. Carlos hesitantly whispered, "I make you that promise, Don Rafael."

"Both men gave the appearance of height. You know what I am saying, Carlos. They talked above my eyes, not looking at me directly. Dressed formally in suits, ties, and shiny expensive shoes, they should have been sweating, but they arrived in an air-conditioned rental car. Their faces were fresh and their clothes were not rumpled. The one named Tomas looked like a blend of Latino and American; dark hair, dark eyes, and thick lips contrasted with pale skin. He talked to me in a Spanish that was too informal for the way he was dressed. His shadow was darker and oilier. He went by the name Roberto. They both looked stiff in their formal garb. Like two pebbles polished to a smooth finish. Shined and tumbled, but hiding a rough inner core. Their eyes were hard as rocks."

"Pedro looked out of place and seemed embarrassed. To tell you the truth Carlos, I was embarrassed for Pedro. He was sweating, and his stocky build looked almost weak next to those two. He was in a hurry to leave and almost pushed his friends out the door. They were reluctant, still hungry for information. As they walked out the door, the one I call the Shadow, asked about a woman named Carmen. Tomas shot him a dirty look, and snarled something about *mujeres*, women knowing more than they should and not remembering to forget what they know. They laughed as if it was all a big joke. Pedro followed them out like a puppy dog."

Carlos tried to assimilate what Don Rafael had just told him. Yesterday, earlier in the day his *pana*, his best friend, Pedro had been with his business contacts from New York. Don Rafael's description was accurate, if biased somewhat. Carlos had seen them as successful well-dressed business associates. Their apparent wealth and willingness to invest in the island development blinded Carlos from seeing them beyond his own need for money and power. Is this what Pedro wanted? Worst of all was Don Rafael's last bit of information. It made it seem that what happened to Carmen and Jesus was no surprise to Pedro. Their comments about women alarmed Carlos the most. How often had he wished Rosie would not know so much? He had just said something like that to Pedro last night. Thinking about last night made his heart race. This news meant Rosie might also be in danger. Danger from what, he wasn't sure, but he felt responsible.

Carlos didn't know what to do first. Finding Pedro and getting an explanation didn't seem likely. He needed to warn Rosie that she was not safe helping Carmen. Don Rafael coughed a few times, and Carlos came back from his somber thoughts. Smiling weakly, Carlos wished Don Rafael had not told him anything. Jesus' death and disappearance had left him confused and worried. Knowledge of Pedro's disloyalty hurt. Instead of pointing him to clarity, his life seemed to be getting darker, more sinister and out of control.

"I don't really want to thank you, Don Rafael. What you have told me doesn't make my life any easier. But thanks anyway. I have to ask another favor of you. Pedro borrowed my truck, could you lend me yours?"

"No problem. I'm in walking distance from home. The truck is in the alley, and the keys are inside. Take these things as well, you may need them."

Don Rafael handed him a flashlight and the *santo* Carlos had been holding when he first came in the store. Bewildered, Carlos stared at the objects in his hand. What possible use could he have for them? Not wanting anymore disturbing information, Carlos headed down the alley. He looked back once to see Don Rafael close the *colmado's* doors and place a sign on the window, "closed for lunch". He saw Don Rafael take a pigeon from the coup near the store's entrance, pat it gently, and then send it off in flight. Not at all sure that all was well, Carlos looked at his watch. It would be hours before lunch. Shrugging, he hurried to find Don Rafael's truck.

SPIRALING DOWN

THE AFTERNOON SUN PENETRATED the thick forest canopy. Monica looked around her. Four years on the island, and not once had she ventured past the town roads or the sandy beaches. Used to the open salty air of the coast, she felt crowded by the tall trees towering above her. All around her she could hear raspy, monotonous calls, "neeeet, neeet," answered by "prrreeeet, prreeeet." Her eyes hurt from searching for the owner of the call, until she caught the fast, flutter of emerald-green wings. Perched a few meters above her head, two *Tody* birds sallied out and with swift graceful movements devoured insect after insect. Their feeding frenzy aided by the insect infested orchids nestled in the crotches of the branches. Milky white orchid blossoms perfumed the air. The smell mixed with of her own fever.

Though it was only a little before noon, the air, already thick with heat, grew denser from the moist air in the forest. She felt the sweat dripping down the front of her shirt and between her breasts. Each drop lazily caressing a nipple, tickling each curve, slowly inching its way down to her naval, and below, to where it finally caught in her own mangled forest. She writhed inside, longing for a lover's sense of fulfillment not yet felt. The sensation teased more at her empty heart than at her desires.

Embarrassed by the timing and inappropriateness of her feelings, she willed it away by concentrating on her steps. They'd left Rosie's two hours ago and had been walking and stopping, walking and stopping, for what seemed twice that time. Her legs ached from the uneven forest floor and her disposition faltered between determined and irritable. Only Carmen's occasional moans kept her decisive and focused.

Abuelita walked at a clipped pace, undeterred by the terrain. She paused suddenly, and pointed up the hillside before them. "There! You see him? Next to the rock ledge, by the grouping of banana trees. There's Don Tuto, the man we are here to meet."

Monica squinted up at the hillside. She strained her eyes searching for movement. Finally she spotted a speck of white, criss-crossing down the hill. As she watched the small white dot grew larger, pausing and moving its way behind one green leaf after another.

"Come, let us make haste," said Abuelita as she started up again on the narrow track they were following. "We'll catch him within the hour if we hurry."

As they walked, Monica adjusted the weight of the stretcher on her shoulders. Since she was taller than Abuelita, their method of carrying Carmen was a little awkward. She had worried that this trek would be too much for Abuelita's small, twisted frame, but slowly they had developed a rhythm. Abuelita's gate showed no stress as she walked with her knees slightly bent. Monica found to her surprise the weight of Carmen rested more on the thighs than on the shoulders or back. Consciously, Monica followed suit and bent her own knees.

Her own body was strong. The beach and fishing area weren't far from where she worked. Daily she made a point to run along the beach and swim out beyond the fishermen's dock. While others in her profession drank and partied with their clients, Monica had always stuck to a regimen of abstinence. Sobriety and physical strength were her only protection against violent over-tures. Even so, her youth and strength did not prepare her for carrying the weight of another person, especially one who tossed and turned in troubled sleep.

Abuelita had done this many times before. Planting

each step firmly and softly, she never lingered more than a second. Monica noted that the stretcher was unlike those used by firemen in New York, or for that matter, any other one that Monica had ever seen. Shaped and whittled into a curve, the bamboo poles molded over her shoulders. It reminded her of a yoke. Stretched between the poles sat a hammock-like net. Having her hands free helped, as she had to steady herself on the bumpy ground. Dodging protruding roots, the thick mesh of leaves and fronds hid them, as they spiraled down the mountain side. She felt joined to Abuelita and Carmen by the silence that surrounded them.

Abuelita's words from earlier in the morning echoed in her head, "What you are witnessing is the unraveling of a web of lies and secrets that up until now cocooned many lives." She wondered if her own silences weren't just a cover for secrets. Up to this point Monica felt that her concealment of truths affected only herself, and were irrelevant to the future. She had been the director of her own life. Now she wasn't so sure.

Monica stumbled and caused the stretcher to tilt to one side. *"Lo siento*, I am sorry, my mind was wondering."

Abuelita turned her head slightly and called back, "Don't worry, I trust that you can hold up your end. Perhaps you want to tell me what is on your mind."

"I overheard you and Rosie this morning, talking about me being a prostitute. I know you understand and aren't judging me, but, but…"

"But what… Monica?"

"For some reason it is important that you understand that I am not really trapped like the other women here. It is my choice."

"Do you mean you aren't like my mother? Monica, I am sure you have your reasons. It is no business of mine. I judge you by your actions toward your friends, not by what others say or think about you."

73

"In high school I was a good student, popular with all the kids my age and I loved studying. It all changed when my parents split up. The world I knew fell apart. I had to pick up the pieces. My sister was only eight at the time. When my parents fought, I would cover my sister's ears. But it was worse after my father left. Without the fighting my mother came unglued. She drank before work, after work, and until there was no work. I'd get up early to dress my sister and make lunches. I'd rush home from school to meet her, and then take the subway to my job at a fancy women's clothing store. I saw how the wealthy lived. I'd trail behind their perfume and pick up strewn clothes they had left behind piled in the dressing rooms. I never talked to them, but obediently I took their rejects back to the main floor. That job taught me a sense of style. I learned how to walk, talk, and dress. It gave me a thirst for freedom and the determination not to pick up someone else's messes."

Abuelita nodded her head as she listened. "So that explains your professional *choice*. You wanted to pretend you were a wealthy lady?"

Monica missed a step. She could feel her face reddening and then she heard Abuelita chuckle.

"Not exactly. I bolted at eighteen. I couldn't take the situation at home any longer.

"Working any job I could find, I paid my way through junior college. One professor in particular impressed me. He was my psychology professor. The art of listening to others and sorting out their problems came naturally to me. At home I performed a similar role. His class gave my actions a framework. One afternoon the professor bumped into me while I was eating alone at the local cafeteria. It was particularly embarrassing, as I had just dumped the entire contents of my purse on the table in order to find enough money to pay for lunch. The professor was kind enough to pay my bill. After that I found myself meeting with him often. I would remain quiet most of the time, just listening to his problems at the college or at home. I'm not sure if it was a conscious decision on my part, but I started to look forward to our meetings. I could forget my own problems and since he paid for our lunches and snacks, I found myself eating better, seeing more sights, and feeling freer. Sex came later. We both understood that our relationship existed only in the professional sense. I knew he didn't love me. I wasn't looking for love. I needed food and mental stimulation. He had a family that he loved. All he needed was someone to take care of his physical hunger. It was a business relationship where we fed each other. Eventually I tired of the professor's stiffness, his narrowness of thinking. It struck me as odd that he had so much knowledge, yet knew so little about other ways of living. But I was grateful for his classes. The classes at the college whet my appetite for more education. The "classes" in bed gave me a means to make myself financially secure."

For a few moments they walked in silence, Abuelita mulling over Monica's explanation. "So I take it you are rich and happy now, living far from your home, courting men. Aren't you still picking up someone else's mess?"

Monica tripped over a root and cursed under her breath. Abuelita's words jabbed at her causing her to lose balance. Stealing herself from reacting, Monica ignored the taunt. "Earlier this morning, Rosie and you were talking about the town believing you were a prostitute when you first arrived here. Were you one?"

"No, we don't have that in common. But I had fewer choices in my life than you. My mother had been a prostitute. She was a wonderful, caring lady. She died at the hands of a jealous lover. I tried to intervene and block the blow. It crushed one of the vertebrae in my upper back. I was left to fend for myself in the jungle."

"How old were you?"

"Too young to feel such pain, but old enough to know the score. I must have been about twelve. Years later, when I finally arrived here, I met Don Tuto and his now deceased wife, Maria. The three of us worked out an arrangement of sorts. Don Tuto built me my home when no one would speak or look at me. My money was not good enough to deflect the fear from anyone else. When Don Tuto found out that I had lived in the jungles of Costa Rico and knew herbal medicines he pleaded with me to nurse his wife, Maria, back to health. Maria and I were like two lost souls. We became close, *pegado*. We could talk about anything. I brought her herbs and brews to relieve the congestion in her lungs. Although Don Tuto finished my home, I was unable to save Maria's life."

"How did you survive the jungle?"

"That is a long story. One of my mother's old friends was a doctor working in the jungle. He found me and wrapped my body in moist banana leaves, filled with powerful brews of jungle herbs, until I healed. I remained with him for years studying the native plants."

"You don't hate your mother, do you?"

"No, *mi hija*, my mother loved me more than she loved herself. I have always known that."

As they had been talking the terrain had changed. They zigzagged along switchbacks covered with thick woody vines. Trees completely obscured the sun. Monica estimated them to be at least ninety feet tall. Without the heat of the sun, her sweat had completely evaporated and now she felt chilled. She looked down at Carmen who had begun to shiver in her sleep. Without any prompting, Abuelita headed off the trail to a large *sapodilla* tree.

"*Tsst*, Monica. We must get Carmen covered up before she is overcome by cold and bad dreams."

Monica immediately stopped at Abuelita's variation of a "cat-call". "*Tsst* was what the macho men called out to women on the street. It was both a derogatory utterance and one of admiration. The call jolted her to awareness. Carefully they removed the stretcher off their shoulders and placed it under the *sapodilla* tree. Looking down at herself and at Abuelita, she realized they were ill prepared for a chilly night in the jungle. "How are we going to cover Carmen without a blanket or even a sweater?"

"Hush your worries, *mi hija*. It's not a problem. We'll make her warm by taking broad leaves from the banana trees and we'll bind them together with the sap from this tree. "Come, *ven aca*, I'll show you some of *my* tricks of the trade."

Abuelita began to break the upper leaves off an old banana tree. Monica started to break the leaves off at the base, but Abuelita's knotted hand, held her firm. "Only take the older leaves from the mature banana plant. The new banana tree sprouts from the rhizomes and the young leaves carry the nutrients necessary to bear fruit. It's fine to take the older leaves as they have already served their purpose and will die as the old stem topples."

The two worked quickly and soon had a pile of thin broad leaves collected. Carmen rested fretfully. She tossed and turned and began to mutter, "Mama, Papa, *lo siento, lo siento*." Shaking her head with worry, Abuelita bent over Carmen's chest and listened.

"What is it, Abuelita? Is Carmen okay?"

"Yes and no. We must hurry." At that point Abuelita scooped a handful of sap from a wounded branch. "Here, put this in your mouth and chew." Abuelita did the same and in a matter of minutes their saliva had changed it into the consistency of gum. With practiced fingers Abuelita spread the gum along the leaf's center. Stacking four leaves together, she then spread the gum along the leaves' edges. Monica did the same. They then attached the sections together in a quilt. When they had completely covered Carmen, Abuelita took a small machete she had tied to her waist, and swiftly cut some vines that hung from the tree. "Here wrap these loosely around Carmen, so the blanket stays in place. Then find us a space to rest while we wait until Don Tuto arrives. While you do that, I'll gather us some food and some healing herbs."

Before Monica could say anything, Abuelita had disappeared in the forest. She held the vines in her hands. They felt light and airy despite their thickness and woody grain. Slowly she wrapped the fibers around Carmen's chest and feet. Carmen slept soundly. The shivers disappeared and her eyelids remained still, signaling the absence of bad dreams.

Looking down at her feet, Monica watched an army of termites emerge from a dead piece of wood. Their activity was frantic. Within minutes they had devoured a whole section of the fallen tree. Amazed, Monica shook her head. She had always thought of termites as destroyers, now she saw them as cleansers, purifying the jungle. Sighing, Monica took one of the vines and brushed the remains of the termites away and sat down. Abuelita's tricks had solved the immediate problem, but Monica still had too many unanswered questions to feel relaxed. How long were they going to have to wait? Where were they going? Why was her friend so troubled? She looked up through the trees, searching for the sky. Following the path of the climbing vines, she found a patch of sunlight. Not much to put your hopes on.

Don Tuto stopped and listened. He had spotted movement further down the hill and needed to center himself. Like the bats he worked with, his ears were highly sensitive. He listened for echoes; trying to determine from where the sounds bounced back. Satisfied that he was headed in the right direction, he resumed his descent. The sunlight had vanished in the jungle and the night sky would soon cover the outlying homes and town center as well. This was the best time to travel. Nightlife in town drew the desperate. Gambling and drinking called the *desperados* to the center of town. They milled the streets and left the hillsides bare. Don Tuto sensed an urgency. Years of silent rescues and intuition made him quicken his pace. Amorous fights gone bad, drunken dares, over-zealous boasts, young girls in trouble, all these he was used to. Tonight he sensed a more ominous call for help.

Mentally he ticked off the supplies he had brought to the caves earlier in the day. The usual fresh fruits, produce, fish, and first aid kits. He smiled thinking of the slab of mahogany he had found. It had been heavy and had almost tipped his skiff over as he had floated down the underground river. The appreciation Don Tuto had seen on his friend Miguel's face had made the difficulties worth the effort. The scarcity of carving material made the mahogany valuable to Miguel. Don Tuto knew he needed to feed Miguel's addiction to carving, his compulsion to create art in the form of a protest.

The sudden flapping of wings in the trees interrupted his thoughts. In the upper canopy, kingfishers and parrots suddenly awakened, took flight. Tuto stopped. The jungle alarm had gone off. Whatever had disturbed the birds was nearby. Apparently the hillside was not abandoned tonight. Someone else was traveling. Noise meant the person or persons were either in a hurry or were strangers. All of his *amigos* knew the routes like the beaten paths to the local barroom, and they kept the code of silence.

Don Tuto debated. He knew that Doña Teresa would be waiting his arrival to help take the "two lost leaves" to safety. He estimated that he was less than a mile from their meeting place. Doña Teresa had helped in hundreds of rescues. He rationalized that she was capable and resourceful. Most likely she could take care of any emergency. He shouldn't worry. But he also knew that a few minutes in times of danger could mean the loss of freedom. How many losses had he witnessed throughout the years? Remembering all the abandoned children, the young adults fleeing their homes from shame, the fights turned ugly due to alcohol or drugs, increased his resolve to continue making changes on the island. Tonight's disturbance troubled him more than usual. No one should be traveling here... unless they were up to no good. He feared discovery.

Bringing his hands up to his mouth, Don Tuto cupped them and made three sharp quick trills, "Whit, Whit, Whit." He waited and repeated the call, "Whit, Whit, Whit." No trills answered his call. Perhaps he was too far from Doña Teresa to hear. Still undecided on whether to pursue the jungle disturbance or to proceed, Don Tuto lowered himself onto his hands and knees and placed his ear on the ground. There was the faintest sound of patter, feet trying to move silently and quickly.

Abruptly Don Tuto stood up and headed back up the hillside. His feet barely touched the ground. His night eyes shifted back and forth. He strained to hear the echoes. Honing in, Don Tuto located the travelers. Grabbing a vine for leverage, he scaled the nearest tree. Perched in the canopy, he peered down on the intruders, watched and listened.

Three men huddled around a mound of cut *liana* vines. Don Tuto tried to see what else was inside, but the mound was camouflaged with leaves. The shortest of the three men had his front to Tuto. He plodded back and forth, shoulders bent over, face puffed up ready to explode. Tuto immediately recognized the heavy stance. It belonged to Pedro, Carlos' jealous friend.

"*Pendejo*, that was stupid! You should never have gotten involved with Jesus. Whatever were you thinking? The police may not take notice of what you did to *la punta*, Carmen, or for that matter, just any macho guy. But Jesus, well I tell you, his spirit is powerful."

The tallest of the three men stared back defiantly. He shook his head, not at all impressed by Pedro's pompous display of anger. Tuto saw strength behind the man's fancy clothing. Although ill prepared for the tropical forest, his eyes and body displayed a readiness for business of another nature. He replied confidently to Pedro, "He might be powerful with a machete, but his heart must be weak. He dropped like a fallen leaf. After he took a jab at my side he just withered. Roberto and I stuffed his dead body between the roots of the *ceiba* tree and left. We won't have any problems from him. You don't have to worry, your secret is still safe with us."

Pedro bent his head down. His feet nervously moved the dirt back and forth. Tuto had to lean forward to hear Pedro's mumbling. "I still think we need to stay low for a while. Carlos will be on the land now. He was close to Jesus. I think he is beginning to have second thoughts about the condominium deal. And if that happens all our plans are ruined. I think you should return to your barge. Maybe take the cargo and disappear."

Pedro's request hung in the air. Flashing a false smile, he came up to Pedro and grabbed him by the shoulders. "Sorry, no can do. We have an old score to settle with Carmen. Just tell us where she is and then we'll make our exit."

Don Tuto had seen and heard enough. He waited until the threesome moved behind the mound of plants to slowly inch himself down the tree. Keeping his eyes on the intruders, he walked backwards until he was out of hearing distance. Then he let his feet fly down the path. Now that he had a name for one of the women he was trying to save, he could almost see the cloud of danger forming overhead. Carmen's story didn't belong to her in isolation. Apparently the strangers had ensnared the honorable Carlos in a business deal and succeeded in feeding Pedro's lust for power. Working in the planning department gave Pedro access to government information and also the authority to discreetly make things happen. Tuto was sure that money had greased Pedro's palm. Bribes, false documents, closed eyes, all these were a part of the island's mode of operation. Although Tuto was accustomed to the double standards, the involvement of outsiders disturbed him. Jesus must have found out something.

Don Tuto mulled over what the intruders had said about Jesus withering and dying. Something didn't ring true. Pedro was right to worry, the spirit of Jesus would not wither. He chuckled imagining the rising spirit coming back to haunt Pedro. Whatever he was involved in; Tuto knew that Pedro, extremely superstitious and religious, feared repercussions from the spirit world. He'd pray to any godly entity that would listen. Jesus might be dead, but Tuto was not ready to believe that as the truth. He sensed Jesus' spirit, alive and active. He scanned the hillside wondering if he had heard his gentle footsteps earlier.

Spotting Doña Teresa's shadowy form kneeling in the distance, Don Tuto quietly approached. Not needing to disturb her rituals, he went immediately over to the beautiful woman seated next to her. Squatting he whispered, "Is your friend Carmen going to survive?"

Monica jumped. "I'm not sure," she stammered to the squatting man who had startled her. "How did you know her name?"

Her head raced with questions as she stared at this man she assumed was Don Tuto. He was neither tall nor small. The evening darkness partially concealed his face, but his eyes shone directly into hers. Pupils, large and open. Immediately she recognized kindness. All her past experience catering to the sexual needs of men, told her not to place faith in men who were incapable of keeping allegiance. But here she discerned a directness that was healing. As uncomfortable as she felt, scared for her own life and Carmen's, she trusted this person.

Don Tuto took her hand and held it close to his mouth. Letting the warmth of his breath touch her. "The jungle has many voices, and I have ears. So far it has not told me your name."

"My name is Monica. You must be Don Tuto."

Bending at the waist in a mock bow he said, "At your service. When Doña Teresa is finished tending to your friend, I'll escort you to the caves."

Monica gave him a quizzical look. "Doña Teresa? I only know her as Abuelita"

"Ah, well the town's people think of her as their grandmother. For the young it is an appropriate title, but for myself, I prefer a different relationship."

Monica looked at Abuelita kneeling over Carmen and back at Don Tuto. She could almost feel the current between them. The energy was tender, warm and comforting. It flowed in a circle moving through her body as well as Carmen's. "Don Tuto, I didn't know where our destination was, only that we were traveling to safety. Are the caves our safety?"

He smiled mischievously, "Doña Teresa has not talked much, I see. She must have her reasons for not sharing more with you." He was about to explain when Carmen let out a whimper. Monica and Don Tuto rushed to Abuelita's side. Abuelita strained a foul-smelling liquid through a cloth and let it drip into Carmen's mouth.

"*Estas bien*. All will be fine. I've given her a mixture of the *zorillo* root and some of the *chicolero* plant. The *zorillo* wards off evil spirits and the *chicolero* removes toxins from her uterine lining. We must heal both the spirit and the body."

"We can't wait too long, as there are others in forest.

I spotted Pedro talking with two strangers. One was named Roberto and I didn't overhear the other's name. They know Carmen and want to do her harm."

Abuelita let the information sink in and then she looked into Don Tuto's eyes. "No one knew we were coming here. I didn't even tell Monica, in case she decided to bolt."

Monica noted the lines of tension crossing Abuelita's face as her mind filled in the blanks between Don Tuto's words.

"You say Pedro was with them and not Carlos? What else are you keeping from me?"

Don Tuto placed himself next to Doña Teresa and affectionately squeezed her shoulders. "I can't keep anything from you. You have already guessed. They've hurt Jesus."

Abuelita's face collapsed. The wrinkles folded in on themselves and her lips narrowed to a thin tight line. Don Tuto gave her another squeeze. This time he held her longer tighter and within seconds Abuelita had regained her composure. Carmen stirred. "Shh, I think Carmen is finally awake and ready to talk."

Carmen opened her eyes and first stared at Monica, then at Abuelita and Don Tuto. She tried to move, but the vines held her down. Abuelita stroked her forehead to calm her. "My child, don't move. We are traveling to safety. Tell me, the dreams are all gone now?"

Carmen stared back at Abuelita. Her jaw was set and her eyes were blank. Her lips had lost most of their rich dark color and her words stumbled out, "Do, do you really believe there is safety in this world?"

Turning her head away from their eyes, she mumbled to herself, "All your kindness can not make my dreams go away." Wrestling to free her hands, Carmen reached out and called, "Monica, *ven aca*. Come here."

Monica slipped in next to Abuelita and grabbed

Carmen's hand from under the banana leaves. Carmen's eyes darkened as she whispered. "I'm not afraid for myself now, I've already experienced the worst. I only worry for my parents."

"Carmen, your parents are a long way from here. What does any of this have to do with them?"

Monica felt the warmth of Don Tuto's body pressing in closer. He was straining to see more of Carmen. She watched his eyes move up and down Carmen's body, as if he were using x-ray vision to see into her soul.

With her free hand, Monica stroked Carmen's forehead as Abuelita had done during their trek. Massaging the centerfolds between the eyes, Monica took her thumb and moved the worry and fear up and away, softening and smoothing the skin. Abuelita gently encouraged her, "That's it *mi hija*, move the evil out, open the space between the eyes, so there can be light."

Carmen swallowed and the stiffness of her jaw slowly eased. With her eyes fixed on Monica, words began tumbling out.

"I left my country because my parents were poor. They didn't agree with the local landowners. You see, my parents were just laborers. They didn't own the land. They were told to burn the jungle ground and grow crops. We all knew that the jungle soil was poor. They didn't listen. They cleared the trees, and slashed and burned large areas. They grew inedible crops. They were drugs, marijuana. I was outraged. Two men from my village, who worked for the landowners, came to pay us a visit. I was young and too stupid to keep my thoughts to myself. Oh, how stupid I was."

Becoming more and more agitated, Carmen closed her eyes and took a breath. Abuelita split a succulent vine open and dabbed the juice on Carmen's lips.

Sighing, Carmen continued, "Like I said. The jungle soil has no nutrients. All the plants have shallow root systems that spread wide to get the food they need. This new crop failed after repeated plantings. The landowners blamed my parents and asked them to pay up. Of course, we had no money. They were going to kill my parents. I walked in on them as they pointed guns at their heads. Staring the two men down, I told them I would work my parents' debt off."

Without shedding a tear, Carmen told her heart-wrenching story in a rush. Monica and Abuelita made no move to interrupt the flow of words. They watched as Carmen's face masked her feelings.

"I haven't seen my parents since that day three years ago. The two men took me outside and raped me in front of my family. They were from my village, but that was of no help to me. I thought I would work my parents' debt off on another field—not with my body. They brought me to the States. I escaped, or so I had thought. I can't believe Roberto and Tomas are here. What do they want from me now?"

Don Tuto stood up. "Shh, *mi hija*, my daughter. We must move you to safety. Your village terrorists miss you. They are still searching. You did right to help your parents. You are the grand protector. Now we must take refuge and perhaps see some justice."

Don Tuto picked up one end of the stretcher and let the curves fall gently on his shoulders. Abuelita did the same. Monica followed behind, watching their easy rhythm. She had been thinking of herself as the protector of Carmen. Carmen the fragile one, Carmen the silent one. Since Carmen had arrived on the island, Monica had watched out for her, making sure that she had the easy customers, except for last night. Monica again felt the shift of perspectives. Now it seems that Carmen had hidden strengths and a few of her own secrets. Who really was the protector? Monica could only shake her head at how little she knew about the people in her care.

STATIONS AND DELIVERIES

ROSIE HAD ALMOST LOST HER RESOLVE to visit the farm and check-up on her crops. Putting the mother pigeon out of her misery had drained her of what energy she had left from the previous evening. But as she toweled herself dry she felt somewhat renewed. She smiled as she caught herself singing an old song that her father used to sing to her before bedtime. The words were simple and endearing. "I have a mother who loves me." Her earlier gloom and physical fatigue slowly lifted. Water, in whatever form, had a way of cleansing her. As a child she had wanted to be a mermaid. Her aunts teased her and declared she'd be a great white whale, traveling the oceans of the world. Moving her now lead-heavy legs, she imagined them as fins, strong, fast and graceful. Keeping this image clearly in her mind's eye, Rosie tried tricking her clumsy body.

As Rosie shook the water from her wet hair, her thoughts swung loose. By now Abuelita, Monica, and Carmen would be well on their way to the caves. With luck the carrier pigeon had arrived safely and Don Tuto understood the message. For now, her role in Carmen's welfare had ended. Free to leave her cabin and attend to her orchid and honey business, she busied herself with preparations.

Going to the farm involved planning. Her present means of transportation was her bike. When she worked at the University as the dean of agriculture, she had traveled the forty-five miles daily in an old battered pickup. Once she gave up that job she retired her keys and took to riding her bike. Glad that she had left her position at the University and proud of her accomplishments, Carlos anxiously anticipated Rosie's application of her knowledge on their own farm. But he had laughed at her and called her *loca* for wanting to ride her bike. Although this amused him, he refused to help her make adaptations to the bicycle. In private it would be just fine, but as in most of their quarrels, Carlos had a different version of what was acceptable for his position in society. It was Jesus and Don Tuto who had helped her convert her bike into a cargo-toting vehicle.

More than two years ago, Jesus had come running up the hillside calling her name. "Rosie, Rosie, *los encontro*. I found them, I found some old tires." Holding an old rusty baby carriage, he proudly blurted out his success. "*Mis bebes*, are good for something, no? All my little babies are grown now. I'd like to give you this."

Normally Jesus and Rosie only worked or discussed matters concerning the farm, but he had overheard her asking Carlos for assistance. Their friendship grew quickly after that. Jesus and Don Tuto found metal scraps and used wooden planks. They fashioned a small trailer that hooked onto the rack at the back of the bike. It was Jesus who found Rosie sprawled on the side of the road after she lost her balance carrying a heavy load up a steep hill. Conspirators, Jesus promised not to tell Carlos about Rosie's spill. Rosie for her part was attentive to Jesus' ideas. He knew more about the land, plants, and animals than anyone at the University.

When she tried growing rice on some of their property, Jesus helped with the irrigation. His advice was to the point and sadly very accurate. "Too much salt here and too many mongoose."

Over time Jesus told her more about his own life. Rosie kept his confidences to herself. She respected him and knew that every action he took was calculated. The town considered him a ruffian for his antics with women, his drunken tendencies and fights. Not doubting his strength, she trusted more in his wisdom.

Thinking about Jesus, she hurried her pace. Grabbing a dress with a wide skirt and short sleeves, she pulled it over her head. She placed a bandanna around her forehead and topped it off with a straw hat. She needed the large brim to shade her eyes. The trailer, already packed with her deliveries, still had space for her mournfully wrapped dead squab she intended to bury. Whenever she went to the farm, she made sure to visit her special customers who wanted the honey from her hives and the medicinal herbs that Abuelita and she had grown. Despite Carlos' concern for appearances, Rosie had acquired a reputation as an eccentric *gringa*. She wore her title as a privilege. Truly of the privileged society, Carlos wore her eccentricity with shame.

Rosie searched the sky for pigeons and perhaps a return message. Seeing none, she mounted her bike and took off. The load was heavy. Her leg muscles slowly responded to the exertion and she began to relax and look around. Nothing about where she lived bored her. She noticed everything. Most of the *jibaros* lived on *parcelas*, government land, with houses made from a collection of what most people consider as junk. Her closest neighbors built their houses out of wood scraps and raised them above the ground on stilts. This was the islander's answer to termites. The roofs were zinc scraps, and often the kitchen area was a simple lean-to. Wire pens for protecting goats and chickens, and coops, housing fighting cocks, surrounded the homes. Oh, how Rosie hated the cock fights.

Not more than a half-mile down the road, Rosie dismounted. She stopped in front of a multi-colored house. Salmon colored walls faced the road with side walls painted powder blue. Pastel green trim framed the house. Rosie called out, "*Hola, hola*, anyone home?"

Not getting a reply, she left a bottle of honey on the

porch step and hung one of the orchids from her green-house on the post. Looking around to see if anyone was watching, Rosie then removed a basket of orchids from the other post and placed it in the back of her trailer. The casual observer would miss the switch, but her friend and client had been trained to notice the exchange as a coded message.

Considered the local expert on the growing and care of orchids, Rosie's fascination with them had come almost as an afterthought while collecting honey from her beehives. The honey she collected had a distinct flavor. Curious as to what nectars the bees chose, Rosie had followed a swarm. Frenzied, the male bees zoomed down with the urgency to mate and buried themselves in what they thought was the warm, brown, fuzzy part of a female bee. Frustrated, they would exit and try another female bee. Rosie had watched, transfixed at nature's trickery.

Each female bee was in fact the petals of the *ophrys apifera*. The "bee orchid," as Rosie called it, acted as a professional teaser. The orchid, out for personal gain, used its body to perpetuate its species. Rosie had taken a few orchids back to her greenhouse to study, and eventually had developed various hybrids by breeding the different petal colorations, which attracted other kinds of insects. While her honey and medicinal plants were more in demand, the market for her orchids continued to grow.

On the road again she heard the motor and honking of a *publico*. Knowing how fast they came down the road, she moved to the side. Cries of greeting came pouring out, *"Buenos dias*, Rosie." Rosie smiled and waved them on shouting after them, *"Vaya con Dios."* To herself, she repeated the saying, "Go with God." Whenever she heard that, she could hear her aunt saying, "May God be with you," and her other aunt saying, "May the spirits be with you, and you be with the spirits." Growing up with her two aunts had assured her of multiple interpretations of the same event. Her mother's sister was a good Catholic. Her father's sister also considered herself a good Catholic, but she believed more in the spirit of the world. She taught Rosie to listen more deeply, to expect the unexpected, for nature's rules followed many different paths. To be spiritual and "with God" held the responsibility of active participation. For Rosie, each version proved correct according to her aunts' gospels, and she merged their world view into her own. Daily she followed their example and made the conscious choice to live with many variations of truth.

Rosie stopped at two more houses but left only honey. Soon she came upon a square cement house tucked back from the road. It too was painted in bright pastel colors, trimmed in green. Wealthy by island standards, a cement house was a step above. The *rejas,* decorative grillwork, also indicated the owners had something worthy of stealing. Rosie loved the brilliant colors. She saw the houses as works of art; each family making their individual statement, no matter how poor they were.

Strips of bark with orchids attached, hung from the grillwork. The orchids lived on airborne moisture and dust particles and had no need for soil. The roots would anchor themselves to trees. Rosie counted. If Don Rafael were home, there would be seven orchids hanging. Today there were eight. According to their code this meant he was traveling and delivering a message to one of the guides. Rosie had wanted to stop and talk. Normally he closed his *colmado* at twelve and came home for a siesta and lunch. No such luck today.

Thinking back on her route, she had collected six orchids. All the homes trimmed in green were her stations of information, part of the network. The guides were busy. Her fugitives, Carmen and Monica, were with Doña Teresa. So much activity was unusual and it left her unsettled. There must be other passengers enroute. Rosie placed one of her orchids next to the eight. At least Don Rafael would know she had stopped.

The rest of the trip to the farm would go quickly. At the top of the hill Rosie veered off the main road. Two *flamboyon* trees concealed the entrance to a smaller path. The trees' flaming red blossoms attracted birds, which circled overhead. Rosie watched for a moment before ducking inside the leaves' fold. This road was bumpier— not well ridden.

Carlos had once told Rosie of the old railroad that had run on the island. As a child he had played on the tracks. After years of struggling, the railroad failed, leaving behind miles of tracks, bridges, and tunnels. Rosie had liked the story. She joked with Carlos, imagining him as a child, less stiff and more playful. He had smiled and responded by pretending to be the conductor. "All aboard, make room for the lady. Next stop my house." They had laughed and ran all the way to their house and made love. It had been a special afternoon.

The next time they talked about the old railroad, they had fought. Carlos wanted to put in a second roadway on their property. The thought of removing any more coconut trees than was necessary, horrified Rosie. She mistakenly suggested clearing off the old railroad to use for the harvesting trucks. His anger echoed in her ears. "This is not a game, Rosie. This is business." Her playful conductor had disappeared and in his place was the efficient businessman's sense of economics. Rosie would not budge from her position. Carlos had never spoken of the old tracks again.

As Rosie rode over rotting wooden planks her wheel caught between the boards. She stopped to pull the rim off the track. She could see clearly through the trees onto the upper part of their farm. Here, the coconut trees parted revealing a space with scattered and infrequent growth. The vegetation held itself back and the greenery abruptly stopped, giving way to an expanse of pure white sand; dunes of refined rock that eventually fell away and flattened into the crystal clear blue of the ocean.

Rosie's chest constricted as her eyes looked out onto the beach. Her breath caught between her clenched teeth. The beach was like a teenage face scarred with holes, pockmarks scattered throughout the dunes. Vast areas of sand had been carted off. Rosie traced the path of a dust cloud only to see Carlos' truck back out and turn up to the main road. Involuntarily her jaws released and her breath turned into yells. She cursed, *"Pendejo*! Carlos, how could you? Carlos, Carlos, Carlos, Carlos!!"

Without thinking Rosie unhitched the trailer from her bike. She sped recklessly down the rutted path. Her worst fears about Carlos had become true. She didn't want to believe that Carlos had violated her trust. They lived separately now, but that did not mean she had stopped loving him. She needed to trust Carlos more than she needed his love. Jesus had warned her something was amiss. As always, Jesus hadn't said much. "Be patient, Rosie, Carlos has problems even he doesn't know about."

How much more patient should she be? Jesus couldn't possibly believe she would allow this to happen.

By the time Rosie made the final turn onto the farm, her anger had turned to confusion, and Carlos' truck had disappeared. She studied the damage. Most of the dunes had been flattened. Only a small ridge-line remained along the beach. With hurricane season not far off, the absence of a barrier could cause major damage to the beach and inland towns.

Totally spent, Rosie leaned up against a coconut tree and slowly sat down. She let her gaze go out to the horizon. Focusing on the waves, she watched as they swelled, crested and rolled into shore. The water lapped at the sands' edge, chaffing back and forth. Sand dollars, sea urchins, and baby crabs landed, only to be pulled back out. The ocean teemed with life, depositing its treasures by her feet.

Holding a piece of driftwood in her hand, Rosie drew in the sand a heart with an arrow running through it. She then systematically erased it with her heel. With one sweeping motion she hurled the driftwood in the air and back to the water. She whispered, *"Adios."*

Not waiting for it to land, Rosie reluctantly stood. Just as she turned to go she noticed a barge and two small skiffs. The nearest loading dock lay miles down the coast. She and Carlos sent all their coconuts by truck to the other end of the island, where large freight ships took in cargo. Rosie tried to think of a logical reason for the barge's presence. Coming up with none, she walked out to the edge of the beach. Distances on water are deceptive, and with the reflection of the sun against the water, she had difficulty seeing more. Relying on one of her dad's many tricks, Rosie brought her hands up to her face and formed circles with her thumb and forefinger. Using her fingers as glasses, Rosie was able to filter out the background and focus on the boats.

She watched as someone transferred large crates from the skiffs onto the barge. Only one person stood on each skiff and from Rosie's view at least two stood on the barge. The crates seemed light weight. Rosie counted ten exchanges, when one of the boats pulled up its anchor and headed back to shore. The skiff rode high on the water, empty.

The wind came from behind the boat. Rowing would be easier and the current would bring the boat and its one crewman back too soon for Rosie. She suddenly grew cold. The sun beat down on her arms, yet her hairs rose up. It was too quiet.

Where was Nada? Frantically she called, "Nada, Naaadaaa, *ven aca*. Nada, come." Mounting her bike, she headed for the loading area. The sand was wet and compact from the receding tide. A long snakelike trail followed her as she headed to one of her hidden paths. Rosie spotted faint paw marks that the waves had not yet washed away. Nada had been down here, but where was she now? She followed the prints until they disappeared.

At the bottom of the main road, where she had seen Carlos' truck, were piles of coconuts. Jesus and the other workers would never leave the coconuts out. Each day they boxed the coconuts that they had felled, preparing them for shipment. The crates were then stacked in the shade to await the next day's trucks.

No crates awaited tomorrow's trucks, only piles of loose and cracked coconuts. Rosie looked back out at the barge. The second skiff headed into shore. She realized she had no time to waste. Walking among the coconut piles, Rosie found Nada. Her tongue hung out of her mouth and she lay immobile. Kneeling beside her, Rosie listened for a heartbeat. Gently she stroked her face and whispered, "Nada, Nada, *estoy aqui*, I'm here." Rosie felt a faint, almost imperceptible pulse below Nada's chin. Nada's body was cool, as if it had already started shutting down. Patiently, Rosie looked for a wound or a bump.

At the base of the neck she found a small needle, much like the one she had used on the mother hen, she had come to bury. Nada was not dead, but almost. The poison in the needle had blocked the receptors of the muscle cells so that muscles began to shut down. If Rosie didn't stimulate the muscles, Nada would die from total relaxation. Using both hands, Rosie pushed down firmly on Nada's chest. "One, two, three, push. Come on, girl. One, two, three, push. You can do it." After four strong pushes, Nada's eyes began to flutter. Rosie felt the urgency of Nada's condition, and the pressing need to discover why someone had tried to harm her dog. She didn't have time to stay if she wanted to escape detection and warn the others. Removing the bandanna from her forehead, Rosie soaked it in the milk of a cracked coconut. She was able to squeeze some milk between Nada's lips, after prying open Nada's mouth.

Rosie walked over to her bike. Looking back, she saw Nada had begun to sit up and lick the remaining coconut milk. Dehydration would no longer be an issue. She knew Nada would hide in the shade and stand guard. Still torn, she took hold of her bike and pedaled. Keeping her mind focused on the task at hand; Rosie refused to look back at the water. She didn't see the skiffs hit the beach. She didn't need to. Her eyes scanned the coconut groves. She noticed the smallest of movements among the palm fronds. A shadowy form clinging to the trunks of each tree seemed to be swinging by. Rosie masked her feelings as best as she could. Poker faced, her lips were held tight in a thin line, not curving up or down. Her eyes held a determination focused on pulling together all the divergent pieces of contrary information. Chin tilted slightly upward; Rosie allowed a slight smile to reach the small corners of her eyes. She blushed with hope and something else.

Rosie took the path that wound above the coconut grove near the end of an old abandoned canal. She considered this the back door to her property and the entrance to many lines of hidden transportation available on the island. This canal paralleled the railroad tracks. When the rains came, it would fill with the overflow of the local lakes, and gush with fast clear water, emptying into the ocean below. Once Carlos had dropped his watch in the canal and days later they found it lying on the beach. The watch had traveled through a series of tunnels. For most of the year, the tunnels were dry and could be walked through.

Rosie remembered her first time traveling in the tunnels. She had been working on her failed rice crop. The island had received less rain than usual and the flooding of the fields, a necessary step in the rice's growth, flowed inadequately. While studying the irrigation system, Rosie suddenly saw Jesus come out of the ground. "Jesus, you scared me! Where did you come from?"

He had given her the widest grin and taken her by the hand. "Come with me. I'll show you one of the island's many secrets." They had entered a semi-darkened tunnel filled with spiders, cockroaches, and bats. They walked for a long time, popping in and out of various tunnels. Some of which were darker than night. Their final exit led to an area not far from Abuelita's house.

They had gone inside her house and it was as if Abuelita had known they were coming. Steamed espresso sat on the table, along with slices of guava and native cheese. They had talked mostly about plants, particularly the herbs and vines that Abuelita dried.

After her father's death, Rosie remembered poring over her father's notes from one of his many trips to the tropics. They described a vine that he hoped could be used in the treatment of multiple sclerosis and Parkinson's disease. Rosie had searched in vain to find more information, and had devoted many years of undergraduate study baffled by the absence of research. Ironically, the vine Abuelita had in her curing house matched the description in her father's notes. Rosie had been shocked, but Jesus and Abuelita had nodded. Abuelita's only comment at the time had been, "We have waited for you a very long time."

At the entrance to the canal, Rosie paused to hide her bike behind some grapefruit trees. Abuelita had been right. Years ago Abuelita had known this day would come. Her warning earlier this morning about the past unraveling had been correct. Nada's poisoning was not random. The venom used to puncture Nada's skin was the same as she had used on her wounded pigeon. Up until today, Rosie had been under the impression that she and Abuelita were the only ones cultivating the vine. Abuelita had taken much care in protecting her discovery of medicinal uses. She was fighting an old battle that started in the jungles of her homeland. The *liana* vine had the potential to unleash toxins that not only poisoned the body but also contaminated some people's mind. Rosie knew there was no antidote for greed.

Thinking of Carmen, Rosie took the dead pigeon from a sack and carefully buried it by her bike. She whispered, "*Lo siento*, I'm sorry. I didn't want it to be this way." The pigeon's death, Carmen's injury, and the destruction of the beaches, merged into a deep loss of innocence. Her best intentions to heal, mend, and create life had been foiled. Their haven had been invaded by a poisonous force.

Before she went inside the tunnel, Rosie glanced upward. Clouds formed in the sky. Clustered in small imperfect convolutions, the white spheres were tightly packed and heavy with moisture. Her resolve to expose Carlos, and all the sinister venom that poisoned the island faltered. Rosie allowed one tear to fall. To the white and pale blue sky, she murmured, "I do this for you, Carlos. Jesus, please guide me." With that she disappeared into darkness.

LA FATINGA

CARLOS FOUND DON RAFAEL'S TRUCK sandwiched between two metal garbage cans at the end of the alley way. He'd forgotten the battered shape of the truck. It was mostly rust, with just enough of the white panels left to hold the junker together. Don Rafael had always affectionately called the truck, *La Fatinga*. Known to have a mind of its own, many a *publico* had rescued Don Rafael from *La Fatinga's* stubbornness. Carlos could only shake his head. He'd need all his faith to coax the truck through the town. To arrive back at Rosie's house, he'd need a miracle.

As Carlos made his way through the alley he noticed the local beggar. His name was Ramon, but most of the village called him Pide, which meant "the requester." When Pide wasn't hunting through the garbage, he was always requesting money, a favor, but never work. As a street person, Pide usually did well. Everyone liked him. Carlos knew he knew more about the workings of the village than their own mayor did.

"*Buenos dias*, Don Carlos, what brings you to my home?"

Carlos laughed. "Pide, your house is everywhere. I'm borrowing Don Rafael's truck."

"I've been guarding it the entire morning. I'll let you take it for a few *pesetas*."

Carlos knew Pide's game. Pide never asked for something directly. He was subtler. Making a face, Carlos held his breath as he approached Pide. His eyes began to smart and he gasped at Pide's smell, a mix of sulfur and feces. "I'll give you two *pesetas* if you'll go get something to eat and take a bath."

"Thank you so much, Don Carlos, for the generous offer. I have been busy and could use some freshening up."

Carlos reached into his pockets and found some change. Quickly he moved away from Pide's offending odor and headed for Don Rafael's truck.

Plastic garbage bags lined the bed of the truck. Carlos could feel his neck and face getting red. Impatient to be on his way, he resented the mess and inconvenience. "*Contra! No me dices.* Don't tell me I'm going to have to haul Don Rafael's garbage through town." Carlos tried to lift one of the bags. He realized immediately that there was no smell. The bag was heavy. Unfastening the knot, he opened the first bag to find it filled with canned goods. The second and third bags held the same. The contents of the fourth bag baffled him. Inside he found a small, collapsible metal ladder, ropes with sling knots, gas lanterns, and a contraption that looked like a rope with a seat sling. Carlos shook his head in bewilderment. Obviously Don Rafael's life held many more surprises, a fact that left him with a sinking feeling. He placed the flashlight Don Rafael had given him in the fourth bag, but decided to keep the *santo* up front with him for good luck. He might need it.

The door of *La Fatinga* refused his attempts at opening it. Carlos tried yanking and pulling. Finally he kicked the door. It swung open so suddenly that the tip banged his head. "*Conjo, corajo,*" he cursed. Rubbing his head, Carlos sat down in the driver's seat. As he adjusted the rearview mirror, he saw Pide staring. Carlos knew he looked ridiculous. He was disheveled and didn't look much better than Pide. Carlos smiled to himself and started to wave, but Pide had disappeared and Carlos remained alone in the alley.

Surprisingly *La Fatinga* started right up. Carlos knocked down one of the garbage cans as he pulled out.

He cringed. Twice he backed up and inched forward to avoid more trash. How he hated the narrow alleys and even the main roads. Crowded streets with everyone strolling after their lunch and siesta made travel painful. Another battered truck tried to pass him. Carlos held back his temptation to shout what was on his mind, but beeped his horn instead, and watched as the driver swerved over the sidewalk, around the pedestrians, and on down the road. It fazed no one. No one knew any different. Having lived off the island for years, this behavior embarrassed and disgusted him. It was one of the improvements he wanted to see if he ever got the condominiums built. Tired of the old, rutted cobblestone, he would widen all the streets and smooth the surfaces.

Carlos could almost hear Rosie's constant mutterings. "Look upward Carlos, the beauty isn't always by your feet or just in front of you." Reluctantly, Carlos glanced up at the balconies surrounding the alleys and road. Half the town lived in these homes above their shops. Ferns and flowers cascaded over each balcony as did the conversations, arguments, and songs of the owners. Once again she was right and this bothered him. Rosie never seemed to care if she was right or wrong, she just stated what she felt. He couldn't argue with her. More importantly, he couldn't win. Despite the poor conditions and debris, Carlos acknowledged these distinctions and acceded to their charm.

He was almost out of town now, and the buildings and people thinned out. *La Fatinga's* engine strained as it climbed toward Rosie's hills. Carlos checked the fuel gauge and pressed harder on the gas. The truck ignored the extra injection and sputtered up the winding road, keeping pace with a meandering herd of cows. *La Fatinga* took the following *lomos* with even less ease. Carlos could feel himself leaning and pressing forward to assist with the rise. He hadn't realized he was holding his breath until he was speeding down the other side. He used this momentum until he had to brake for a flock of frantic chickens that decided to cross the road. Screeching to a stop, *La Fatinga* rested, halfway up the last of the hills from Rosie's house. It was just a mile or so away, but the truck refused to budge.

Carlos looked down at his shoes, once polished to a sheen; the tight pointy loafers now failed to give even a dull reflection. Each pebble from the road pushed up into the thinned soles, as if to poke fun. Walking was not Carlos's choice. If only he had his own reliable truck with him. But Pedro had taken it to go find help for Jesus. Who knew what Pedro was up to, now that he had betrayed him? Getting out of the truck, Carlos unbuttoned his shirt, sat down by the side of the road, and waited. The sounds of squawking roosters filled the air. Carlos recognized those disquieting sounds. They came from an old dilapidated wood barn that housed the local cockfighting arena.

Despite Carlos's irritation at having lost his momentum due to the wandering chickens, and ultimately stalling out, he mentally paid the hens a sympathetic tribute for traveling as far away from the cocks as possible. Carlos recalled the first time he had been to this barn, the first time he'd gone to a cockfight. He had snuck out of his house to go with his neighbor and best friend, Pedro. He was about fifteen, rebelling from his father's strict rules, but not wanting to be caught. Even though they had arrived early, the arena had been dark and loud, filled with drunks and an excited crowd. Two cocks with metal gaffs placed on their claws, paired up and weighed-in. When the birds set in the pit, everyone had yelled out their bets, "twenty on the green!" Carlos had thought twenty dollars on the green-banded cock was extravagant. He had only brought a dollar and had placed it on the biggest cock.

As the roosters faced off, the arena had quieted down to whispers. The tension had been more than Carlos could bear. After one lunge, his cock had fatally stabbed the other rooster in the neck. Carlos hadn't known whether to be elated or disappointed. The crowds had starting yelling again. He had looked up from the pit and had spotted the local banker sneaking off with a lady. They were laughing and kissing, their own blood running fast with the adrenaline of competition. Another set of cocks had been put in the pit and Carlos had gone to place his bet of two dollars, when he'd seen Jesus vomiting in the corner. Jesus did little to hide his visceral reaction to the brutality.

Carlos had stopped visiting the cockfights after he came back from college. Pedro had continued to go, as had the banker and most of the town's businessmen. It just occurred to Carlos, that after that first time years ago, he'd never seen Jesus there again. Jesus had been smart and stayed away, like the hens.

Sweating impatiently, Carlos now waited for the barn doors to open. Even on Sundays, the crowds couldn't resist a good cockfight. After they thanked the lord, confessed their sins, the day of rest translated into a day perfect for wining or losing hard-earned money. Any minute someone would walk out and be able to give Carlos a ride up to Rosie's. The doors did open, however Carlos had forgotten one consistent pattern. Every time anyone came out, they stumbled over his or her own feet. The last thing he wanted to do was bring a bunch of inebriated men up to Rosie's. Carlos jumped to his feet when he saw the door swing open again. To his dismay, Roberto and Tomas, his business partners, sauntered out with Pancho—an old *campesino* whose house neighbored Rosie's—in their arms. Pancho struggled to get loose. They lifted Pancho up by his armpits and placed him in their car. The car sped off, going up the hill.

Carlos kicked *La Fatinga* and a voice from the back of the truck admonished him. "Don Carlos, didn't Don Rafael instruct you on how to care for *La Fatinga?*" Carlos didn't want to believe his ears, but the stench told him it was Pide.

Pide raised himself up from between the garbage bags and jumped down from the bed of the pickup. Without a word he lifted the hood of the truck and fiddled. *La Fatinga's* engine alternated between rattling and choking until it miraculously started. Pide hopped into the driver's seat, reached over to the passenger's side, and opened the door. Carlos just stared.

"Get in. Hurry, Don Carlos, we must catch the strangers." Carlos got inside. Before the door was even shut, Pide took off. With Pide at the wheel, *La Fatinga* came back to life. Dark black clouds followed them as they careened forward, taking each curve as they hugged the mountainside. Carlos coughed. "Pide, where are we going?"

"The strangers are going to Doña Rosie's house. They are looking for the lady you brought to Doña Rosie's last night, to heal. They won't find her, but we'll go just in case."

Carlos rolled down the car window. He fumbled for the seat belt. Not finding anything to secure himself in, he grabbed the strap dangling from the truck door. Once again he felt like life was taking him for a ride. Death could be lurking just over the next hill. Pide, oblivious to Carlos' fear, hummed while tapping his free hand on the dash. The tune linked together a series of monotonous, repetitive sounds, almost a chant.

Through clenched teeth, Carlos whispered, "Stop that, you are driving me crazy. Rosie might be in trouble. The people you just called strangers are my business partners. They just took Pancho against his will. Pancho is just a drunk, not worth messing with. They want to get information from him about Rosie and her patient. I regret ever taking that woman to her house."

Pide quieted, but his fingers still tapped a silent rhythm that ran through his head. To Carlos, the silence was worse. He wondered if he had offended Pide, of all people. They had traveled close to five miles before Pide resumed humming. This time Carlos didn't say anything realizing the humming as Pide's futile attempt to calm him down. As they pulled up in front of Rosie's house, Pide turned to Carlos and put his hand on his shoulder. "Get a hold of yourself, Don Carlos. The strangers aren't here, but I don't know what we'll find."

Carlos looked into Pide's eyes and saw concern and respect. Although the look made him feel uncomfortable, somehow less powerful and more in need of sympathy, he nodded and stepped out of the car. Pide was quicker and had already entered the cabin through a door left ajar. Carlos had always insisted on locking their doors when they had lived together, but Rosie was of the belief that if danger were knocking, nothing could get in its way. A locked door only deterred friends, she said. Enemies needed no excuses for destruction.

Carlos didn't have to go far to find the destruction that Roberto and Tomas had left behind. A hushed silence lingered in the house, as if the cabin were holding its breath, waiting for the intruders to leave. The only noise Carlos could hear was the sound of cracking glass. He rushed to the greenhouse where Rosie had set up Carmen's sick bed. Pide was standing in the center of the room, surrounded by slivers of broken glass. Roberto and Tomas had shattered every windowpane in the greenhouse. The floor crunched as Carlos walked in. Strewn amongst the debris were all of Rosie's orchids. They had ripped the plants from their bark and baskets and had stomped on them, grinding their beauty and life into the floor. Squatting down to study the mess, Pide looked up at Carlos. Pide's face had taken on an ashen pallor, and tears formed in the corners of his eyes.

Carlos nauseated at the image of Pide's implied intimacy, exploded. Rushing into the room he toppled Carmen's make shift bed. He threw a small statue of Don Quixote against the wall. More glass shattered on the floor. Carlos's blood raged; pulsated. He knelt next to Pide and grabbed his shirt. "It's only Rosie's hobby that is ruined. You have no right to cry for Rosie. She is *my* wife. I've been violated. What a waste. Pide, wipe your pitiful tears. Tell me where Rosie is. You knew she wouldn't be here. You seem to know everything I don't. Tell me, Pide. Who are Roberto and Tomas? I've talked business with them, but it appears that you have better judgment than I. Let me in on some of the secrets."

Pide stood up from the floor. His color had returned. Before facing Carlos, he retrieved the statue and righted the bed. Even in his bedraggled clothes Pide took on the air of correctness. His chest and shoulders filled with pride. His eyes were dry. "I listen, Don Carlos, do you?"

It was Carlos's turn to go pale. He thought back on all the times that he had dismissed Rosie's concerns. He had heard her. He could repeat back her ramblings about the farm, preserving the land and the coconut palms. He had heard different ramblings from Roberto and Tomas, all of which pleased his ear more. By choice he had chosen deafness and blindness. He was losing his relationship with Rosie to those who could see her more clearly. Carlos closed his eyes against the pain. His head fell and his shoulders drooped, as he let out a deep sigh.

"What now, Pide? You must have a plan or you wouldn't have hidden in the truck."

"First we must check the pigeons, to see if there are any messages, and then we'll decide."

Carlos nodded and followed Pide out to the coop. Pide knew his way around the property better than Carlos.

It was obvious that he had visited often and Rosie had welcomed him. Carlos had stayed away to give Rosie the space he thought she needed. To be more honest he had stayed away because he didn't feel comfortable. They had shared a beautiful home together. This cabin was Rosie's alone. It was an embarrassment to him.

Out of the coop, the pigeons flew around in circles over head. Even Carlos knew this was wrong. Rosie only let the pigeons fly in the early morning. She kept them in the coop away from their natural predators. Her pigeons were her pets, but they also were well-trained messengers. Carlos remembered his fight with Rosie over the isolation of the cabin. Rosie had answered his arguments by explaining how homing pigeons work. Carlos had called her silly. Rosie's words echoed in his mind, "Homing pigeons are loyal. If you treat them right, they will always return. They are more dependable than you, Carlos, and the island's failing phone system."

Rosie had tried to make a joke, but Carlos flinched as he recalled his retort. "Go ahead, Rosie, play with the pigeons if you like." Carlos could tell by the way that Pide approached the pigeons that this was no game. Pide put his arm out and three of the pigeons landed. He studied each of them and then placed them back in the coop. Carefully he repeated this procedure until he had the entire flock back safely inside the coop. Only one pigeon remained. Wrapped around its leg was a red metal band. Pide held the bird and slid a piece of paper out from the band. Pide read aloud, "Move fast. Strangers."

"I don't understand the message, Pide. None of it makes sense to me. Rosie and the women are gone. They were gone before the strangers even arrived. I'm smart enough to figure out that Pedro must have told Roberto and Tomas about Carmen. But it doesn't explain what Roberto and Tomas are after, and how Rosie got Carmen away from here. Carmen was wounded and bleeding. She couldn't leave without transportation. Rosie's truck is still here."

Pide didn't look at Carlos. Carlos' fingers curled tightly at Pide's silence. He knew Pide had heard him, by the way Pide nodded his head and made small snorting sounds. Carlos paced back and forth, waiting for Pide's reply. Pide weighed his trustworthiness, just as Don Rafael had done at his store. Carlos flexed his fingers and held back the hot words that passed through his mind.

Finally Pide faced Carlos and asked, "Do you think you can drive over to Doña Teresa's house and then to your farm?" Without waiting for a reply, Pide handed Carlos the keys.

At the thought of his farm, Carlos mouth went dry. His hands went up to his throbbing head, cradling the twisted associations that Pide's question provoked. He wanted a drink. He wanted to go to the bar and forget everything. He wanted to forget the image of Jesus' body stuffed between the *ceiba* tree's roots. Carlos wanted to disappear.

Trembling, Carlos answered, *"Esta loco.* I found Jesus' body at the farm. I can't make sense of it. Part of me thinks I dreamed it, that I had a bad nightmare. I just don't know."

Carlos expected Pide to react to the news of Jesus' death, but Pide only shrugged as he walked over to *La Fatinga*, and sat in the passenger seat.

"Say something, Pide. Did you know that too?"

In answer, Pide shrugged his shoulders again and stared ahead. Carlos took his place behind the wheel and silently prayed that he could start *La Fatinga*. His hand shook as he turned the key. The truck refused to turn over. Silence lay between them. He tried again, pumping the gas slowly. The motor made a stifled cough and went dead. Carlos's fingers tensed and curled into a fist as he began pounding on the dashboard. He continued hammering until Pide reached over and grabbed his hand.

"Carlos, listen. Always listen to the motor. Wait for the catch, then press the gas."

Carlos did just that and *La Fatinga* sputtered to life. Embarrassed, Carlos looked over to Pide, to say thank you, but Pide's face had closed down. He continued staring straight ahead. His eyes seem glazed and his mind had drifted off as he began humming his slow repetitive chant.

The drive to Doña Teresa's house required traveling a long winding route. Although Rosie and Doña Teresa lived deceptively close, with their properties butting one another, walking was actually easier than traveling by car. Poorly maintained roads made travel bumpy, dusty and awkward. *La Fatinga* sputtered erratically. The motor's drone created a hypnotic calm. Carlos' hands softened their grip on the steering wheel and he eased himself back against the seat.

He reasoned it was natural for Rosie to ask Doña Teresa for help. When Rosie had moved out from their house, Doña Teresa and Rosie had become close friends. The friendship had been against his wishes. He had told Rosie about the stories he'd heard when he was growing up. Doña Teresa had been accused of being a voodoo priestess who had come to seduce all the men away from their wives and leave their homes. At first the town had shunned her, but now they considered her the official healer. Carlos claimed he didn't believe either of the stories, but preferred that Rosie keep her distance. Rosie ignored his wishes. Fascinated by both stories, she discovered that Doña Teresa used many of the island's plants for medicinal purposes. The two collaborated, with Rosie scientifically verifying the cures that the townspeople already accepted as truths.

Carlos knew Rosie had stopped seeing her colleagues from the University on a social basis. Occasionally she would consult with department heads, but in the past year or so she had become less open. Carlos had taken this as another personal snub. The more Rosie slipped out of society's view and his grasp, the more Carlos resented Rosie's friendship with Doña Teresa. Her loyalty should be to him, not to an old woman, even if his associates secretly believed in the power of spirits. They appreciated a dedicated wife and a family. As he pulled up to Doña Teresa's house, Carlos pushed aside his resentment. He wanted Rosie to be here. It would mean that everything was okay.

Butterflies fluttered inside him. It was as if he were approaching a haunted house. In all the years Carlos had lived on the island, he had never actually been to Doña Teresa's house. When he was younger, his parents had forbidden it. Even his daring friends stayed away. They said there was too much power coming from the house. When Doña Teresa took Jesus in after his parents' death, the house became even more of a mystery. Jesus never invited people over. At first his friends were curious, but after their questions went unanswered they told stories instead. As time went on Jesus became devoted to Doña Teresa, her work with plants, and less open to his friends.

Carlos' mouth felt like paste. His emotions caught in his throat and his lips puckered with judgement. All the islanders called Doña Teresa, Abuelita, but his parents had always insisted on him calling her the more formal name. They had created a distance of superiority. Abuelita was everyone's grandmother, but not his. He had never questioned his parents' decision until this moment. He had assumed it was only based on their social standing. The unspoken rules of social status were rules that he had followed his entire life. Carlos closed his eyes, seeing Jesus and himself as children.

They were playing in the sugarcane fields, when he heard his mother call. "Carlos, *ven aca*, come home now. Stop playing with your imaginary friend, you have to come in for dinner."

Often Carlos ignored her calls when he was playing with Jesus, the only *amigo* who didn't make fun of him for his imaginary friend. One day the sugarcane field caught fire. His mother and father came running, knowing on Sundays no one would be harvesting.

Carlos had tried to explain to his parents what had happened, but they hadn't believed him. "It was an accident. My friend didn't mean to do it."

"Which friend is that, Carlos? We know that Jesus comes to these fields. He did it, didn't he?"

Carlos had only shaken his head no. He couldn't admit that his imaginary friend had started the fire, because it would mean that *he* had really lit the match. After that day, Jesus never came back to play. He only came to work.

Carlos opened his eyes. He could see now that Jesus had not closed himself off from his friends. Wrongly accused, he had protected himself. Unspoken rules stacked themselves high, creating a wall of isolation. It was Carlos who was quarantined, not Jesus. Carlos had been feeling that separation all day, first from Rosie, then Don Rafael, and now Pide. Oddly enough he even felt it from his *pana,* Pedro.

Carlos stared down on Doña Teresa's property. Situated slightly uphill, one looked down on a wall of greenery. Graceful fronds of ferns obscured the house. Carlos felt a breeze as their whirling leaves swayed with the wind. Their fluctuation made each leaf stand out. Usually indifferent to plants, Carlos noted their delicacy as contrasted with the hairy broad trunks from which they sprouted. Giant tree ferns lined Doña Teresa's land. Their profile formed an imposing defense. They stood as guards over the mossy green carpet. Paths had been created with slats of bamboo, so that as one walked, the moss covering remained untouched. The three separate bamboo paths all led to a walled trellis. Carlos took the path closest to where he had parked the truck. Arriving at the wall, Carlos saw that the trellis, which was covered with meandering vines, oleander, ferns, and orchids, hid the metal *rejas* which barred him from entrance. Futilely, Carlos searched for a way to open the metal gate. He spotted what he thought was a handle and reached his hand through the trellis. Immediately he pulled his hand back. "Shit! These vines have thorns." In pain, Carlos headed back to the truck. Blood trickled down his arm and onto the green moss carpet. As he walked he noticed other dark red droppings. Apparently he wasn't the only one not welcomed.

Although it was warm out, his hands became clammy, and the hair on his arm began to slowly rise. Up until this moment he truly believed that the happenings of the last two days had been isolated incidents. Mistakes easily explained, easily fixed. The thorns had only scratched his arm, but their meaning penetrated and burst the images he had of everyone he thought he knew. Suddenly remembering Pide, Carlos ran the rest of hundred yards to the truck.

La Fatinga was empty. Carlos stared at the passenger's seat. With Pide's disappearance all that remained was the *santo* Don Rafael had given him. The eyes of the woman carved so meticulously, haunted Carlos. The easy expression of joy was that of Rosie's, wide pupils filled with life. It was Rosie, when she was open and dedicated to him. He missed that Rosie. Carlos averted his own eyes as the stares of the *santo* pierced his heart. Rosie had failed to give him the joy of a family. Looking into Rosie's eyes now, he would only see his own emptiness. He turned his back to the truck and faced Doña Teresa's property. Carlos searched the periphery of the greenery.

The giant tree ferns drew his eyes across the center of the property. It was an illusion of force, just as the bamboo pathways were. The paths drew the unknowing towards a promise of entrance that didn't exist.

Slowly scanning, Carlos spotted a darker green color along the trellis, off to the side, outside of the triangular points of the pathways. He felt the spring of the moss under his feet, as he crossed the carpet. Each footprint bounced back, disappearing as he progressed toward the green hole. Carlos slid his body through the narrow passage he found. His first sight was that of Pide busily gathering plants into a burlap bag.

Pide didn't look up. He continued to gather plants. Carlos strode in front of him, blocking his way. The two faced off. With no more than a grunt as an acknowledgement, Pide handed him another burlap bag.

"Your friends have broken in again. Abuelita would never have left these vines lying on the ground. Most of the curing houses are empty, but we can salvage these plants."

Carlos studied Pide's face. He held the lines from his jaw to his mouth taught, keeping words and thoughts inside. Pide's eyes, now clear, lacked any light. Knowing it would be useless to badger Pide with more questions, Carlos stuffed the vines into the bag.

He was amazed at the world within Doña Teresa's compound. Her home was surrounded by various outbuildings. Carlos counted nine. They were small wood structures with slatted walls. Each slat acted as a ventilator, opening and closing to let in more or less air. Strips of tin from a discarded roof, lay in front of them; raised off the ground by concrete blocks. One strip held leaves and peelings from plants. Another contained stems cut on the diagonal. Most of the tin beds held dark red roots. Doña Teresa's sun-drying technique was simple. Carlos assumed these plants had been left because they were not fully dry. He noticed four other curing houses that still held plants. These had been left alone. Only some of the plants had been tampered with. Curiosity finally got the best of him, but instead of asking Pide, he studied the plant in his hand.

The vines were sticky. It was as if their life juices were seeping into his palm. A strange tingling sensation pulsated in his palm and worked its way to the tips of his fingers and branched out to crawl up his arm. He felt no pain. In fact he sensed only the absence of feeling. His hand and arm seemed detached from the rest of his body. Carlos let his mind travel with the same detachment.

The plant he held, a strong woody vine with soft broad leaves, was commonly found in the hills and deeper into the forest. He'd used them as rope swings when he was a child. Carlos paused at the image of himself as a child. The word "child" kept creeping into his thoughts. Simple images made connections that tied knots in his mind. From thoughts of childhood he'd jump to thoughts of Rosie and the pain at his loss of becoming a father. Holding the vines in his palm, rolling it around, he could feel the unraveling of one knot. Rosie's time passed with Doña Teresa involved this vine. Somehow Roberto and Tomas had twisted themselves into his life, more insidiously than he suspected.

Carlos thought he heard his name being called—an echo and a stretching of his name, "C aa arlos, C aaarlos." It was as if he were in a tunnel, hearing unintelligible words. Straining to make out the sounds, Carlos turned toward the direction of the call. Pide was standing by his side yelling at him. Words streamed together, finally forming a comprehensible sentence.

"Don Carlos, *cuidate*! Be careful with those vines. They contain a sap that quiets the nerve messages. Soon you won't be able to use your hands."

It was true. Carlos' hands were beyond numb. They

were limp and difficult to direct. He had only gathered a handful of vines compared to Pide's full sack. Pide's hands were covered by thick gloves.

As if in apology, Pide lifted his sack in salute. His lips parted showing his broken teeth and what Carols interpreted as a smile. "Strong medicine Abuelita and your Rosie make."

As Pide's words began to blur again, Carlos' mind drifted back to a conversation he had had with Rosie almost a year ago. One night he had come home late from a meeting with the town council to find Rosie lying on the floor dragging her body. Carlos had been disgusted at the sight and had thought she had been drinking. Rosie had said this was her "twilight zone of repose." Carlos frowned at the joke, but Rosie had spoken in earnest. She often claimed her muscles became so relaxed they were almost paralyzed. The signals between her brain and her muscles became fuzzy, sometimes dying. Quickly Rosie had pulled herself up on the couch and tucked her feet under her body. She immediately started reading a book. She held the book close to her face, but Carlos had seen the tears. In a voice that was threatening to crack, she had whispered, "It runs in my family, but I'll find the cure."

"Concentrate, Don Carlos, concentrate. Make your hands work. Don't let them die."

Carlos shook each hand. He watched as his arms flailed, but still he felt nothing. Pide pulled him over to a birdbath and placed his hands in the cool water. He felt the first twitches of life as his hands made hypnotic jerks.

"Pide, what is the name of this vine?"

"Your Rosie calls it *curare*."

"Tell me, Pide, can you die from this medicine?"

Pide took his time in answering. He looked at the sky, the plants, and finally back at Carlos. "Some birds are beautiful to watch, but they eat all the berries from a tree. Bees make the sweetest honey, but their sting can kill. The medicine from this vine is very powerful, but death comes in many forms. The strength of this vine is in its power to heal. Only another man's greed can kill."

Carlos had never heard Pide talk so profoundly. It was suddenly clear to him that Roberto and Tomas were not beautiful birds. They appeared more like vultures coming in for the kill, or perhaps they scavenged off of someone else's greed, leading them to the kill.

Carlos thought of Pedro. He thought of himself. All he wanted was the best for himself and the island. Was that so wrong? His hands tingled, every nerve desperately trying to come back to life. He saw without seeing, his excessive pride; it lay over everything. Deals that would bring money and prestige carried a price. How far did this numbness penetrate. He had blocked the death of Jesus, preferred to see it as a dream. He loved Rosie, but barely understood her. Why, if he were such an important person, did he feel so small?

RIVER OF ANGELS

DON TUTO, ABUELITA, AND MONICA had been moving steadily now for more than an hour. Monica's heart and mind no longer jumped at the sight of shadows, as the shadows had taken over the day. She could discern the leaves and vines that hung from the many trees. Her ears heard beyond the touch of their feet to the music of the katydids, *coquitos,* and the occasional bird. For the most part they moved easily in the dark silence.

Don Tuto had taken her place and carried the stretcher with Abuelita. Carmen remained asleep. Monica had only to walk and think. She found herself listening to her surroundings, with the same attention she had once listened to her old professor. The darkness filled her heart with a sense of mystery and mysticism. Simple wonders she would have missed or ignored, accompanied their procession. Monica smiled to herself. She was getting used to the unexpected, almost welcomed the chance to not be in control.

Yet the very thought of losing complete control sent her heart racing again. She wasn't fool enough to believe that Don Tuto and Abuelita experienced the same sensation. They were in control—knowing the destination, the plants, animals and even the birds that inhabited the forest. Every movement they took showed years of preparation.

At the sound of wings flapping overhead, Don Tuto and Abuelita veered off their path and set the stretcher down. Monica felt the swish of wings close to her head and there deafening noise. Bats swarmed everywhere. They had arrived at the caves.

Monica remained quiet, listening for Don Tuto's and

Abuelita's movements. Hordes of bats obscured all other sounds. She had a moment's panic until she could make out Don Tuto's and Abuelita's forms dragging thickly woven vines over towards Carmen, which they attached to each side of the stretcher. Monica stared at the darkness looking for the entrance to the caves. Not spotting one, she momentarily panicked. To reassure her, Don Tuto placed his hands on her shoulders.

"Be careful where you step. The caves are below us. I'll climb down first and you and Abuelita will ease Carmen down with the pulley. Once I have her situated, you will follow on the cable ladder."

Confused, Monica had expected to walk straight into the caves. She imagined a narrow doorway in the mountainside, something they could easily slip into. The assumption in retrospect had no basis in reality, but spoke to her need for hope and easy answers. Her imagined entrance certainly wouldn't have afforded a secret hiding place. Closing her eyes, Monica reviewed the sensation of walking up a steep incline, down again and then climbing slowly back up. She envisioned the cone-like hills, *mogotes*, that had brought them to this spot.

Buried below them was a black hole, fringed with greenery. The hole, enormous in diameter, had been carved out of a mass of rock, both solid and porous, and had created a spatial vacuum; their promised safe haven. Even though unsure about what lay ahead, Monica did not have time to agree or disagree with Don Tuto. His head disappeared over the black abyss. It seemed an eternity until they felt a tug on the rope, their signal to lead Carmen down.

"*Mi hija*, brace your feet and lean back with the rope. Gravity will do most of the work. We must counter the pull so that we don't topple over the edge. The drop is a long one."

Monica took a wide stance and dug her heels into

the rich earth. Leaning back she took hold of the rope. Abuelita called, "*Ahora*, loosen your grip now. Keep your breath even and let it be the guide."

Monica breathed deeply and with each exhalation the stretcher slowly inched its way down. They continued until they heard the echo of its landing. Monica hesitated for a moment and took one long breath. Courage filled her lungs and she began her descent.

The cable ladder hung along the shaft wall. Moisture from the walls seeped into her hair and clothes. At first the smells were a mixture of earth, water and air. As Monica stepped closer to the bottom, the stench of bat guano filled the space. She felt the heat of the rotting and poisonous gases and gasped for air. Don Tuto was there to hold her and guided her to a section of shelf where less stale air came flowing in from another chamber. Monica waited in the darkness for Abuelita.

The darkness affected her profoundly. Monica felt her breath stop. It caught in her throat, refusing to move. Her eyes were of no use. She listened. She smelled the moisture. The darkness entered her ears and mouth and nose. She felt it in her skin. The bats had quieted down, but she could feel the breeze as their wings brushed by her. Their presence comforted her. This was their home.

Abuelita's feet touched the cave shelf. Her landing created a slight vibration, a rippling that repeated itself over and over. Disoriented, Monica made no move. She waited, trying to relax and breathe normally. Between the echoes Monica heard moaning. It was Carmen. The bats hovered over her stretcher. The moans turned into cries and screams that reverberated against the walls of the cave and penetrated the darkness more dramatically than a beam of light. Monica felt a wave of evil pass through the screams.

The bats had stirred up the air, but edginess echoed back and forth, so that the moans created a current of wicked guttural sounds. Repelled, the bats flew off to some height above where they hung and rested. The cave returned to quiet.

Monica didn't see Don Tuto come up next to her. She felt his warm breath by her ear and immediately felt the rhythm of her breath return. "Don Tuto, was that normal for the bats to hover over Carmen. Is she all right?"

"The bats reacted to sounds we couldn't hear. The sounds disturbed their space. I don't think Carmen ever woke up. The screams you heard came from a darker place than this, somewhere deep inside of her. I don't think she is all right. The bats sensed something wrong, something not visible to us. When we get to the chamber I call 'The Hall of the White Maidens,' we'll wake her and perhaps she'll give us another version of her story. We must be patient. We still have a way to go. Abuelita and I will carry Carmen to the river. You will follow us."

Monica did as she was told. Without light she could not see her way. Her own movements were sporadic. Walking, shuffling her feet to each side, she felt for the width of the cave floor, moving forward, reaching her hands above and around to find the height and distance between the cave walls. Every muscle tightened with anxiety. Abuelita and Don Tuto traveled at an even pace, flowing easily along the uneven shelf floor. Abruptly they stopped. Abuelita whispered, "Stop trying to see. Close your eyes. This is a place where no light has ever existed. No object has ever been seen. No creature has ever gazed at another creature. Eyes have no value here; just use intuition as your guide."

Monica closed her eyes and they moved on. She had been straining to see what didn't exist. The strain behind her eyes eased, but her arms and legs still moved stiffly with pent up tension. The passageway seemed to go on forever with the only disturbance a current of cool air. The breeze stopped as they turned. The passageway narrowed and Monica felt the walls brush against her shoulders, jolting her sense of time and space. Without markers, time held no meaning; hidden in a perpetual state with no beginning or end. In the caves the darkness existed physically.

Monica had no sense of the hour. She couldn't remember the last time she had eaten and the bar where she worked was more a memory than a fact. She wondered what else was hidden, what other darkness lurked inside of herself. She felt alone, knowing that she hadn't notified anyone of her whereabouts. No one knew she was here. She had vanished into a world she couldn't see. Involuntarily she smiled, remembering what people could see of her; only a beautiful body to hide in.

The passage opened and Monica found herself breathing fresh moist air. The sounds of water falling filled her ears. She guessed they were by the river. Moments later, Abuelita called out to her, "*Mi hija*, we are at the *Rio de Los Angeles*, the River of the Angels."

Don Tuto moved off the narrow shelf they had been walking on and lit a lantern. The small light created a glow in the blackness. Gradually Monica's eyes adjusted, first seeing only shadows and finally focusing on forms. Surely, what lay before her eyes had to be an apparition? Nothing Abuelita or Don Tuto could have said would have prepared her for the beauty that surrounded her. Sculptured stalactites decorated the curved ceiling.

Monica felt as if she were in a sanctuary created by the most talented artist. The shapes and textures spoke to her body, which swelled in sensuous anticipation. Monica's face turned red surprised by her own reaction. She placed her hand along the wall, absorbing the smoothness and coolness of each formation. She could not remember when she had last caressed anything or anyone with such awe.

Below them flowed a narrow river. Don Tuto and

Abuelita had already placed Carmen in a small skiff, which Don Tuto pulled out from behind a small dip in the cave wall. Monica slipped on the mud covered floor, sliding down from the cave shelf and into the water, which barely covered her ankles. It was cool and inviting. After splashing herself everywhere, she reluctantly climbed aboard. It was a tight squeeze.

Don Tuto began paddling. With each stroke he seemed to become younger to Monica. Abuelita held the lantern high in the air to guide them. The light fell on Don Tuto, lighting up his face. The deeply imbedded creases seemed to melt away and Monica saw a young man, proud and passionately focused. Don Tuto must have sensed her staring. "These caves are my true home. All that I love is here. *Bien venido*, welcome, I hope you enjoy them as we do."

Monica had hoped he would tell her more. Before she could ask anything, lights distracted her. Lanterns, randomly spaced, hung along the cave walls. The river had changed, widened, and deepened. Merging passageways came from all directions. Monica realized the placement of the lanterns served as lights to guide them. Their glow gave the effect of a warm parlor, inviting the guest to enter.

The river moved faster. Monica first sensed and then heard the roar of water rushing. From the cave wall, water spouted and cascaded down, creating a waterfall of spiraling short, narrow twists. Above the din, Monica thought she heard voices. She nearly fell out of the boat turning her body to listen, but the walls distorted the sound and she could not tell whether she actually heard voices or not. She settled back into the boat. Once past the waterfall, the river narrowed again and silence returned to the cave. Off to her right, Monica saw movement. She thought it was someone walking on a shelf above them, but the lanterns' light created shadows and

Monica didn't trust her vision. Then to her left she heard the pattern of feet stepping lightly along side of them. Monica didn't need to look to know the smell of another person.

"Don Tuto, how many people are here inside the caves? Do they live here?

"How observant you are, Monica. The question needs lots of explaining. For now I will give you simple answers. The number changes daily. Most of the time people come and go. Some are longer residents, depending on their needs. Those walking along the cave shelves are lookouts. Everyone here needs some form of protection. I come here daily, Abuelita less often. Only a very few people in the town know of the existence of this section of the caves."

The next curve of the river brought them to a chamber that reeked of bat guano. Three men with dust masks raked through a deep, rich mound of the dried bat excrement; the remains of thousands of insects piled upon one another. It was the leavings of the entire bat colony and food for creatures Monica couldn't see, the silent ones lurking on the cave floor. Monica felt sick. The smells caused her to gasp. Her breath felt tight within her chest. "How can you make them do this? Don Tuto, are you punishing these people?"

Don Tuto's back stiffened at the accusation. His hand went to his throat and a loud gulping sound followed. He did not turn to speak to Monica. He waved at the three men, who waved back. Moments later they disappeared and three other men came to replace them. They too had masks on. As their skiff passed the chamber, Monica's hair blew in all directions. She felt air circulating above her. The smells seemed to dissipate, and with it her nausea.

They traveled on in silence, passing various small uninhabited chambers. The stagnating air made Monica feel closed in for the first time. Don Tuto turned and nodded to Monica. "To work in *these* chambers would be punishment. There are no vents and little air enters from outside. I know about punishment. My wife Maria died because of these fumes."

Again Monica heard the gulping sounds from Don Tuto. Her own throat felt raw from his attempts to clear his pain. More gently than before she probed, "What was her illness?"

"It was the bat guano that made my precious Maria ill. She had inhaled the dust from their droppings, which contained spores of fungus. We were down here too long without ventilation. The exposure weakened her system, overpowering her lungs. Eventually the sickness moved through her blood system and liver. She had ulcerations on her ears, nose and lips. I unknowingly killed her."

Monica bit her tongue, holding back words, feeling the sting of loss. She had nothing to reply to Don Tuto's confession. She had overstepped her bounds, speaking out, judging, before she thought.

But Don Tuto paused only to smile at her.

"Maria forgave me long ago. The men you watched have all volunteered to make black gold. From the bat guano they take turns sifting through the droppings, until they have a fine powder which is used as fertilizer. The fertilizer is very beneficial to our farmers and we are trying to export it around the world. Your friend Rosie uses the fertilizer on her orchids and she has been very helpful. The men you see working with the bat guano rotate every half-hour so that the fumes do not over power their lungs. They only pass one day a week down here. It is a labor of necessity and perhaps the only way they can provide for their families. Most of the men have been denied jobs for various reasons. Some are uneducated, some too educated. What they have in common is their love of country and family, and the unforgiving habit of questioning society."

Monica listened to Don Tuto in disbelief. She couldn't comprehend what he was telling her. She looked down at Carmen still wrapped in the stretcher. Carmen had not stirred since the bats had flown around her. Maybe Carmen had a place in the caves, but Monica wasn't so sure about herself. "What are you asking of me, Don Tuto?"

Don Tuto began paddling again. Abuelita was smiling and nodding as they glided through the river. The water deepened and the air grew cooler. Monica looked back and only saw darkness. The glow of the lanterns was gone. The only light was ahead. Wrapping her arms around herself, Monica hugged her chest tightly. She felt her heart beating, her nipples stiff with cold, and the soft cushion of her breasts. Abuelita wrapped a shawl around Monica's shoulders, but offered no words of encouragement.

With that simple gesture, Monica chest swelled. She held herself tighter feeling her own strong arms encircling her soft body. Monica had been comforting herself for years. It was a skill learned from childhood. She could see her mother naked in the bathroom after a drinking binge. Her mother would be folded in a corner, with her knees brought up to her chest, arms pressing her body inward. Monica would watch, as her mother would rock herself back and forth. Not knowing what else to do, Monica would wrap a towel around her mother and leave her to her own healing.

Lost in her own thoughts, Monica felt disoriented. The past distracted her, leaving her meandering in dark bathrooms with no particular insight. Momentarily she had lost her cave focus and in that short time the river had changed. Don Tuto was paddling faster and in deep concentration. Abuelita had picked up a paddle and paddled on one side trying to guide the boat against an oncoming swell.

Monica spotted another paddle and mimicked Abuelita's strokes, matching her strength against the surge of the water. Abuelita nodded at Monica. Her lips were moving, but Monica could barely make out what she was saying. The only word she heard was *"la lluvia,"* the rain. A storm above ground created huge flows in the underground streams. With each slice of the paddle Monica's determination increased. The water level rose, pushing the skiff into narrowing passageways. Above her, Monica sensed a swirl of activity. People scurried along unseen paths to avoid the rising water. Don Tuto's back muscles flowed, rippling up and down like the river. His power and control acted as an example that Monica set her mind to pattern. The skiff moved as an entity. All its energy focused on a point around some corner, where something different would occur. They traveled without dissension, accepting what must be done.

Just as suddenly as the water rose, it seemed to even out. Don Tuto placed his paddle on his lap and let the river guide the skiff. Abuelita replaced her paddle for a lantern, holding it close to the waterline. Monica stopped paddling and watched as the path they followed became pencil thin. The walls of the cave converged in a point. She felt them scrape the side of the skiff and rub against her shoulders. The force of the river shot them through the small space and delivered them to a haven.

A wall of about a hundred feet stood beside the river. At the very top Monica spotted a series of lanterns which faintly illuminated the wall. There was a long, level, natural shelf about fifty feet wide. Monica guessed that it was about forty feet above the river, which appeared to have vanished into a shallow pool. Don Tuto tied off the skiff and threw up a set of thick ropes. Immediately hands from above reached for them. Monica stared up at a platform and felt many eyes peering down on her.

First Abuelita ascended the ropes. Once Abuelita

made it to the top, Monica followed. Arms and bodies accompanied the eyes, which quickly came to the edge and helped hoist Carmen up in the stretcher. No one had spoken a word, filling the silence with a sense of order and knowledge. Monica stepped back to get a better view, her legs wobbling beneath her. Except for one wall, lanterns lit the entire chamber. A statue like formation in the shape of three women emerged from the center of the untouched wall. White stalactites dripped down from the ceiling giving the illusion of women nude from the waste upward. Part of the drippings appeared to veil the women's breasts. The feeling was one of sensuality and purity. Monica found herself moving slowly towards the underworld goddesses. An energy force drew her in. As she approached the wall to touch the statues, a hand gently pulled her back and moved her own hand away.

"This is the Hall of the White Maidens. Not everyone feels their energy. You must be one of the gifted."

Monica didn't know what to respond. The woman who stood before her was small in stature. She seemed young, but Monica couldn't be sure. She held a small baby in a sling and smiled openly. No one else had come over to speak to Monica; instead, they attended to Carmen and conferred with Abuelita. Monica felt the strain of the last two days. Energy quickly evaporated. Her unsteady legs began to buckle underneath her. She reached out to steady herself and the small woman leaned forward catching her arm and side, breaking her fall. Together they walked to the far side of the chamber, where Monica eased herself onto a wooden bench.

"I didn't mean to be rude. Thanks for your help. I am suddenly so tired and disoriented. My name is Monica. Who are you?"

"They call me *Jovencita*, the young one, but my real name is Carmela. This is my son; he is four months old. His name is Dominique Jesus Guadeloupe."

Monica stared at the baby in Carmela's arms. The baby was tiny, almost scrawny. All that peaked out from the sling wrapped around Carmela's shoulder was a nest of black curls and two round eyes framed by dark brows. Amassed with wrinkles, Dominique's face and eyes spoke of the wisdom of an old man. He was silent, watching, taking in the movements and words of those surrounding him.

Monica smiled back at Carmela, "That's a long name for such a little boy. You must have big plans for him."

Carmela's own smile vanished. Her eyes moved away from Monica's face and she looked down at the cave floor. It was then that Monica realized that Carmela was only a child herself. Judging from her slight build, lack of hips, and the smallness of the nursing breasts, she couldn't be more than fifteen years old. Monica watched as Carmela brought Dominique closer into her hips. The sling enclosed him in a warm cocoon, but Carmela encircled him with her arms—arms that reached around the baby and back around Carmela. The two were inseparable. It appeared to Monica that Carmela's embrace was also meant to hold herself together. She seemed to cling to Dominique's small life, pressing him into her heart, scared to let go for fear they both would fall.

Carmela raised her head up slowly and continued until her chin was higher than her nose. It was a gesture of defiance, done to mask moist eyes that held tears not ready to be shed. Monica felt her own tears come as she watched Carmela focus and stare so directly that the emotions evaporated, leaving Carmela with eyes hardened with purpose. Eyes that dared Monica to care, pleaded with her to understand, and challenged any judgment. Monica's heart began to race. Her breath caught first in her chest and then in her throat. No words came as she felt the guilt run through her blood.

Instead of seeing Carmela, Monica suddenly saw her

own sister. Monica had finally escaped her home when her sister was twelve years old. That was four years ago. Her mother never wrote, but her sister would write cheerful letters about school and the prizes she had won at art shows. Looking at Carmela's brave stance, Monica realized now that they were all lies. Just as Carmela fiercely protected Dominique, her sister had taken to protecting Monica. Monica thought that by sending money, providing the economic base for her sister, she'd been the protector. Who embraced her sister now that she was gone? Who gave her love when her mother was making love with a stranger or with the bottle? Where was her sister's refuge?

Dominique began to fuss. Carmela softened her stance as she began to sway back and forth. Not only did the baby quiet down, but Carmela's eyes brightened. Monica witnessed the joy they exchanged in a synchronization of movement and thought. Carmela's lips turned upward in happiness, feeling love. She cooed the baby's name over and over. "Dominique Jesus Guadeloupe, Dominique, Jesus, Guadeloupe, *mi amor, mi amor.*"

Carmela whispered to Monica, "Someday soon my son and I will be leaving here. I know he will have a good life; a life better than my own. Don Tuto, Jesus, and Abuelita have helped me so much. They say I can't stay here long because of the fumes, but there is another island not far from here where I will be safe and can raise Dominique."

At the mentioning of Jesus' name, Monica became alert. She hadn't thought of him since two nights before at the bar. She'd cursed him then with his drunken macho behavior. Carmen had indicated that he had not hurt her, but Monica was not convinced of any story, especially since she now heard only gratitude in Carmela's voice when she spoke Jesus' name. Jesus' double image puzzled her. Monica realized from the affectionate way Carmela paused when speaking about Jesus that her son was partly named for him. Monica didn't dare ask why.

Almost simultaneously with thoughts of the previous night, Monica heard the moans of Carmen. The cries surrounded her. Eerie moans bounced behind Monica and above her. This time Carmen was wide-awake. Her eyes were open, but whatever she was experiencing was a waking nightmare. Monica kept her distance. The other women hummed while Abuelita held Carmen's hands. Monica counted four women in all. Each appeared relaxed, but focused. One massaged Carmen's feet, another stroked her forehead and, the other two women stood behind Abuelita waiting for directions. The vines that had held Carmen to the stretcher had been removed and blankets had been placed on top to maintain her warmth.

Carmela watched the scene and slowly inched toward Monica. She pulled Dominique in closer to her hip as she searched the cave walls, looking all around. Monica followed her movements, feeling her unease. Although Carmela clung to Monica's side, she too started to hum. The song they were humming had no words, but each of the women took different parts as if they were singing a round; altos, sopranos, baritones, joining to create one voice. The women's voices filled the chamber creating a blend of music that resonated in waves. The richness of their harmony penetrated her being. With each ripple, the moans lessened, until Carmen fell silent.

Gradually the women helped Carmen sit up. They whispered and Carmen listened. From where she stood, Monica couldn't hear their conversation. She walked over slowly, not sure of how she felt. The eerie, animal-like moans and Carmela's apparent unease had unsettled Monica. Carmen's eyes no longer held fear, but looked like those of a cat ready to pounce, sharp and calculating. This was not something Monica had noticed before.

Carmen had always seemed fragile. Monica had

watched out for her, making sure that she worked the easy clients. Carmen's eyes appeared too alert for someone who had been so ill. A knot began to form in Monica's stomach. The knot inside tightened and twisted as Monica stepped into Carmen's vision. Carmen stared at her and then beyond.

Monica turned to follow Carmen's gaze. She saw Carmela scrambling up one of the makeshift ladders set against the cave's wall. Guadeloupe was crying as Carmela struggled with his weight. Instead of comforting the baby, Carmela nudged herself up onto another shelf and instantly disappeared behind a column.

Turning back, Monica noticed the clenched hands and tight set to Carmen's face. And then the smile, the soft innocent smiles that Carmen gave to her friends. The sudden switch in demeanor sent chills through Monica. Only with the return of Carmen's childlike smile, could Monica relax.

Immediately the knot in her stomach began to dissolve. Carmen's sweetness always had that effect on her. Words came rushing out, "*Oye,* Carmen, I'm here. You must be so confused. I've been so worried about you. You've been sleeping for so long. And your sleep has been filled with bad dreams. *Me alegra,* I am so happy to see you sit up and be so alert."

"Oh, Monica, *mi hermana,* my sister, thank God you are here with me. My head and my body hurt so much. Everything hurts. Tell me why we are in this horrid place."

Monica sat down beside Carmen and gave her a hug. She felt her friend's body against her own. Surprisingly it was stiff and guarded. Monica expected to have her melt into her arms and see tears. Instead she felt passive arms and shoulders held precisely in place. Monica gave out hugs sparingly, a precautionary result of her job, and expected a sense of gratitude or appreciation when she did extend herself. This hug felt worse than empty. Even Carmen's heartbeat felt hard and too calm. Her own pulse raced. Looking into Carmen's eyes she said, "We are here for your safety, Carmen. The men from your home village are searching for you."

Carmen looked down at the floor. "How do you know this place is safe? Who are all these people and where precisely are we?"

Monica didn't have any of the answers, and up until that moment had not been in a hurry to find out. Taken by surprise by all the events, she had given up her usual tight control. It had been enough to know that Rosie and her friends would help Carmen. She trusted their judgement, their kindness. Carmen seemed ungrateful and Monica was at odds. Had she misjudged the situation and her response? For the first time she wondered if Carmen had played the role of victim.

The women had stopped humming and Abuelita had let go of Carmen's hands. Abuelita's face had lost its softness and the smile lines around her eyes and lips tightened so that Abuelita's ears moved back and her nostrils began to flare. Monica, noting Abuelita's anger, felt even more ambivalent. Abuelita stood up and walked in front of Monica. She stared at Carmen, walked back and forth, and just stared. The chamber fell silent. It reminded Monica of playing chess with her father when she was younger. Just before he'd checkmate, there would be a silence, a calculating silence that would determine the fate of the game. But this was real. Abuelita stopped and smiled, "*Digame*, tell me, Carmen who here don't you trust?"

All eyes were on Carmen. The four women who had been attending Carmen stood with their hands folded across their chests, their legs spread apart. Besides Abuelita and Monica, no one else remained in the chamber. Carmela and Don Tuto both had disappeared.

Carmen scanned the room. She looked at each of the women, and then stared at the vacant upper shelf. Although Monica couldn't see anyone she sensed they were being watched, just as they had been watched as they traveled along the river. For some reason Carmela had disappeared in a hurry. They really weren't alone. Anyone could be monitoring the scene and reappear at anytime.

Carmen turned her eyes back at Abuelita. She shrugged her shoulders and shook her head. "I really don't trust people I can't see. Too much has happened and I am tired. I don't want to be hunted or questioned. I am grateful for your help, but I don't want to be here. I'm sure the men from my village have given up on me, and I have matters that I must attend to."

Monica listened and strained to hear the truth in Carmen's words. The new edge to her voice, even the words she used, made Monica question their past relationship. She took both of Carmen's hands in her own. They were cold, clammy and callused.

"*Contra*, Carmen. Everything you are doing confuses me. I don't know what to believe. Even holding your hands makes me wonder. The palms are rough and torn. They feel like the hands of a farmer. Who are you kidding? I'm a prostitute just like you. You know the first rule is to keep the merchandise unblemished."

"What I do on my own time is my own business. I don't have to explain anything to you."

"But you are wrong about that. How many times have I had to save your ass? In our business no one protects us but ourselves. And now everyone here has risked their life for you. You owe it to me and them to tell the truth."

"What truth do you want to hear, Monica? That you are the hero? That I depend on you? I don't think you have stomach enough to hear my truth."

"The truth I do know is that you are not physically

or mentally ready to go anywhere. You need to rest. *Tu sabes*, you know that I'm you friend."

At first, Carmen didn't respond. She squinted at the dimness and searched around the chamber room, debating her options. Apparently satisfied, she cleared her throat. "Monica you are my friend. You have watched out for me, and I am tired. I have no place to go. What was I thinking? You are right, as always. I should rest. This place is as good as anywhere. Abuelita what is your plan?"

Somewhat annoyed, Monica dropped Carmen's hands. "What did you mean by saying I'm right as always? I can't tell if you really agree with me, or if you are resigned to your fate. Your voice is so flat that I feel ashamed for even questioning your motives. Maybe I am expecting too much too soon, or too little too late."

Carmen bent her head downward, clasped and re-clasped her hands. "I need to know what Abuelita's plans are."

Abuelita responded slowly to Carmen's question. She seemed reluctant to answer. Their relationship had changed. Neither trusted the other. Monica no longer felt comfortable. The silence she had experienced with Don Tuto and Abuelita on the journey into the caves had been one of sharing. Now the air was thick with distrust. In the semi-darkness the smile lines, which had fascinated Monica when she first met Abuelita, had vanished, leaving her skin pulled tightly across her cheekbones and her lips sealed in a frown. She no longer appeared like a kindly old healer. She seemed more like a fighter. Monica didn't know what the battle was about. Only that the lines had been drawn.

Abuelita's voice was almost a whisper when she finally answered Carmen. "These caves are good for hiding. But you can't hide forever, Carmen. Your nightmares and screams are with you wherever you go. Perhaps you'd like to leave them within these damp walls and let the river carry them away. I suspect you have told us only one version of truth, and that the other version is giving you bad dreams."

The torches along the upper shelf suddenly went out. A cool breeze swept by Monica's face. The air had moved in quickly from above. Monica couldn't visualize a shaft, but the air felt fresh and cool. Only a fierce storm above ground could cause this much of a breeze down below. The very thought of a storm caused the hair on Monica's arms to rise. The sudden and complete removal of light left Monica feeling less safe.

Even in the caves, the rain reached down stirring her own nightmares about her mother and sister. She remembered one night when it had been raining. The wind blew her window open and the rain and wind howled inside. Her journals had gone flying, and she tried to catch them as the wind blew them out the window. Monica ran out in the rain only to find her mother dressed in a negligee crying and screaming. A man backed out of their driveway. Monica asked no questions, walked back inside, and closed her bedroom window. Her windows always remained locked after that night so as to keep the wind and rain and the sounds of her mother screaming firmly outside.

Helpers within minutes re-lit the torchlights. Monica secretly wished that Carmen had vanished in the darkness, disappeared like an apparition. Her ambivalent behavior weighed on Monica's conscience. She understood less and felt more out of control. But Carmen hadn't moved. The only reaction Carmen had was to again scan the upper shelf. Monica also looked along the perimeter of the walls. She detected the shadows of the guards and felt their footsteps. She wondered where Carmela had disappeared to, and if she was with Don Tuto. Monica wanted to be with them and leave Carmen. But if she left Carmen she would feel guilty. The same guilt she felt for abandoning her mother and sister. Yet Carmen didn't seem to need her anymore, making Monica feel useless and also guilty for having abandoned her to Jesus the previous evening.

Abuelita stepped forward and approached Carmen, "Enough talking for now. The truth can wait. It is time for all of us to eat."

Two of the other women stood up. The placed their hands under Carmen's armpits and gently lifted her to her feet. Carmen stumbled at first, but then slowly walked around the chamber. She made her way to the unlit wall where the white maidens' statue took center stage. Carmen made no move to touch the stalactites. Her mouth was a straight line. She stared for a long while, her lips circled downward. The statue seemed to repel her and she turned away. Monica watched as Carmen's legs began to buckle. Abuelita was immediately by her side.

"Carmen you need our help even if you don't like it. I'll help you walk to the other chamber where our meal has been prepared."

"Do it quickly. I don't want to be in here anymore. This placed is haunted."

They walked in a procession along a narrow passage, barely wide enough for two people. They were walking single file except for Carmen. Abuelita was supporting her. Monica pushed ahead of the other women to be nearer Carmen. "I can do that Abuelita. Carmen I can help you."

Monica reached out for Carmen's arm. Carmen stumbled and moved away. "I don't need your help. I'll be fine."

They walked on in silence after that.

Less well lit, the hallways and the cave became depressingly dismal. Monica counted the lanterns on the wall. She could walk twenty-five strides before another lantern appeared. The spacing was almost exact. She had fallen behind everyone else but felt the presence of something behind her. She turned back to look, there was nothing but blackness. All the lanterns had been put out. Monica walked another twenty-five strides to the next light. She turned again. The last lantern darkened. Monica could almost make out the form of the person putting out the lights. She had to know who it was. Nothing in the caves was left to chance. In a whisper Monica called out, "*Oye,* listen to me. Who are you? Why are you turning out the lanterns? I won't tell."

After walking past the next lantern, Monica turned again. This time she stepped back and pressed herself into the cool cave wall. She listened for footsteps, but heard nothing. As she started to walk again an arm reached to hold her back. "*Callate,* keep quiet. You must stay with the others for everyone's good. I turn out the lights so no one gets lost or strays. It is my job to keep you safe."

Before Monica could respond the figure had vanished. Stumbling in the darkness Monica had to hurry to catch the group. She shuddered with a sense of *déjà vu.* Something familiar nagged at her. It was silly, but she recognized the smell of the voice. Monica never forgot the smell of her clients. It was what left the largest impression on her. The talking, the foreplay, the actual act of intercourse, she erased immediately from her mind. But the smell of a client stuck. The perfumes could never hide the tensions, anger, and fear. She had just smelled untainted sweat... the sweat from an individual who was clean, not perverted by liquor. She smelled purpose. Obviously his purpose centered on keeping her with the group. Monica couldn't break away if she wanted to. She'd be lost in a maze of blindness.

Smells of food came wafting through the corridor. They all quickened their pace. The aromas led them into a large chamber filled with light. Monica's hand immediately hooded her eyes. Blinking she tried to focus. Don Tuto sat with another man at a long table laid out with gourds filled with rice, *platanos*, and *gondules*. The two men stood as the women filed in, taking their places at the table. Don Tuto smiled with his arm around the other man. "Miguel and I welcome you to our table of plenty. *Buen provecho*, eat."

Food equated to peace. The tension slowly dissipated as the women took their places. They all looked to Miguel, "Let's have a toast, to the prettiest sights I've seen in a long while."

Monica had to laugh with everyone else because of the comical face Miguel made. He had raised one eyebrow and tipped his soiled Panama hat in a gesture of appreciation. Even Monica could feel his honest gratitude for all women. She blushed, feeling like a royal guest. One of the women gave him a kiss on the cheek and another shouted from across the table. "I'm next. You've been in the fresh air and look so handsome."

"What, you only like me when I have been above. You are all so narrow-minded, I might have to find myself a new hiding place."

The friendly batter continued while they were eating. They were almost done when Miguel stood up and went around to each of the women. Monica could tell that this was a ritual. These women were hungry for information. Miguel whispered into each of their ears. Their responses varied. Two of the women laughed and the other two cried.

Eavesdropping is a skill that Monica had mastered at an early age. People misunderstood her aptitude, thinking she gained insights from her intelligence alone, but she picked up interesting facts from conversations never meant for her ears.

The women who were laughing and embracing

repeated over and over, *"Me alegra,* I'm so happy. She has finally found work and is settled. She has found work." The two who were crying mumbled, *"Adios mio,* oh my God, may they rest in peace." Freedom and death delivered in a whisper.

Monica realized that Carmen and she were not the only ones with stories. It took her by surprise when Miguel walked up to her. He smiled slowly, letting the lips tease her heart, parting slowly, moistening, closing, and finally opening wide. He came close and brushed his cheek next to hers. His warm breath tickled at her ear. Monica could barely make out his murmurs. *"Mirate,* watch her. Your friend is trouble."

Monica had no response. During the meal she had watched Carmen. Carmen had eaten an entire plate of food and had laughed at the antics of Miguel. Had Miguel said Carmen was in trouble, or *is* trouble? It was obvious Carmen was in trouble. Monica forced herself to laugh. She didn't know if this was a game or a command. She felt herself drawn by his insistent whisper. Trying to keep in role, and happy to do it, she pulled Miguel to her face and kissed him fully on the lips. She whispered, "You have my attention."

Everyone had gotten up and Carmen walked slowly with Abuelita. Peace appeared to have continued after their meal. Monica tried to relax but she watched them, following her own curiosity, she told herself, not Miguel's murmurs. The group looked at a table of wooden statues. Monica stood next to Carmen and admired a wooden statue of a nude Don Quixote, a humorous rendition of the traditional hero. Monica smiled. She knew immediately that it represented Miguel's handiwork. Another statue of the city hall, showed three monkeys sitting on the steps. One had its hands covering his eyes, the other covering his ears and the last his heart. On a table off to the side, Monica noticed Miguel's tools and a statue in the process of being carved. Monica found the scene more gruesome, depicting a *ceiba* tree with a person pushed in between the roots. Carmen spotted it at the same time. She broke away from Abuelita and picked it up and screamed "*Adios mio*, how could you know?"

Miguel took the statue from Carmen's hand. "What do I know, Carmen?"

Carmen's face went white. Her shoulders shook. "I left him there. I ran and left him there."

Don Tuto came up behind Carmen. "Whom did you leave?"

"It's a trick, isn't it? You all know don't you? I am such a fool."

Monica watched as Carmen started to laugh, a delirious cackle that echoed back from the cave's walls. She looked like mad a woman. She walked in circles laughing and then she turned and faced them all. "You all thought he was a bad man. He was a joke. He actually tried to help me. Jesus is dead."

The news left everyone in the caves breathless and silent, suspending grief and disbelief; creating an atmosphere of uncertainty and confusion. Abuelita walked slowly from the back of the room, controlled and purposeful. Monica pictured her in Rosie's kitchen when she first sensed that Jesus was in trouble. Abuelita's original concern for Carmen had been genuine, but the fear of old lies being exposed and the fear of losing Jesus had also brought them to the caves. Abuelita stood in front of Carmen. She held her bent back erect and said in a firm calm voice, "Now, Carmen, would be the appropriate time for the truth."

"I don't know what happened. He was drunk, well not really. Men came. Jesus didn't want me. He loved the farm. How did you all find out? He isn't a real man, not like the others. I can't be here any longer."

Carmen babbled for awhile longer not making sense,

going in circles. As Monica listened she became distracted by a familiar smell. It was the same scent she smelled as they walked through the cave's corridors to eat. Without a voice Monica couldn't be sure, but her memory brought her back to the day she had arrived on the island.

She had been walking down the street, sizing up the town. Two drunken men had approached her. Monica could have handled the situation, but a tough, handsome fellow had shooed the drunks away. Monica had been annoyed at the loss of business and barely thanked him. She remembered the incident because that evening the same man came into the bar where she had procured work. She had expected him to make a pass and want her services and when he ignored her, she actually became slightly offended with hurt pride.

As a prostitute Monica never let her emotions show. The rejection stung less and less over the years. The man was no longer a stranger. He would come in nightly drinking way too much. Monica tried to make sense of what she was remembering. Never having slept with him, Monica was unsure of the scent. But something made Monica believe that the person she smelled was Jesus. She was sure he was in the caves, just as Carmen was declaring him dead. The Jesus from years ago, before he was tainted with alcohol and anger.

LIES OR OMISSIONS

GRADUALLY ROSIE'S EYES ADJUSTED to the black of the tunnel. A small amount of light seeped through the cracks turning the darkness a hazy gray. As long as it was daylight outside Rosie wouldn't have to take out the flashlight she had stowed in her backpack. She tried to move fast, not liking the cobwebs overhead or the cockroaches that brushed against her sandals as they climbed along the canal's floors and walls. Her feet betrayed her once again. The numbness had returned so that each step felt like she was dragging a heavy chain and lead ball.

Her body always reacted first to stress and now the full weight of what she had witnessed at the farm, sunk in. Carlos had betrayed her, gone behind her back to sell sand from their property, and more frightening and disturbing was the implication of drug smuggling, a drug she and Abuelita had developed. She had abandoned her bike at the farm, and ducked into the canal to warn Don Tuto and Abuelita at the caves, but she hadn't abandoned her dread, which continued to numb her heart.

Twenty-five tunnels made up the old canal system. Rosie did not know them all. The most familiar tunnels led to Abuelita's house, her property, and the caves. Don Tuto, Don Rafael, Abuelita, Jesus, and her crazy friend, Pide acted as the official runners, and they considered these pathways emergency routes. They traveled in the darkness of night guiding the town's *undesirables* to safety.

Undesirable held many connotations. The town feared people that didn't conform. Jesus called them misfits. Women—once your neighbors and friends—who became mothers out of wedlock no longer fit neatly into the system. Their voices called out in pain and the town's people shunned and ostracized them for having brought shame to their families. Political dissidents openly disapproved the system and their punishment left spaces and unanswered questions. And some like Abuelita, Don Tuto, and Jesus knew too much of the system. They knew about the bribes, the double accounting system and the more far-reaching abuses to the people, but were wise enough to find ways to work around the injustices. They continued on above ground, making themselves fit into the daily routine by behaving according to the rules.

Rosie lifted her feet up; right, left, right, left, stepping purposefully, connecting them with her body and within the confined black space. The effort drained her of energy. Fearing failure in her unassigned job as a *runner,* she fought the physically disassociated sensation. Never intending to be a *misfit* or *undesirable*, she shook her head trying to shake herself free of self-pity. Unwittingly she had made herself just that, undesirable. Carlos no longer looked to her as a woman. She felt sexless, not having felt the warmth of his body next to her own for longer than she cared to remember. She never intended to fall out of his favor.

Tears slid along her cheeks as she continued walking in the dark tunnel. She found herself weeping; not wanting to be in the canal. The darkness seeped into her skin and bones, making her own thoughts morose. She remembered their last attempt at making love. Carlos had come home late from a meeting. She couldn't remember if it had been with the local politicians deciding on zoning or if he had been drinking with his buddies.

He came in without a word, but his alcohol-laden breath nudged Rosie from her sleep. Almost immediately she heard his inevitable snoring. Refusing to feel rejected Rosie had cocooned her body against Carlos' curled body. She positioned her belly under his buttocks creating a cupped affect, which also left a place for her head to rest along his back. Her simple act of affection backfired. Carlos had pushed her away as he had done so many other evenings. Not knowing what else to do Rosie had pushed back with her words, "Carlos, stop punishing me for the loss of our baby."

His reply had been worse than his physical rejection. "Your passion has gone to your head. All you think of is the land and plants. You have left me nothing."

In the morning when she woke, Carlos had already gone. He'd left no note.

Rosie's foot hit the side of the canal. She cried out in pain. She couldn't help herself. She yelled the word "undesirable" over and over. The walls of the canal echoed back, "undesirable, undesirable." She didn't fit into Carlos' life as snuggly as he wanted. Carlos feared her unpredictable will, her refusal to conform. Carlos didn't know of her desire to fit, that her body didn't listen to rules. Rosie's cry turned to laughter verging on hysteria. Feeling desperate, she had to keep moving. Perhaps they should call the misfits, *desperados,* the hopeless.

Her own hysteria aroused her from her gloomy thoughts. Rosie had to warn Abuelita and Don Tuto about the skiff and barge she'd seen by their farm. Somehow she fit into their life and goals more easily than into Carlos'. Rosie stumbled forward and slipped, falling down. Mud and debris made the canal floor slippery. Just like the life she lived. Life shouldn't be this complicated.

Despite her hurry Rosie again thought of her father. He came to her in waves, usually at her worst moments. She wondered if he had felt displaced living between the jungle and their home. In part she blamed him for complicating her life. It was his discovery of the *liana* vine that had put them all in danger, and his obsessive nature for the truth Rosie suspected killed him and her mother.

All these years the stigma of suicide had haunted her, but before now she had never thought of murder. Murder made more sense than suicide, but if that were true, the danger still existed.

Rosie tried to quicken her pace but her legs failed. She tried to conjure an image of Jesus. She thought she had seen his shadow along the beach. Hopefully he lingered near by. Rosie suddenly wanted out. She didn't want to save anyone. She only wanted to see the assured face of Jesus.

Rosie smiled, remembering some of the conversations she had had with Jesus. At first they would just work side by side with an invisible line dividing them. Jesus had kept his head down, weeding or digging. Sometimes he would look out at the land and stare. Once, Rosie had asked him questions concerning the health of the soil. Not one to use many words, Jesus had bent down on his knees and started rummaging in the dirt. Rosie stood transfixed as this large man delicately lifted worms out of the earth. His large hands, roasted a deep brown on the outside, placed the worms gently down. Rosie stared at his palms, marred with deep black lines. "The earth looks good. There are ten earthworms in this small section. See the ones with the red stripes it means that the soil is rich with nutrients."

Rosie had nodded, pleased. She had tried to scoop some earthworms out herself. Jesus had chuckled. "Don't laugh Jesus. Tell me how you can find them and I can't."

Jesus had smiled back, his smooth caramel skin glistening and his eyes winking. "They can tell you are coming Rosie. They feel your vibrations and run. You must be quicker."

Another time Rosie had been looking at the rice fields worried at what she saw. The plants weren't thriving. It had been five months since they had planted them and the weeds had overtaken the fields. Each day Jesus had been coming to weed, but when the coconut season began he'd been called off to help Carlos. Rosie, frustrated, had passed each afternoon weeding. One time, as the sun set, Jesus had appeared.

Rosie had been squatting over the rice plants tugging at the weeds. She had tucked her left hand under her armpit, and the right hand pulled the invasive plants in short swift strokes. Occasionally she'd shake her right hand in the air, flexing her dirty fingers. She'd resumed her steady process until her hand hadn't been able to do more. Then Rosie had switched the positions of her hands, so that the right hand was tucked under her armpit and the left hand continued the weeding. Eventually piles of weeds had accumulated on both sides of Rosie and her shirt displayed criss-crossed lines of dirt. Most of her clothes had this same streaked pattern; evidence of her numbness, the loss of feeling. Rosie had been ashamed. Her shirts decorated like a banner, reminded her of too many loses. Tired and feeling hopeless, Rosie had wiped her tears of frustration from her face leaving brown stains.

Jesus' voice had startled her. He seemed to have appeared out of nowhere yet he had been breathless, as if he had been running. "*Hola*, Rosie. I came as soon as the coconuts were all loaded. It looks like the weeds have gotten the better of you."

"I'll be okay. The weeds are taking over the rice paddies and my hands are playing their games again. I'm afraid we'll lose this year's crop. Even the worms are unhappy. I've only found a few amongst my weeding and this one is split in half."

Rosie had turned her head away when she had felt Jesus' eyes studying her face. He had taken a pure white handkerchief from his back pocket and guided her head back to face him. Softly Jesus had cupped her chin in his hand and wiped her right cheek. Rosie had smelled his sweat and had felt the gentle strokes of caring. Embarrassed, she had grabbed the handkerchief from his hands and rapidly wiped the other side of her face. The awkwardness would almost have been funny, except for the fact that Rosie had found herself continuously touching her right cheek and clinging to the handkerchief.

The awkward moment disappeared as Jesus had taken the halves of the earthworm from Rosie's hand and bored a small hole in the ground and covered it. "Worms have five hearts. This worm won't die. It will try to regenerate its head and tail. But you may be right about the rice. The mongooses hide in the weeds, and eat the rice plants that have survived the strangling weeds."

They had worked weeding the hopeless plot until dark. Rosie had watched Jesus leave and stayed awhile thinking about having five hearts. Holding the handkerchief up to the stars, Rosie watched the night breeze ripple through the white cloth. She had thought about letting it go, but instead she had tucked it inside the top of her soiled shirt.

Rosie searched the canal walls for clues of how far she had come. Decorated with mud streaks and tear stains, her appearance reflected her state of mind. Lacking a handkerchief, she took the edge of her skirt and wiped her face. Nothing registered her progress. Breathing slowly, she forced herself to regain her composure, inhaling the stagnant smell of the tunnel and exhaling stale, insipid thoughts. More tormenting memories came as well.

The conversation most painful to remember happened the very next time Rosie had seen Jesus. He had been re-digging irrigation ditches destroyed by the mongoose, when Rosie confronted him. She hadn't even said hello. "Jesus, I've always thought you such a kind man. How could you play with the lives of so many women and father their children? You're being irresponsible."

Jesus hadn't looked up and had continued digging dirt. When he had completed two more rows, he put down his shovel and had faced Rosie. *"Buenos dias*, Rosie. But from the tone of your voice it is not a good day. Is it?"

Rosie noted his formal voice, so unlike the friendly soft whispers she was accustomed to hear. She had crossed the line with Jesus. "I was being rude. I apologize. My only excuse is that Carlos and I fought this morning. He says I look like a peasant, that I work too hard on the farm. He thinks I should go back to teaching at the University. I am used to him criticizing me for my appearance, but he warned me against you. Carlos told me you were a ladies man and had fathered at least ten children."

At this Jesus had cocked his head and stared at Rosie almost mockingly. "You of all people shouldn't be fooled by appearances. I am the father of every child who needs me. I do love women, but I have no children of my own."

Confused, Rosie had stood back and studied Jesus as if he were a stranger. She could see why women found him attractive. His broad shoulders framed his muscular body and strong arms extended down to his large agile hands. She had witnessed their nimbleness time and time again in the plantings. Never concerned with his looks, he had always been generous towards her, always giving, never asking for anything in return. His physique looked comfortable; not made to be anything but strong and soft. Strong shoulders, arms, and legs, with a soft center.

The wrinkles around his smile and the creases around his large twinkling blue eyes had caught Rosie's breath. He would be easy to love, but Rosie couldn't be sure. He could be playing her for the fool.

Rosie had countered his statement. "Jesus you are

talking riddles. If you aren't the father why does the town believe it? Is everyone wrong?"

At this Jesus had shook his head and the smile had slowly disappeared from his face. "I love women way too much to hurt them. I am a man of many hearts. I'll become the father of their children when there is no father. It makes life easier."

Rosie kept hearing in the back of her mind Carlos' chiding. She had held back on believing Jesus. Carlos and the town gossip had told her otherwise. There might have been some truth to what Jesus had said, but she wondered why he felt compelled to make life easier for these women? Without thinking Rosie had taken the shovel from Jesus and started digging the next ditch. Jesus had stared at her while she dug, which had made her feel self-conscious but somehow authentic, capable. Jesus' approval for some reason mattered.

But the anger she had felt from Carlos and the fear that he might be correct made Rosie bluntly ask Jesus about his own parents. "I heard that your parents were killed because you got the neighbor girl pregnant."

Jesus' eyes never left hers. His face muscles had twitched slightly until he finally spoke. "You are partially right. My parents were killed." Rosie still could hear the pain Jesus held in his voice. He had grabbed the shovel from her hands and had dug furiously as he continued to talk. "They were killed defending my honor. I had told them that the girl's father had raped her and I was only her friend. It didn't matter because the uncles came to kill me. But I was out the night my house burned. I made a promise to my dead parents and myself that I would never let this happen again to anyone I knew."

Rosie dragged her legs along as she reflected on Jesus' words. Jesus would never have told her the truth if he hadn't thought she would believe him. It took many months before he told her about the caves. Rosie thought about the worms buried in the ground, worms with five hearts. Carlos had been wrong last night with his evaluation. She did know who Jesus was.

Rosie suddenly felt very tired. She wanted to sit down. Her legs could hardly move. Her sandals sloshed through pools of water, from what Rosie believed to be a bursting of the rain clouds she had seen before she entered the tunnel. In a fit of desperation she took off her sandals and let her feet touch the water. Relief came almost immediately, first to her toes, then to the soles of her feet. She didn't really want to walk without shoes, but she had no choice if she expected to arrive at the caves.

Rosie walked faster. Her dress hem absorbed water as the rain overflow from Lake Guajataca spilled into the canals. She wished she had worn shorts. But once again she had tried to honor Carlos in his need for appropriateness. Looking around Rosie tried again to get a sense of how far she had traveled. The smells of the canal had changed. The last time she had actually been down in the tunnel Jesus had told her that after you traveled to the older section the smell would change to that of rust. Rosie smelled rust and decay. She knew that she must find the correct channel or else she'd get lost in the maze.

Luck accompanied her. Rosie spotted one of the two inner tubes used to float down the canal when the water rose high enough to make walking difficult. Two years ago, during Hurricane Hugo, Rosie and Jesus had been forced to float down the canal. Carlos had been away on a business trip in Central America. The winds ripped through the house and Rosie had feared for her orchids and the pigeons. Outside, she tried to board up the pigeon coup when Jesus had arrived. Together they nailed down both houses.

Crazed, Jesus talked incessantly about the people

caught in the caves. Without thinking Rosie had offered to help. All night they traveled through the canals, ferrying young mothers, political dissidents, and so called criminals into safe homes. The river that flowed through the caves became violent with a hydraulic force too powerful to navigate safely. Don Tuto and Abuelita had to literally lift each person on a pulley to ground level as none of the chambers were sufficiently safe from the outpouring of water. Rosie had collapsed at Abuelita's house, not returning home for another two nights.

When she did arrive home it was to Carlos' wrath. He had been gone three weeks and hadn't phoned but twice. Rosie had tried to get word to him but each time she had called he had been out late with clients. She had wanted to discuss the irrigation system and her success with a new orchid. And more important, she had been feeling lonely and was worried about her health. When she finally spoke with Carlos, he had talked about the investors he had met. She had kept silent about her health. Apparently Carlos' trip had been cut short by the hurricane.

Rosie found herself the direct target of his anger and frustration. She had walked into the dark, damp house, looking a mess, just as Carlos flung open the door. She had automatically raised her arms to embrace him but had stepped back after she had seen his face.

Those two nights seemed so long ago. Rosie realized that the present rainstorm would soon blow over. The hurricane season had already ended and the island's weather behaved less erratically. She wanted Jesus to appear though, like he had done that night. Rosie scanned the walls and floor, searching for a sign; some indicator to help break through her reluctance to float down the canal. Once she committed, she wouldn't be able to turn back.

Rosie stood there feeling like a coward. Logic told

her to go forward but her intuition drew her out. With guilt she turned herself around and headed back to the opening. The light had all but disappeared. Despite the darkness she traveled quickly, drawn to the entrance by an unknown force. Even her feet felt the power. The cockroaches scattered and the cobwebs melted away as she trekked through the tunnel. In less than thirty minutes she found herself back at the entrance to the canals.

Before stepping out onto the path, Rosie listened. The wind came off the ocean whispering the word *patience*. Or at least Rosie thought she heard the word patience float by. It could have been her own thoughts replaying Jesus' words. He had said to be patient with Carlos the two nights she had remained at his and Abuelita's house. He had said it again just last week.

With frayed nerves, Rosie didn't know how much longer she could suppress her frustrations. Loneliness, anger, and fear tangled around her heart. Skillful at healing others, she had closed the doors to her own heart. The art of healing came from caring, but she cared from a distance as the pain became unbearable up close. Rosie wished she could regenerate new arms and legs that functioned normally, able to feel and touch, but she wasn't sure that this would open her heart.

This time Rosie heard for sure the word patience. She heard three voices raised and hushed and raised. She sensed an argument, one she wanted to hear.

Quietly Rosie walked further down the path and slipped behind some brush. She held her breath when she spotted Pedro. Even with the late afternoon sun fading, she noted his red face and raised arms. He leaned up against Carlos' truck, but Carlos was nowhere in sight. In his place, Pedro fought with two strangers. Rosie stared at the truck. In her mind she reviewed the time she last saw it speeding away from the farm, not far from this spot, the ruined dunes, the dust, the destruction.

Perhaps Carlos had never been down here. Maybe it had been Pedro driving the truck. Rosie felt relief until she wondered why Pedro had Carlos' truck.

Pedro pleaded, "You must leave now. Carlos is gone and so is Jesus. I don't know what any of this means, but I know that no good can come of this now."

Rosie couldn't see the other men without revealing her position, but she heard their response.

"Money is always good. That has not changed. Let's get these vines on the ship. We were lucky to find so many already cured at your Abuelita's house. It's a shame we didn't find our friend Carmen."

Pedro shook his head. "You shouldn't waste your time on her. She caused all these problems."

Rosie stood frozen in place, but her mind bounced back and forth trying to piece their conversation together with what she knew. Her hands and feet started to tremble. Pedro had been with Carlos when he brought Carmen to her house. Rosie racked her brains trying to remember the scene. Pedro had waited impatiently outside while Carlos had talked with her. Rosie knew Carlos had come to her house out of compassion, trying to help. He wouldn't have brought strangers to her if he knew of any danger. Pedro—his best friend, his *pana*—had intentionally lied. Rosie bristled at the betrayal.

Abuelita had been right to take Monica and Carmen to the caves. These people had a vendetta against Carmen and nowhere above ground afforded her safety. The complexities made Rosie dizzy. She knew that Monica and Carmen were in good hands, but Rosie sensed something else amiss.

The obvious connection between these men, Pedro, the stealing of sand, and the barge anchored off shore only made sense if the talk about land development and condominiums was a pretext, diverting Carlos and herself from something bigger. Carlos' and Jesus' disappearances worried her.

Rosie knew Jesus' patterns. He should be wandering around the property securing the crops and coconut shipments. Rosie faltered thinking of Carlos' habits since his whereabouts had become a mystery to her. Before Rosie could connect any other thoughts her left leg collapsed from under her. She tried to remain upright and quiet, but her skirt caught on a branch. The three men turned to face the rustling noise.

Angry at her clumsiness, Rosie managed to lift herself up without revealing her hiding space. She harnessed her fury, breathing deeply, envisioning once again her father as he centered himself. Rosie was the only one who knew his secret as she had watched him many times summon strength when there was none. Her father faltered mostly at night after a strenuous day at the lab. She had noticed after his last trip to the jungle, that his concentration had dwindled and that his legs and hands often didn't respond as well. Rosie flashed back to the night of the car accident. Had her father been able to focus and control his body or had someone or something distracted him. She would never know.

Rosie steadied herself on a branch. As she touched the branch, Rosie also reached for her father. She imagined the limbs as his hands bringing warmth and energy. Her own heart pounded. She worried what Pedro and the others could see. But by the time Pedro's gaze found the position of the noise, Rosie blended in with the trees. Balancing most of her weight on her right foot, Rosie dug her roots into the ground below her, lifted her head up, sending her hopes up toward the sky. Camouflaged by her very stillness, her pose fooled even herself.

Hidden from view, Rosie ignored everyone but Pedro. She focused her eyes on him alone. Under her steady gaze, Pedro's face turned ashen, sweat began to drip down his forehead. He turned his head away, but Rosie's glare brought his attention back. The sun's rays seemed to be coming from Rosie's eyes. Pedro burned inside. Rosie beamed fire and Pedro stumbled back into his comrades. Rosie knew she had no real power, except that which Pedro allowed her. His own fears reflected back to haunt him. Rosie's deep concentration had to be selfless to be effective. Her thoughts had to come from her core, taking all that was important to her and funneling it outward.

A cloud moved in over them and the heat subsided. Rosie sensed her energy waning and had to concentrate to remain standing. Pedro shivered and inched his way further back. "I told you. We must run from here. I feel him. I feel Jesus and he will have no mercy."

Still hidden partially by the brush, Rosie felt Jesus' presence as well but said nothing. Pedro's friends looked at Pedro strangely and abruptly pushed him aside. "You fool, Jesus is gone. You are too superstitious. We have wasted too much time and now we have a visitor coming out of the bushes."

Rosie fixed her gaze beyond the men and watched as a familiar shaped shadow passed along the hillside, and with it a sense of relief washed over her. Slowly she walked somewhat unsteadily out from behind green leaves towards her intruders and extended her hand. "*Hola,* you must be Roberto and Tomas, the business men my husband, Carlos, has been working with."

Rosie, ignoring her disheveled appearance, smiled her most charming smile, the one she had used at the University when the administrators had tried to cut her budget. "I didn't expect you. Carlos said nothing of a personal visit. I must chide him when he returns. He has had much on his mind these last few weeks."

Roberto and Tomas brushed dirt off their hands and returned the handshake. Rosie couldn't tell if she was convincing in her role, but she hoped that whatever

Latino upbringing they had would force them to be gracious, anything to give her more time to get information or to make her escape.

"I was just searching for my dog, Nada. She is usually here with Jesus. Have you seen them?"

Not waiting for an answer Rosie started calling, "Nada, Naaada, Naaada, *donde estas?*" From the corner of her eye she glanced at her intruders. They stood upright, at attention. They looked silly. The stiff unbelieving look disappeared quickly when they spotted Nada running down the hillside towards them.

Rosie almost chuckled at their ghostlike faces. Nada ran into Rosie's arms and she gave Nada a hug and ruffled her hair. Nada turned away from Rosie and snarled at Roberto and Tomas. The dog growled at their feet when Rosie called, "Nada, *ven aca,* come. Stand by me."

"I don't know what has gotten into her. Pedro don't look so frighten, Nada wouldn't hurt anyone unless they would try to hurt me."

Pedro cleared his throat and stepped a little further back. "Rosie I know how loyal Nada is to you. Maybe I should take my friends and make an appointment with you and Carlos later."

Rosie couldn't make up her mind what would be best. The appearance of Nada certainly had taken the men by surprise. But Rosie had no more surprises. With her energy depleting quickly she had to find out more about Carlos and Jesus. Taking a risk, Rosie tried to glean more information from Pedro. "That might be a good idea Pedro. I take it you will be seeing Carlos soon, since you have his truck. Will you give him a message for me?"

The color had returned to Pedro's face although it was now redder than normal. Pedro turned back to look at Roberto and Tomas, waiting for some cue. They too had regained their composure although they paced in circles, looking first at Nada and then out at the ocean. Rosie could tell that they felt penned in.

Tomas found his voice first. "Pedro, we have intruded too much already, let's go."

Relieved Pedro breathed a deep sigh. "Rosie what message would you like me to give my friend Carlos?"

The word friend echoed in Rosie's ear and almost made her falter. How she hated lies.

"Tell him that I will sign the papers for the condominiums to be built. We can work out the details later. I trust his judgement. Also tell him that I am to meet Jesus, as I have seen him on the hillside."

With that said, Rosie nodded an *adios* to the group, and trudged up the hillside with Nada. She knew of a good vantage point a little higher up where she could rest and watch. She walked slowly; feeling six eyes following her every move.

Everyone's thoughts centered on Carmen, harmful thoughts and healing thoughts. Rosie no longer knew what her own thoughts should be.

MEANDERING

CARLOS FOUND HIMSELF BACK IN *La Fatinga*. His hands were still shaking with twinges of returning life. Pide was seated on the driver's side. Carlos had put up little resistance. With his hands and arms recovering from the poisonous prick of the vine, Carlos could barely open the car's door.

"Tell me again Pide why we are going back to *La Finca*. I feel like we are going in circles... chasing our tails."

Pide didn't even bother to turn his head toward him as he answered. "Your business friends are *perros*. Dogs that need a lesson. We must make them put their tails between their legs. I've seen them at the farm many times before. They will ship Abuelita's vines somewhere else to make money."

Carlos glared at Pide. "How many times have you seen Roberto and Tomas there? Why didn't anyone tell me about this?

"What can anyone tell you Don Carlos? You travel a lot. Your job is to make money. How do we know what you see or turn your back to? Who do you listen to?"

Carlos had had enough of Pide. This nightmare was more than he could take. *La Fatinga* continued on its uneven but steady pace up the hillside. The sun was low in the sky, hidden partially by clouds. The air smelled damp and earthy, like it always did after a quick shower. Normally he'd be ending his day at the bar, reviewing with friends the day's occurrences. Carlos shook his head. The nightmare really had begun the night before, at the bar with Carmen. Everything had appeared so innocent. Carmen leaving with Jesus.

"*Digame* Pide. Tell me what you think of these events. I can't figure out why Jesus would take Carmen up to *La Finca.*"

Carlos wasn't sure if Pide had heard him. The drone of the overworked motor of *La Fatinga*, was the only sound present. They had meandered around two hillsides, before Pide replied. "What makes you think he took her there?"

Of course Pide always stated the obvious. His words were like darts attacking an assumption. "Be clear with me, Pide. My mind is still in a fog. I can't tell if the poison from the vines has affected my brain as well as my hands. Are you saying that Jesus didn't take Carmen to the farm?"

"I am saying nothing. Think it through. Where does your distrust toward Jesus come from?"

Carlos knew Jesus loved the farm, that he worked it for years, and felt a part of its vitality. More important, Jesus was the guardian. Even if Carlos could magnify Jesus' shortcomings—alcohol, women, his temper—none of these would get in the way of protecting the farm. Jesus' loyalties extended deeply and Carlos knew Jesus would never let Rosie down. In a way, Carlos now associated the farm more with Rosie and Jesus, than with himself. He distrusted Jesus' intentions toward Rosie, but never the farm.

The heat in *La Fatinga* became unbearable. Awkwardly Carlos fumbled with the window's handle trying to let some fresh air in. His hand and arm still tingled. These sensations tugged at his brain as well. Abuelita and Rosie had been secretly working with potent vines, trying to find cures for a disease he refused to believe or notice that Rosie suffered from. His head ached, straining to get beyond his own hurt. He stretched his arm out of the car window, trying to let the warm air filter through his fingers. Everything seemed just beyond his grasp. For a brief moment the twinges sparked his memory.

The image of Jesus and Carmen from the bar burned through the convoluted twists of events. He had been talking with Pedro not really paying attention to anyone in the bar, but he did remember seeing Jesus talking with Monica and then Carmen. At first he had appeared demanding and macho calling out to Monica, but he calmed down once he was with Carmen. Carlos vaguely remembered looking over and seeing Jesus' eyes locked with Carmen's. He had his arm around her until Carmen had jumped up abruptly and stormed out the door. Jesus had quickly followed.

Carlos turned away from the window and brought his hand back inside. The tingling sensation was completely gone and his confusion was slowly disappearing. Excitedly he faced Pide, "Maybe Carmen forced Jesus to go to the farm. I don't think any of this was an accident."

They were just passing the last bend in the road before they turned into the farm. "Pide, *por favor,* please slow down. This is the spot where Sanchez's sugarcane truck was turned over last night, by Roberto and Tomas' rental car. Don't you think it is odd that the entire road had been swept clean?"

Pide smiled crookedly. "There might have been an accident, but who would know now? Are you sure, Don Carlos that an accident happened?"

The vein on Carlos' forehead began pulsating. "You don't believe me?"

Pide stared ahead, blaring his horn as they came around a sharp bend in the road. It was a local custom to warn other drivers where there were blind spots. But Pide wasn't just tapping on his horn; he was holding it down as if it were a siren. "Calm down, Don Carlos. Of course I believe you. But look below us. Your truck is speeding up the road and if we aren't careful, we might wind up on the side of the road just like Sanchez's truck."

"Shouldn't we surprise them Pide and approach them quietly?"

Pide turned to look at Carlos. His grin stretched from his eyes to his chin. The look was humorous and conniving. "I am warning them. *La Fatinga* is so noisy with its sputtering motor and screeching brakes; they would hear us in a few minutes anyway. This way they will have time to prepare their lies if they decide not to kill us."

Carlos frowned at Pide's logic. "Contra, this car is worthless. Why don't you just pull off the road? Unless you are enjoying this game?"

Abruptly Pide swerved off the road and *La Fatinga* screeched to a halt beside two coconut trees. He got out, slamming the door behind him and walked away from the car.

Carlos slumped down in his seat and placed his hands over his eyes. His fingers and palms felt foreign to him. The touch was light and soft against his face, which was covered with stubble. Unwelcomed whiskers bristling against unmanly hands. What he needed was the strength of callused, working hands, capable of action. He felt weak and insubstantial, incapable of making a difference. Slowly, Carlos sat up and walked over to Pide. "Why would they want to kill us Pide? You are talking about people I know."

"People you know are robbing you and the island. They know you better than you know yourself. If you don't believe their lies, you might find out the truth and try to stop them."

"Stop them from what? All I want is to improve the island, not hurt it. These vines they are stealing, what really does that have to do with me?"

"Suddenly you are blind again. Money is everything to these people. You know about money, don't you? This isn't just a business deal. I have seen them smuggling not only these vines, but the sand from your land as well. They are using you as a front."

Carlos' hands began to shake, but not from the poison. He folded his arms across his chest and then pushed back his hair and paced. "So what I am to say to them? Do you have some sort of a plan."

"You are the gambler Carlos. Remember your college days when you played poker. You don't have to say anything, but use your face wisely. If I remember correctly you only lost once."

"How dare you talk about my past." Carlos felt the veins across his forehead throbbing. Before he realized what he was doing he found his hands wrapped around Pide's neck. Pide's face had turned red before Carlos stopped. For once Pide's smell had saved him. Carlos dropped his hands and backed away. "I didn't know anyone on the island knew about that. I earned back my tuition without my family knowing. I don't want to hear how you knew. Obviously I wasn't that careful."

"Secrets come easy on the island. You should know that. I am like an invisible wall, a wall with ears. No one pays attention to me so I hear common knowledge, which I store. My kind of information is just truer gossip. It is harmless, not like what the government collects. You didn't know that the police have a secret file on you too, Don Carlos? No one on the island is exempt. You have been lucky these years. I am sure that the mail and customs officials if they chose to, could cause you trouble."

Carlos was dumbfounded. Unconsciously he stood taller and drew his shoulders down and back. He lifted his chin slightly and stared down on Pide. Pide looked pathetic. His shorts were old pants, sizes too big for him. Pide had created his own style by chopping off the legs of a pair of pants and leaving strands of thread dangling.

The pants were held up with a twisted vine knotted in front. A shirt hung over his torso like a net. There were more holes than material. Dark hairs and skin protruded, embarrassing Carlos with its intimacy. Spit formed in Carlos' mouth, he swallowed it.

"There is no reason to spy on me. I am a hard working person."

Pide turned his head slightly and spat on the ground before he answered.

"So am I, Don Carlos. Should they spy on me, Abuelita, Rosie, Jesus? Who would be the right person for them to spy on?"

"Okay Pide, I get your point."

"I am not sure that you do, Don Carlos. Watch me for a minute."

Pide took a deep breath and filled his chest. He rolled his shoulders back, mimicking Carlos' stance. Carlos watched, as Pide seemed to grow taller. Pide's facial expression became stern, losing all vacantness. His eyes, dark and menacing, bore into Carlos with an intensity that demanded respect. Carlos found himself actually stepping back. But just as quickly as the transformation had happen, Pide relaxed his stance and shrugged.

"It is all a show isn't it, Pide? Who were you just now? I don't know you anymore."

"I am only me. The same as I have always been. But you, Don Carlos, who are you?"

Carlos found himself staring into Pide's crooked smile. Hatred filled him as well as an insane need to laugh. Once again Pide was disarming him. Logic, reason, salesmanship were weak armor against Pide's truths. Carlo felt the distaste of lies in his mouth, but this time he did not swallow them down. He answered Pide, by spitting on the ground beside him.

With his bare foot, Pide flicked sand over the dribble.

"Secrets are never buried too deep on the island. They

are just brushed under the carpet until they become useful. The *carpetas* pay friends and relatives for secrets. Trust is bought easily. Wipe the worry off your face. Here comes your truck."

It took all Carlos' control not to reveal his indignation and sense of being violated. The sight of his truck and Pedro repelled him. The fact that Roberto and Tomas were with Pedro, cemented his anger. Carlos looked over at Pide, took a deep breath, and willed himself calm.

The three men were staring and trying to look casual. The back of the truck was filled with sealed coconut crates. Pedro was in the driver's seat. Roberto and Tomas stayed inside as Pedro rushed to get out and greet Carlos.

"Carlos, Carlos, *mi pana,* I have looked all over the farm for you. Where did you get to? I was worried and found your business partners to help search. You don't look so good. What happened last night? We couldn't find you or Jesus' body. You must have buried Jesus by yourself to look so bad."

"I went into town when you didn't return, Pedro. Pide was kind enough to bring me back to the farm. I am glad to see you."

Carlos walked up to his truck and opened the door. Roberto and Tomas quickly came out and extended their hands. Without hesitating Carlos nodded his greeting, but kept his hands by his side. From the corner of his eye, Carlos watched Pide move into the background, making himself invisible. Carlos' slight snub of Roberto and Tomas brought fear into Pedro's eyes. Carlos had known him way too long to miss the signs. His pupils were enlarged, darting back and forth, going nowhere. When they were younger, Carlos had called him frog eyes.

Pedro was acting guilty and suspicious. Carlos wasn't sure if Pedro was afraid for Carlos or himself. Pedro's behavior reminded him of when they had raided a roadside cemetery when they were in their teens. Pedro had stolen some of the gifts left at the grave sites. For weeks afterwards, Pedro had nightmares. His parents had been beside themselves with worry, but Pedro wouldn't confess his actions. All he had talked about since that night twenty years ago was the spirits seeking their revenge.

"Whatever made you think I buried Jesus? Are you sure he was ever there, Pedro? I fell asleep waiting for your return and when I woke up he was gone. I thought maybe you and I dreamed the whole thing."

Pedro had no answer. His eyes bulged and then glazed over. He finally closed his lids and his body started to tremble. Roberto and Tomas were better at hiding their thoughts. Their faces remained stoic, but Carlos noticed Tomas place his hand over his left thigh and wince. It was probably where Jesus had wounded him.

Carlos just stood there waiting for their next move. Poker, chess, business they were all games he played well. He was good at waiting and risking. Patience where money was concerned was a virtue that had created much of his success. He was proud of this, but he could feel his heart beating irregularly. The stakes were higher. He felt that if he did anything wrong, he would lose more than he could imagine.

Roberto made the next move. He went over to Pedro and shook him. "Pedro get a hold of yourself. We knew you were upset when you found us. How can we help?"

Roberto's words weren't sinking in. Pedro was lost to his fears of voodoo and spirits and bad omens. He was powerless. Carlos dug his heel into the ground, disgusted by his friend's weakness and his superstitions. "Can you take him home?"

By the look Roberto gave Tomas, Carlos knew that they too were weighing the odds of discovery. The two of them still thought their escapades had gone undiscovered.

Tomas was fidgeting, looking out towards the ocean. The two of them were beginning to posture; straddling their legs wide and placing their hands folded behind them. Together they rocked on their heels, back and forth, taunting their bodies as a challenge. Carlos sensed that they were just as confused about Jesus' disappearance as he was. He wanted them to leave so he could find Rosie to sort out what was happening.

"You can take him home in my truck. Pide is still here and he can give me a ride back later. I really must get home and clean up. I'd go with you, but the truck only holds three people."

As if on cue, Pide started the engine of *La Fatinga*. Carlos began walking over to the old truck, not waiting for a reply. Just as he was getting in Roberto strode over.

"We met your charming wife, down on the beach. She asked us to deliver a message to you."

It was as if Roberto had stepped inside his mind. Were his thoughts that obvious. Although his pulse was throbbing in his ears Carlos forced himself to turn slowly. All he could picture was the chaos Pide and he had found in Rosie's greenhouse. Where was she? He had assumed that Roberto and Tomas had been unsuccessful in finding Rosie and Carmen. What if these bastards were holding her hostage? He could never forgive himself for endangering her. But it wasn't really his fault. If only Rosie would follow the rules. She was always so contrary. Carlos never knew what to expect. How could he protect Rosie, if he couldn't control her?

As casually as he could, with his heart pounding in fear and anger, Carlos spoke. "She must have been taking a stroll. What did she say?'

"Actually she was looking for your dog. She said she'd sign the papers for our deal. All that worry for nothing. She didn't seem upset."

It had to be some sort of a trick. Rosie would never

give in. He knew her. The coconuts and land were more important to her than he was. Hadn't she proven this to him over and over by her obstinate behavior? Even as he stood there sure that these were not Rosie's words, Carlos was hopeful. Maybe it was a signal of change from Rosie.

Carlos simply shrugged at Roberto's observation, "Rosie always surprises me. She's unpredictable. I guess that is good news for you. We'll all have to get together to sign papers later this week."

Roberto offered his hand and Carlos had no choice but to shake it. Pide pushed down on the accelerator and Carlos slammed the door as he got in.

LA PUNTA DE VISTA –
POINT OF VIEW

FROM HER PERCH ROSIE COULD SEE ALL THE WAY out to the island where the military conducted its bombing practice. The barge she had seen earlier was not far from its shores. The ocean was flat, showing no emotions. The waves had died down with the absence of wind, even the sparkle from the sun's reflection was empty. The two small skiffs she had seen taking her stolen coconut crates were either long gone or hidden on the opposite side of the barge.

Rosie only had to turn her body halfway around and she could see down to where she and Pedro had talked. She followed Carlos' truck as it made its way up from the beach and towards the main road. For some reason Pedro, Roberto, and Tomas had stopped along the road. Rosie watched as Pedro got out and rushed over to a parked truck. At first Rosie thought that it was a planned rendezvous until she recognized the car. A momentary smile crossed Rosie's lips when she saw Carlos get out of *La Fatinga*; Carlos with his pride, his need to impress. Well, the sight of Carlos driving in the dilapidated metal shell greatly impressed her.

Rosie could only hear the sound of gentle waves hitting sandy beaches. All conversations were carried out to the water and Rosie found herself watching a silent movie. From what Rosie could see, everyone wanted to be somewhere else. Roberto was shaking Pedro as everyone looked on. She could have predicted that. The poor man was overcome by fear, even seeing Nada had set him off. Rosie suspected his guilt was more a factor than the workings of voodoo. Pedro was too set on the dark side.

Whatever good he held inside was taken over by negative powers. Even she believed in the spiritual side of voodoo. It was closely related to healing.

Nada's paws dug into Rosie's thigh. She had been lying at Rosie's feet, but something made her jump up on all four. After all these years, when unsure of herself, Rosie had learned to rely on Nada. Nada had a dog's sense of rightness, simple and pure. Both paws were now on her thighs and Nada whimpered in her face. It didn't take a shaman to realize that something was wrong.

The air was still warm but with the falling sun, darkness fell on Rosie. Shadows caught between night and day, the twilight of emotions. Rosie could feel the pull of evil. Black magic worked best in shadows with dubious forms. There was no mystery why healing was always associated with white light.

Rosie paid attention to Nada and followed her lead, turning her back on the men below. At least she knew where Carlos was. Lately she had felt that she and Carlos were walking in shadows. The pull of black magic seemed to have inhabited her island. Pedro was under its spell, but she sensed that his voodoo was more imagined than real. She worried more about Carlos with his haunting need for economic gain and rising social status.

Their relationship had changed. Carlos had once looked upon her with love. They were bound by what Rosie believed to be a passion for the island and intensity for life. As she walked up the hillside, following Nada, Rosie wondered if she was different in Carlos' eyes. If anything Rosie loved the island more than ever. She craved touching the soil, growing new species of plants. It seemed the more she loved all that surrounded her, the less beautiful she became to Carlos. She didn't doubt Carlos' love for the island but her innocence was gone. The island must produce, she must produce, or they were not useful.

Rosie felt the encroaching feelings of distrust. They gnawed at her insides and violated her sense of well being. The sight of Carlos in *La Fatinga* meant that Don Rafael had judged Carlos to be safe. The oddness of that thought struck Rosie hard. Safe enough to use the truck, safe enough to talk to, but was he safe enough to love? Rosie's insides churned, as her own spirit battled. She felt impure, a hypocrite. How could she expect Carlos to be different when she herself looked elsewhere for connections?

To combat the evil of voodoo or black magic, a true healer had to be empty of the desire for power or need of greed. They worked their spells as empty vessels. The spirits of either evil or good passed through them and were reflected back on the patient or victim. If a shaman were to appear at this very moment, what would be mirrored back to her? She could only imagine her own reflection, sandwiched between Jesus and Carlos.

By now Rosie guessed where Nada was heading. She was going to hers and Carlos' favorite spot on the farm. When they had first bought the farm they had often come to sit there at the end of a day, dreaming of a family and a future.

At the sight of the *ceiba* trees, Nada whimpered. She walked around and around the wide trunks sniffing and whimpering. Rosie bent down and patted Nada's head and held her tight. There was a slight trembling in Nada's legs and Rosie could feel her fear. Rosie kept Nada close to her side until she found the space between the trees where she could sit. Rosie nestled herself amongst the roots of two old *ceiba* trees. The large canopy of leaves felt like a shroud, protecting her from the sun and rain. She placed her hands on the skin of the trunk, letting its coolness filter onto her palms. She often came here so she could feel the solidness of the tree's life. The two trunks massive bases were intertwined and offered a place to hide and listen to one's own heartbeat. Rosie slowly emptied her mind so the tree could perform its magic.

A surge of pain passed through her body. Tears came from a well of sorrow Rosie didn't know existed. The skin on her arms felt like that of the chicken, *piel de gallino,* bumpy with the hairs standing straight up. Her body became rigid. She hugged the *ceiba's* trunk and found her arms quivering like Nada's legs. The peace she sought was shattered by the sensation of violence. Rosie knew without knowing. She could feel Jesus all around her. And despite these frenzied sensations, Rosie forced herself to be calm. She uncurled her body from the trees' trunks and slowly began to walk around, searching.

By now Nada was pawing at the dirt. Her tail was down and she was moving in a wide circle sniffing, pawing, and sniffing. Rosie let her do the work. Instead of looking at the ground Rosie focused on the tree. A dark red stain was smeared along the bark. It was dry and odd looking. While Nada circled around, she studied the design. Crude as the spattering was, Rosie could see the outline of the cave. Its meaning was unclear, but Rosie knew she must go to the caves. Her tranquil spot had been violated and Jesus had made a sign. Rosie didn't know if it was a warning or a more pointed directive.

She thought about Carmen and the violence surrounding her. She wondered whose blood was smeared on the *ceiba* tree. Jesus' absence bothered her. It was so unlike him to disappear when anyone was in need. And as much as she hated to admit it to herself, she was in need. Not like Carmen or the other women who they helped, but she felt her needs of passion and nurturing rising to the surface of her face. Her eyes brimmed with emotion.

Nada was perfectly still, her tail pointing straight up. Rosie bent down to where Nada was pointing. Tears distorting her vision, blurred her eyes, but her fingers fumbled through the dirt. A small prick to her finger let Rosie find the needle. It was one just like she used on the pigeons, one similar to the one found in Nada's neck. Rosie waited for a loss of sensation, but her finger felt normal. There was no poison left.

Abruptly Nada started barking again. Rosie froze, scared to see who was behind her. Nada's barking subsided and all she heard was the swishing of a tail and Carlos' murmuring, "Good dog, Nada, you found her for me." Rosie turned to face Carlos. Seeing him there was almost too much. The tears were coming down full force as she walked towards him. Nada jumped playfully between them. Carlos reached out to embrace her. Rosie stood still, holding back words and letting his familiar arms encircle her.

"Rosie I have been worried about you. Your place is in a shambles. I've been looking for you everywhere. What have you been up to?"

Despite his arms holding her in a tight embrace, she could sense his disapproval. She wasn't where he expected. He had been inconvenienced and worse yet she had left her home a mess. Rosie closed her eyes and let Nada's joyful nudging calm her.

Before releasing Rosie, Carlos pulled her in tighter, pressing her face into his chest. Rosie felt like she was suffocating with her nose smashed and her lungs constricted. She ignored the discomfort. What stunned her more was Carlos' smell.

In all the years they had been together she had walked behind a trail of 'Old Spice'. Immaculate, orderly, and tidy were all words she associated with her husband. When they had lived together, she would often wake to a whiff of cologne as Carlos left in the morning or his stale smell when he returned at night.

Now she smelled sweat, grime and fear. As she pushed away from Carlos' arms and tucked her head to avoid his gentle kiss to the top of her head; Rosie realized she had never truly smelled Carlos.

"From the looks of you, a lot has happened since you dropped off Carmen. You look like you haven't slept since then. I can't remember ever having seen your *Guayabara* looking wrinkled."

Carlos stood facing Rosie with his hands dangling by his side. His face was shadowed by whiskers, which grew unevenly around his lips. He looked soured and irritable. Rosie almost felt pity, until he looked at her and gave her his familiar stony stare.

"Jesus is dead. I found him here the night I left Carmen with you. He was stuffed in between the trunks of the *ceiba*. I tried to watch over him and sent Pedro for help. I am so sorry Rosie. I must have fallen asleep and when I woke his body was gone."

The hardness behind Carlos' stare crumbled and Rosie ran to his side as he cried. His entire chest was heaving, shaking with emotion. "I am so sorry, Rosie, so sorry." They dropped to the ground and rocking back and forth, Rosie cradled Carlos until his breathing became normal.

"Shhh, Carlos, it will be okay. I am here now, safe and sound. You don't have to worry about *me* now, do you?"

"Didn't you hear me Rosie, Jesus is dead. You can't just sit there. Where is your compassion? You are so distant. React, please, react. This is a nightmare and I don't want to be dreaming this alone."

Rosie lifted Carlos' head off her lap and stood up. She closed her eyes and sighed. She opened her lips as if to speak, but instead she pursed them, holding back her thoughts.

Carlos clenched his fists above his head and began pacing. "Rosie, Jesus died because of me and my crazy schemes to make money. Everything is *not* okay. I thought I had lost you when I went searching and your greenhouse had been ransacked. Don't you see I have ruined everything?"

Rosie froze. The news of Jesus was no news. She had already figured out that there had been a fight. She suspected that Jesus was still alive and the fact that Carlos couldn't find him actually made her feel secure. But the news of the destruction of her greenhouse left her feeling fragmented. All her confidence was shattered.

Her face was red and her tongue caught in her mouth trying to break the seal on her lips. Spit formed on the sides as she blurted out her anger. "I trusted you. What have you done? Your friends from New York are behind this aren't they? Carlos, you with honor, when will you tell me the truth?"

"I am trying to tell it to you now. But you aren't listening."

"What did they take from the greenhouse?"

Carlos looked into Rosie's eyes. "They were looking for Carmen, but when they didn't find her, they ripped apart your orchids."

Rosie nodded her head up and down, exhaled and in the smallest of whispers she said, "Is that all?"

"No, the glass was shattered."

"Did they find the starts?"

"What starts?"

Rosie felt her stomach knotting up. "It isn't a hobby Carlos. Each orchid takes years to propagate. I was working on hybrids."

"You don't have to lecture me, Rosie. I care about Jesus' death and you are only worried about your orchids. Let me speak."

"Go ahead."

Carlos took a deep breath and moved in closer. His breath came out slowly as his eyes went from Rosie's head to her feet. Rosie could feel every tangle, every hair out of place. She dug her feet in and widened her stance.

She was still barefoot from her walk in the tunnels and she wiggled each toe until she could actually feel the dirt beneath her. Rosie felt Carlos' hands on her waist. With a tug, he pulled the back hem of her dress out from the front of her belt. The modified shorts she had made fell away and she stood in her proper dress. The cloth was silky and brushed against her ankles, sending chills up her legs. Involuntarily, Rosie flinched, and drew her feet together. Carlos removed his hands and stepped back.

"Pide and I found a note with the pigeons warning against strangers. I guess the warning came too late. We went to Abuelita's house looking for you. Pide seemed to know exactly what to do. Rosie I almost died thinking they had hurt you. Whatever you and Abuelita were working on they stole."

Rosie turned her head away. She couldn't look at Carlos. Somehow even with all his gentleness Carlos made her feel wrong. She didn't want to fight their old battles. Rosie shook her head trying to get rid of her anger. "I tried to tell you about our experiments, but you were busy with finding new markets. It doesn't matter. I am glad you know. The strangers I assume are your business friends Roberto and Tomas. I caught them stealing sand from our beaches and they have a barge out on the ocean, probably filled with Abuelita's vines."

"Rosie, you have to believe me I had no idea what they were up to. I have always accused you of being naive. I've been a blind fool. Do you trust me enough to explain what is going on?"

Rosie stood still thinking of the late nights spent alone, dinners missed, fights about the land. She felt a black hole where her heart should be. No lightness or clarity, just the murky feelings of lost love.

"I know Carlos, even with all our problems; I never truly believed that you wanted to harm the farm. We are wasting time. We have to warn Don Tuto, Abuelita, and the others. I have a feeling that Carmen when she is healed will bring more problems."

"Where are you hiding them Rosie? Pide has told me a lot about your vines and the experiments. He had to after my hands went numb. But he refuses to tell me anything else. You have been keeping so much from me.

"I had to Carlos. I am not even sure you are ready to hear about your island now."

"Nothing will surprise me after today. Pide has shown me more than I have seen in years. I had no idea that he was so close to you. I don't remember you ever talking about him."

"Pide is like a shadow. He is always there. When times are harder for his friends he is bigger than life. He seems to disappear when all is bright. I depend on him."

Carlos' face went pale, and he bent his head. "You haven't depended on me for a long time now."

Rosie let his words hang in the air as she busied herself with the buckles of her sandals. "We shouldn't linger any longer. I don't think your friends will let us get far if they really want to find Carmen. You better stop by the house and get a different pair of shoes. We'll be doing lots of walking."

"You are acting just like Pide. Ordering me around with no explanation."

"Did you have something to say to me, Don Carlos? I heard my name mentioned."

Carlos turned to find Pide standing behind him, patting Nada. Nada hadn't even barked as Pide approached. Rosie was grinning and ran to give Pide a warm embrace. It was the first time he had seen her smile since before they had separated.

"Rosie is right, you are like a shadow. What is that in your hands?"

"A pair of boots. You'll need them to walk through the jungle."

Carlos kept his mouth shut as they walked. Rosie and Pide surrounded him with an impenetrable silence. The two of them didn't need to converse. Each anticipated the other's moves. Rosie led the way and he was stuck in between with Pide closing in on him from behind. He felt like a prisoner. Without words to distract him, Carlos studied Rosie's back.

Despite his disapproval of shorts, Rosie had tucked her dress back up between her legs and hooked the hem into her belt. Her pace was fast, but uneven. Her legs were strong and shapely. Veins protruded from her calves, which were tight with muscles and little skin. Her thighs curved above her knees with a slight indentation, small dimples. Carlos' thought about those dimples. He had no recollection of having kissed them or of having traced the dip. His groin felt thick and heavy and he cursed under his breath. How many times had he told her to cover up? She should listen to him.

Rosie was oblivious to the world and him. Even now she was studying the plants and searching on the ground. He had no idea what she saw. It was hot out and his feet hurt. The boots Pide had brought him made blisters, but he knew better than to complain.

He could hardly see with the sun's retreat and the thick canopy of plants. The darkness became rooted inside and he wanted to run. Shadows hovered over him and he felt watched. Neither Rosie nor Pide faltered, but he could sense their apprehension. They were looking for some sign. Rosie cocked her head towards every noise.

Rosie's uneven pace became hypnotic. She would take a long stride with her right foot and the left would follow somewhat stiffly and slowly. Her hips compensated with a sway and Carlos kept his eyes focused on them. Even in the failing light, the oscillation drew him in. He remembered making love, but he couldn't put a face to the woman. It had been months ago on one of his trips away from the island. Dinner meetings with associates always ended with drinking and dancing. This woman had been with them the entire week and one night she returned with him to his hotel. She was shy and hardly talked. All Carlos remembered now was her hips and how they swayed. He had come from behind and she continued her swaying until he had collapsed on top of her. He was drunk and talked about the island, Rosie, and her plants and his frustrations. In the morning when he had awakened she was gone. It was what he had wanted.

Carlos stumbled and fell, barely catching himself with his hands as he hit the ground. Furious, he reached out for help. From behind him, Pide took both of his arms and lifted him up, supporting Carlos' back against his chest. Carlos felt the full length of Pide's body. His face reddened and he pulled away. "*Contra* Pide let me go."

At the sound of Carlos' voice, Rosie finally turned and stared. She noted the flush on Carlos' face, the look of embarrassment, the look of being caught at something naughty. Rosie tilted her head from side to side. "Shh, I am listening."

All Carlos heard was the call of some bird, "Whit, Whit, Whit." And then Rosie and Pide both brought their hands up to their mouths and in unison whistled a returning call. "Whit, Whit, Whit."

"Who are you two signaling to? Who is out there?"

Neither Pide nor Rosie answered. But the birdcall repeated itself. "Whit, Whit, Whit." It seemed closer. Rosie smiled at Pide. "We might as well make ourselves comfortable, while we wait." As an after thought she put her hands on Carlos' shoulders and tried to move his body towards the ground. "Have a seat Carlos."

"Rosie you have to be insane. There is no place comfortable in this jungle."

"Suit yourself, Carlos, but I think that banana tree will make a nice resting spot."

Rosie moved the dirt around with her foot, sweeping away insects and leaves, crossed her legs, sat down, and closed her eyes. Pide leaned against the banana trunk. Carlos paced back and forth.

Rosie looked like she was dozing, but her eyelids were barely touching one another and she watched from the slits. She wanted to ignore Carlos. He seemed so pathetic pacing like a penned in tiger, with his maleness weighing him down. In the past she had seen him as protective, conservative, conscious of society, but now she knew the truth. He was an adolescent playing the part of a businessman who was politically powerful. His immaturity made him impotent, unnatural. Perhaps she had fallen in love with the adolescent, but an immature man was something different. She was too old to raise an adolescent into manhood. She didn't have the energy.

Pide peeled back a banana and handed it to Rosie. "*Gracias,* Pide, but no thanks. I'm not hungry."

Carlos walked over and pulled a banana from a dangling bunch. "I can't remember the last time I ate one of our bananas right off the stem. I am so hungry."

The banana went down in almost one swallow. Rosie watched as it moved down Carlos' throat. He dropped the peel on the ground and reached for another. Pide cleared his throat, "mmgham". Carlos pulled his arm down so fast that Rosie had to laugh.

"Go ahead Carlos, there are plenty. Pide was only making fun of you, your inhibitions and your lack of control."

"I am trying to control my hunger. I can't remember the last time I ate."

"I forgot how literal you are Carlos. But your hunger in some form has always been what we have fought over. Dinners missed, because you were late or had no appetite. Late because you filled your hunger differently than I did. It doesn't take much to fill my needs. But you *never* seem to be satiated. Funny I'd never thought about us that way. We just have different appetites. It sounds so simple doesn't it?"

"Too simple. You make me sound like I am greedy and selfish. I have sacrificed so much for you."

"I am too tired to have this conversation. Maybe you are right, but I don't see you as a helpless victim. All that you have *ever* relinquished is your pride. I have always been an extension of that."

"You are my wife. I am proud of you. There are expectations. You are supposed to help me and be by my side."

"You are also embarrassed by me when I am most myself. You are my husband and you are supposed to help me and stand by me."

"I have also provided for you."

"I am not talking about money. I am talking about lost babies and empty hugs. I am talking about my love for your island and the people who live here. I am talking about something so simple there are no words."

"No words. You and I have been silent for so long. That is the problem. You keep so much from me. You have been living another life. Even now you have secrets. Pide knows you better than I do."

"Jealousy doesn't become you, Carlos. I think we are both missing love."

Even with the sun down and a cool jungle breeze, Carlos' face was hot. He might be missing love, but all he felt was anger. Once again Rosie had humiliated him. It was bad enough she made him feel guilty with all her questions, but to say these things in front of Pide was unforgivable. Their problems were private.

Rosie couldn't help but see Carlos' reaction to her words. The signs of his anger were predictable. Flushed face, tense jaws, front teeth dragging over his bottom lip, snagging the skin. His emotions were raw. "I know what you are thinking, Carlos. He's gone. Pide always disappears at the right moments. I apologize for my timing, but not for what I've said. We do have different appetites. I don't want to talk about us now. I am more worried about what Carmen's friends are up to. Pide should be back soon with Don Rafael. His signaling sounded close by."

"Don Rafael is in on this too? I knew he was testing me when I went to talk with him at the *colmado*. I felt like a stranger with him, begging for information."

"He wouldn't have lent you *La Fatinga* if he considered you a stranger. *La Fatinga* carries all our supplies."

"So that is what those garbage bags contained. I almost tossed them out. Are you ready to tell me who or what you are supplying?"

Rosie didn't answer at first. Carlos appeared so sincere. She needed to separate her personal issues of trust from those concerning the island. "Have you ever noticed people disappearing from the island?"

"The only disappearance that seems strange to me, is that of Jesus. People come and go all the time Rosie."

"You know what I mean, Carlos. Have you ever wondered where Isabelle, or Carina, or that sweet girl Carmela went? Have you noticed a lot of the younger kids leaving our town?"

"They leave to find jobs or because they get pregnant, Rosie. What is your point?"

"My point is that if these people aren't important to you, you don't notice. There are problems on this island, Carlos, but you are too busy to see this. If someone disagrees too loudly, they are gone. If you weren't my husband, I too might disappear."

Carlos felt the same chill run up his spine and down his arms as when he had sat with Jesus' body, only to find it gone in the morning. He'd had these same thoughts the other night.

"*Contra,* Rosie, you don't have the good sense to be

quiet. I know it is difficult to make changes, I know there is a double standard on the island. You just have to play the game and know the right people."

"Miguel knew the right people but he is gone."

"He had a nervous breakdown and was hospitalized."

Rosie stood up and brushed the dirt off her makeshift shorts. "We supply Miguel."

Carlos remembered the *santo* that Don Rafael had handed him when he was leaving the *colmado*. It was of young girls, huddled together. All of them were giving birth. The meaning of the bats hovering over head suddenly made sense to him. In disbelief he whispered, "Carmen is in the caves."

Rosie never thought of Carlos as ignorant. She knew he would eventually put the clues together, but she still held back. Her outburst was done more to shock than to inform. Angry with herself for trying to impress Carlos, she abruptly turned away and walked behind the banana tree.

"Stop hiding from me, Rosie. You are doling out information... teasing me. Just tell me what is going on. I hate not knowing."

"For the longest time I thought that I could help those less fortunate than us. I have always felt alienated, but since we have money and power, my alienation belonged to me alone. I wanted to help others."

"So you alienated me?"

"No, Carlos, that wasn't my intention. We just grew apart. Even now, when I am trying to tell you about what has been going on for years below your very feet, you want to talk about us. You want to place blame."

"You don't love me."

"Carlos, *caye la boca,* please be quiet and let me talk. Miguel and many other people are hiding inside the caves. We have developed a system where they can hide and also learn skills until it is safe for them to leave the island. We earn money by making fertilizer and shipping it overseas. We provide food, shelter, and support."

"Who is this *we* you are talking about. It sounds like you are planning a revolution."

"Not the kind of revolution you would imagine. It isn't about independence or ownership, it is more about fairness."

"Why did you bring Carmen down there? How will that help her?"

"I misjudged her. You brought her to me injured, and she was being harassed. Now I think she came to this island to make trouble."

Carlos had had enough. He was impatient and tired. Rosie was talking in circles and not telling him anything. She still hadn't spelled out who actually knew about the caves. Obviously, Don Tuto and Abuelita were the instigators, odd loners, whom everybody loved. This was his island and he would not be made to feel a stranger. He was convinced that Rosie was in shock. She still hadn't reacted to Jesus' death.

Darkness had set in and the jungle air was cooling. The stillness and silence that fell between them was cold. It was like a draft coming off a wall of ice. Nothing he could do now would thaw Rosie. The wall was for him alone. Her intimacy was for others. He had a hard time remembering her in his own arms with any warmth or passion. Now he saw her body and so did everyone else. The wall that had been building between them, separated them not just physically, but acted as a barrier to all thoughts and sounds.

He listened to the night and heard nothing. The sky had disappeared above layers of vines and even if there had been stars, no light could filter down. Yet Carlos could feel something about to happen. The lack of noise was eerie. He could no longer tell if Rosie was standing by the banana tree or if she too had disappeared. Out of nowhere came a wave of swooshing. A breeze passed over his head and with it a mass of black night moved forward.

The bats were coming out.

The roar was deafening. Carlos covered his ears thinking he could block out the sounds. But there were no real sounds. The sweep of the bats took only seconds. The movement ceased almost as soon as it started. His ears prickled from the high pitches of noise that he knew were in the air, but felt more like bolts of lightning jolting the senses and then leaving a void. His heart pounded as he let his hands drop from his ears. What he heard was his own fear, and it did not disappear as the bats flew past. It was a miracle that there were no collisions.

The blackness moved in on Carlos, shutting him inside his own dark closet of anxieties. This was the second night he had passed outdoors. Unlike the bats with their special radar, Carlos couldn't steer clear of obstacles. Every thought collided with another. It seemed that the island spirits were conspiring. The people he thought he knew intimately had changed form and he felt jostled and disoriented. Jesus, Rosie, Pedro, Pide, Carmen, Roberto, Tomas, Don Tuto, Abuelita, Don Rafael, and Miguel: the names thrashed inside his mind. He felt bruised.

From the blackness Rosie emerged. Carlos first felt, and then noticed, two shadows following her. He immediately thought that Roberto and Tomas had found them. A wave of relief fell over him when he heard Pide's voice and then Don Rafael's.

"Rosie, *lo siento,* I am sorry that it took so long for me to come. I got your delivery, but was detained."

Rosie had her arm around Don Rafael. She gave him a hug and stepped back. Carlos wondered if they had forgotten him. He didn't really care. Their voices gave shape to the darkness and calmed him. At least now he would learn what was really happening.

"It doesn't matter Don Rafael, I knew you were busy with other people. When I dropped off all of my orchids I suspected that you were delivering a message. Do you have any idea why there is so much activity on the island?"

"Other than Carlos' business friends, Roberto and Tomas, trying to steal from our island and their ransacking of your place and Abuelita's for plants? Perhaps you mean the barge that is traveling back and forth from your property stealing the sand and carrying away our native plants. Or are you asking about the rumor that Jesus has disappeared? No, I am sure you already know these things. Carlos must have shared all of this with you. Am I not right Carlos, you have told Rosie everything?"

At the mention of his name Carlos realized that he wasn't invisible. He so much wanted to be like Pide, forgotten and left to be an observer. Once again he felt that Don Rafael was challenging his honesty. He had promised him when they had talked in the *colmado,* that he would make things clear. Now Carlos felt more lost, and he resented Don Rafael's assumption that he had not told the truth. Thankful that the night covered his red face, Carlos answered the accusation.

"I have tried to make sense of everything, but Rosie keeps so much information to herself, I am not sure that she knows what I have told her. She interprets things differently than I do."

"Carlos, we don't have time for interpretations. I have only asked that you be truthful. I am disappointed that you are still caught up figuring things out by being right or wrong. Miguel sent one of the guides to let me know that Carmen has created some problems in the cave. She tried to strangle Carmela and then she escaped from the main chamber."

LIVING IN DYING

"QUICK, FOLLOW HER."

"Someone go up a level."

"Sound the alarms."

"Shh, you'll be alright. She won't hurt you."

Monica listened to the clamor of rushing feet and the hushed voices. Everyone seemed to have vanished. She watched as Miguel scanned the chamber walls and then climbed up to the shelf above. He too disappeared, but the voices continued echoing off the chamber walls, "Follow her, follow her."

She turned to do just that, only to stumble. Carmela was sprawled on the cave floor. Her eyes were closed. Her body was twisted, listless. Carefully, Monica lifted Carmela's head. The skin along her neck was raised, red and swollen. She could actually see handprints and moved her own fingers along until she felt Carmela's pulse. It was weak but at least she was alive.

Monica looked around the chamber for something soft to prop up Carmela's head. The tables and chairs from the dining area were hard. She didn't want to risk moving her, so she sat in silence with Carmela's head on her lap. In the shadows of the chamber she could sense movement. All the torchlights, except those in this chamber, had been turned off to make Carmen's escape more difficult. Although the voices had ceased, the silence was anything but quiet.

She heard a faint pounding sound, which she decided was her own heart. To calm herself, Monica found herself staring into the torchlight. The flame flickered and danced along the wall. First it rose tall and thin, then it wavered back and forth, tilted to one side, almost extinguishing itself, until it rose tall again. But for this light, they would be in total darkness. Monica had the urge to blow the flame out, to obliterate the scene before her. The darkness would blanket the horrors that Monica felt. Carmen had actually attacked Carmela, tried to strangle her. If Miguel hadn't pulled her off, Carmela would be dead.

Suddenly wails startled her. Dominique, where was Carmela's baby? The cries became louder and louder until Abuelita appeared. Dominique was in her arms. Monica had completely forgotten the baby. She sighed in relief.

"Where have you been? I thought everyone had abandoned me?"

"I was holding Dominique when Carmen attacked. Carmela had just come to eat after everyone was over by the statues."

Dominique's wails drowned out Abuelita's words. Abuelita motioned her to get up. As Monica stood, Abuelita thrust the baby into her arms. The wails slowly settled down to small whimpers as Monica swayed back and forth holding him close into her chest.

She was surprised at the baby's lightness. There was no real weight to the body, just the sense of its will to live. Dominique was squirming, moving his lips wordlessly, kissing the air. Monica panicked and stared down into his dark eyes. Behind the pleading intensity, the flames of the torchlight reflected back. Monica had to close her eyes. The pull was so great. She squeezed back her own tears as she cradled Dominique's head. So much love and need poured out from such a tiny form. His pleas jabbed against her chest, poking at her ribs. She felt tightness inside.

"Abuelita, the baby is so fussy. I can't seem to calm him down."

"He is only hungry."

Hunger. Monica hadn't realized how hungry she was.

Although they had just eaten, holding Dominique made her feel empty. She had nothing to satisfy his basic need, nor her own. She felt lifeless against his spirit. Her body had always been a source of comfort, but it had nothing to offer now.

"Abuelita, I am sorry. Dominique doesn't want me."

"Of course he doesn't want you. He needs his mother. Keep him close until Carmela can nurse."

And as if on cue, Carmela began to stir. Her moans bounced from the cave walls, hollow and forlorn. Abuelita held her head gently and applied a poultice to her neck.

"My baby, my baby. Where is my baby?"

"Quick, bring Dominique over."

"Will she be alright?"

"Not if you don't bring that child over here in a hurry."

Monica knelt down next to Abuelita and reluctantly handed her the baby. Abuelita opened the front of Carmela's dress and placed Dominique on her chest. Instinctively he found his mother's breast. Carmela had closed her eyes again and seemed to drift off. The rise and fall of her torso mesmerized Monica. Each breath lifted Dominique up and then slowly back down. His small body covered Carmela's heart. Sucking sounds came from beneath the crown of his black curls. Monica laced one of the curls around her finger before she abruptly stood up.

"They both seem happy."

"Content would be a better word. Their ultimate happiness is so unsure."

"Carmela is so young. How can she possibly be in so much danger?"

"Young and tough. With some rest I think she'll recover from her physical injury, but I am afraid of her other scars. She has witnessed so much brutality in her life."

"I should have guessed that she was afraid of Carmen.

The signs were all there, but they made no sense. When we were in the Hall of the White Maidens, I could tell that Carmela was disturbed. As soon as Carmen awoke she scrambled up the sidewalls. I remember Carmen staring at where she had been. Her look was menacing. I think they recognized each other."

Abuelita walked over to the table where they had had their dinner. She removed some of the plates and took the flimsy table cloth. With care she placed it over Carmela and Dominique.

"I want to keep them warm. That is all we can do now. I wish we could have protected her more. But even the caves aren't safe."

"Abuelita, you are scaring me now. Surely just because Carmen tried to hurt Carmela, doesn't mean the caves are unsafe."

"We can't forget her assailants. They will come for her, and perhaps Carmela, too."

Monica thought long and hard about what Abuelita had just said. How would Carmen's assailants come? How would these strangers find out about these caves? It had taken them hours to travel to the entrance. Only locals would be able to bring them here. Who else didn't Abuelita trust? A chill passed through Monica. She could feel the damp air penetrate her skin. The shadowy darkness blanketed her, but gave her no warmth or security.

Monica looked first at Carmela and Dominique and then at Abuelita. The contrast was sobering. Abuelita, the wise one, the healer, the elder, was pacing in front of the *jovencitas*, the young and innocent. Her fretting seemed out of place, making Monica lose her patience and confidence.

Despite her annoyance, Monica placed her arms around Abuelita's small frame. Abuelita's body felt bony. Her skin was cool and clammy like she was an extension of the cave walls. There was almost no reaction to her hug, just a slight pushing away. Abuelita had no time to acknowledge her. She talked to the cave walls, but Monica knew every word was meant to convince her of some other reality.

"I don't trust Carmen's story. I think she borrowed it from Carmela. We found Carmela on the beach. She was left there in the night. She was badly beaten and had been raped. Jesus found her and nursed her back to health. Apparently Carmela was taken from her family in trade for a debt. She traveled here with other girls her own age. But she was too stubborn and wouldn't listen. Carmela said that one of the girls was older and ran the operation. The men even listened to her. She knew everything about the island."

"That doesn't make sense. Carmen could have escaped. She is a victim just like Carmela."

"Monica use your head. Would a victim try to strangle another victim? Would she hurt her protectors? I think Carmen has played us all the fool, even her assailants. You heard Carmen's hysterical confession, just like I did, at the sight of Miguel's statue. She left Jesus wounded on purpose."

Monica no longer heard the calm voice of Abuelita. The voice that had led her through the jungle, that soothed her fears as they had entered the caves. There was a strained almost pleading tone behind Abuelita's words now. Monica could feel the nervousness of someone trying to explain too much. It was as if Abuelita had to convince herself.

Whatever the cause, it was infectious, and Monica nervously wrung her hands. To regain her own composure Monica stuffed her hands inside the large pockets of the pants she wore. Having slept in them through their jungle walk, she felt leaves and twigs, which she rolled over and over enjoying the crumbling. She dug deeper and her fingers latched onto a packet of matches and a small ball of string. Whatever chore Carlos had been doing when he last wore these pants, Monica silently thanked him. Already she could feel a plan formulating in her mind.

Still not sure of what she felt, Monica tried to answer Abuelita with reasoning. "Carmen said Jesus was dead, not wounded. Maybe she ran because she was afraid she would be accused of murdering him. They were both left for dead."

Abuelita shook her head back and forth. "No, Monica. Carmen's friends are only chasing after her. I think Jesus just got in the way."

Monica turned her back, closed her eyes, and started to walk away.

"Where are you going, Monica?"

"Away. I've had enough. No matter what I say, you have some other story or twist to the truth I think I know. I can't be of help to you here. I don't even believe you anymore. We are talking about Jesus being dead and you aren't even upset."

Abuelita walked over to the table with all of Miguel's statues. She picked up the half-carved *ceiba* tree and fingered the form that depicted Jesus. She caressed his face and body. The tears streamed down silently. Abuelita bent her face to the statue and held it to her lips. Monica stared. Abuelita looked so old and deformed. Her twisted spine collapsed into itself, balling up in knot. She looked weak, miserable.

Monica rubbed her eyes, not quite understanding what she was seeing. Perhaps the shadows of light were playing tricks on her. She blinked and looked again. Abuelita had hobbled over to Carmela. Her back muscles were tensed and cramped. Her spine was caught in a ripple of pain. "Abuelita what is happening? Are you okay?"

"Weariness, I am just weary."

Monica watched as Abuelita removed a vile from the front of her shirt. She took what looked like a fine sewing needle and dipped it inside of the vile. Reaching behind her own head, Abuelita bent her arm back and pricked the skin below her neck and above her shoulders. Almost immediately the knot of muscle relaxed and Abuelita slowly straightened her upper torso. Her back was still somewhat crooked, but Abuelita's face had lost its luster. The wrinkle lines of past smiles seemed frozen in place. No warmth came from them.

Filled with sympathy, Monica wanted to help, but Abuelita's demeanor warned her off. Stone-faced, Abuelita's mask concealed all her thoughts and feelings. Instead of offering comfort, Monica had the urge to pull at Abuelita's long gray hair. Neatly coiled in a bun, each strain of hair was precise and perfect. Monica resented the days of stress that seemed to have left Abuelita untouched. She fumbled with her own hair and haphazardly twisted the matted strains into a knot at the nape of her neck.

Abuelita tried to continue her conversation as if nothing unusual had occurred. She turned towards Monica, but Monica had moved off, inched herself nearer the sleeping Carmela.

"You should stay with me. You won't be able to find your way through the chambers. It would be safer."

"Safer than what? You yourself said the caves weren't safe anymore. I don't mind walking in dark corridors, but I sense you want to keep me in the dark longer than necessary. How can I ignore what just happened to your back? What else are you hiding from me?"

"Monica, you are just angry. You feel betrayed, but you don't know where you are going."

"I am going to find Carmen. I am going to get out of the caves and I am going back to work. I trusted you. You are no different than the hypocrites that come to the bar. For some reason you think your secrets are more righteous, more noble. Who are you to judge people's motives?"

The word righteous hung in the rank air of the caves. It lingered and bounced from wall to wall. Almost as soon as Monica had said the words she wanted to take them back. Being right, honorable, helping. What was so wrong in that?

"Mi hija, lo siento. I apologize."

"I don't want your apologizes. I want to understand what is going on. I want to know what happened to Jesus. I want the truth."

"You have heard the same things that I have from Carmen. Neither of us understands, but Jesus can't be dead. My heart would hurt too much. It only feels heavy now, so he must be alive. Whatever Carmen saw isn't true. I used to know the truth, but time does funny things with that."

Monica looked around her again. Something was different. The flames from the torches had nearly burned out and there were formless shadows that were shrinking. She could feel a breeze, but nothing moved. It was more a smell; a whiff of air that drew her in. Someone had entered the chamber. The smell was familiar. Without her eyes to identify who was there, she relied on her memory. The scent was fresh to her. She immediately thought of Miguel, but there were too many layers of fragrance. Whoever was there, smelled like manure. She wanted to alert Abuelita, but she thought better of it. Scanning the walls and quietly sniffing, Monica pushed Abuelita in conversation. "I remember the first morning I was at Rosie's house and I sat with you drinking coffee. You pulled out Jesus' lottery ticket. It had a picture of a *liana* vine. Why was that so important?"

Abuelita tried to straighten her back with little success. She lifted her chin and dropped her shoulders.

Although she was looking straight at Monica, her eyes were vacant. Hypnotized in thought.

"The vine is a miracle. You just witnessed its power. I brought the *liana* vine with me when I came to this island. Drug companies and drug dealers were after me."

"So all of this is about drugs? This whole set up of the caves is a front for drugs?

"No, no... of course not. The cave is a refuge. The use of the *liana* vine has nothing to do with the caves. This plant isn't like heroin or pot. But it has properties that still the nerves. When I lived in the jungle I worked with a doctor who was trying to use it to stop nerve spasms and help with rigid joints. I think the drug companies had him killed because he wouldn't sell them the rights to use his discoveries."

"So Jesus sent you a message with a picture of a *liana* vine by carrier pigeon, and you think that after, how many years, 20, these same people are still after you?"

Abuelita's eyes snapped back into focus. It was as if she had been slapped.

"I hear disbelief in your voice. When I fled my home country I had to create a new life for myself. I promised the doctor who had saved me from the evil men who raped and murdered my mother, who nursed me with my broken back until I had healed, that I would continue to do experiments during his absence. He gave me my life, and my purpose. Since his death, Rosie and I have made some wonderful discoveries."

"Where do we fit into all of this? Carmen had never met you or Rosie before. I only just met you and I have been living here for over a year. How would we ever find out about these vines?"

Abuelita came up so close to Monica's face that she could smell her hair, a mixture of oranges and coconut. The skin above Abuelita's lips began to tremble. Anger, frustration, strain... Monica couldn't tell what the cause was for the muscle to spasm like that. And then it hit her. "You're telling me the truth aren't you?"

Abuelita only nodded and then placed her right hand over her lip. She massaged awhile and finally gave Monica a somewhat twisted smile.

"I never lie. I just held onto my secret too long. When Rosie discovered her father's old medical notes in a trunk last year, I realized that her father was the doctor who had saved my life. The pieces just began to fit into the puzzle she and I both had about our pasts. Every year her father would take a sabbatical to work in the jungle. He had just returned to the States with good news, but within days he committed suicide. Rosie was haunted by his death not only because it was a supposed suicide, but that he took her mother with him, leaving her an orphan. Back in the jungles, I waited a full year for his return only to find out about his death. He was like a grand-father to me, but I had no time to mourn. The jungle was crawling with men who wanted his research. I left every-thing behind and came here to start all over again. Rosie never knew about me as she was growing up, but the doctor had pictures of her as a small child. I recognized her years ago, when she first arrived on the island, but waited until she came to me with Jesus."

"I still don't see the connection to Carmen or Carmela or to myself."

"Rosie is a renowned scientist. Her work at the University has been published in journals all over the world. Carlos is a businessman who travels to all Latin countries. Rosie has always used her maiden name for any of her work. It makes sense that the pharmaceutical companies would follow up on Rosie, even if Rosie had no idea of her importance. I suspect Carlos even bragged about her on one of his many trips."

"Abuelita, you really don't know how all this is related, do you?"

"I only know that fate is patient. My old fears have never gone away. I now know more about the *liana* vine and if it gets into the wrong hands it could be used harmfully. Jesus sent that message as a warning. Jesus was with Carmen."

Already Monica had tired of the story, any story. She couldn't hold on to the strains of importance, who was friend or foe, who was in danger now or in the past. Her thoughts were distracted by the presence of a distinct smell of someone. They were not alone. Monica no longer cared if there were guards watching over them. Everyone was there to control. She needed to break free from the restraints of misplaced goodwill.

"Abuelita, I believe everything you have to say. But it doesn't change anything. Someone has to take care of Carmela and the baby and someone has to find Carmen. I am going to find Carmen and probably the person who is watching us from somewhere in this room will either stay with you or follow me."

Having said that, Monica pulled the matchbox from her pocket. The offending smell of burning sulfur accompanied the small flame. Monica followed with her eyes the shadow that was creeping along the upper shelf. As she left she heard Abuelita whisper, "*Vaya con Dios.*"

Before Monica could reply, words filtered down from above. "She doesn't need *Dios*, I'll be with her." The mocking tone infuriated Monica, but she had to smile. She had suspected that Miguel was in the room. She called up to him, "If you insist on protecting me, you could at least help me up to where you are standing."

Obligingly a hand reached down from above. Monica blew out the match and grasped Miguel's arm and was hoisted up to a narrow landing. With no space to move, Monica felt her body pressed into that of Miguel's. She couldn't tell if the heat she felt was coming off of Miguel or if her own body was reacting to him. She dismissed the sensation and tried to focus on finding a way out.

"I assume you know the way out of here?"

"*A sus ordenes.* I am at your command. I will lead you where you want to go, but I must warn you that you may change your goal. Leave Carmen to her own devices. I have already sent others to retrieve Abuelita, Carmela and the baby."

"So why are you here? Do I need special protection or are you all hiding something that you are afraid I will find?"

"Yes… to all of your questions."

Monica had been half teasing when she asked the questions, but now she felt unease creeping along the walls of the cave. She began to lose her nerve, and her perspective. She closed her eyes and ignored Miguel's proximity. She tried to focus on her surroundings. The smells of Miguel were mixed with something beyond dampness. The odor was mixed with earthiness, like the smells after a fresh rain. But there was no rain in the caves. And then Monica heard it, the dull roar of water. Water was moving quickly further back in the caves. It would soon be literally creeping up the walls.

Miguel slowly turned himself so he was faced away from her. "I knew you would sense the danger, once your frustration was gone. You guessed right. The river is rising quickly outside. I came back to get you. Others will come to help Abuelita."

POWDER KEG

THE DROPS WERE HEAVY, bending the leaves overhead, drenching not only the tops of trees, but also all the understory of plants. Although it was not the rainy season, the tropical forest paid no attention. Rosie tried to see the sky through the canopy, but all was dark.

They were all drenched and uncomfortable. With the news of Carmen's escape, Pide and Don Rafael had run ahead to the mouth of the cave. But now with the heavy rainfall the cave became a trap. Rosie mentally tallied how many boats they would need to transport everyone to safety. She had no idea of how many other people were down there with Abuelita and Don Tuto. With all the recent activity and messages, Rosie knew that the rains would put everyone's life in jeopardy.

Rosie had grabbed onto Carlos' hand as she walked. She did it mindlessly to hurry him along, but now she felt his fingers squeezing hers. There was no power or strength to the squeeze, just a demand. The fingers were soft and long, almost flawless. They felt like that of a petulant child's.

It was too dark to see his eyes, but Rosie knew that his long eyelashes held the raindrops. She used to love how they would shimmer in the rain. But the shimmering was an allusion, for no real tears were ever shed. When she had lost their baby, her own eyes pleaded with tears; Carlos' had become hard. The sky blue twinkle was replaced by the cold deep blue of disgust. Without looking she knew that his thin body was shivering. His hand was cold, clingy. Twice he had rearranged his fingers to entwine in hers. Twice she disentangled them and now finally she dropped his hand entirely.

"Carlos, rub you hands together to create some warmth. You'll be needing them to paddle."

It was the first words they had spoken since Pide and Don Rafael had taken off. Carlos pulled his hands back and blew warm air into them. His words were muffled, but clear enough for Rosie to hear. *"Contra, Mujer."*

"If you have something to say, Carlos, say it."

"You exasperate me. What ever happened to the Rosie I married? You pass your time trying to save the world, strangers. What about us?"

Rosie let out a deep sigh. Despite her calm, her determination, Carlos' pointed questions tugged. Her head throbbed at the pulling of past attempts at explaining, spent tears, silent battles. "I don't think I ever changed. You just saw me differently than I was."

"We had dreams together. *La Finca* was where we were going to raise a family, grow old together. Isn't that what you wanted?"

Rosie tried not to hear the words, or feel the wet drops against her cheeks. She swallowed hard before she spoke. "I don't think the dream has changed for either of us. We'll just dream them separately. As a couple we don't exist anymore. You abandoned me to rules, when I needed you."

"I still need you, Rosie."

"I know. You need me to help you out of here. You need me not to embarrass you. You need me to make everyone believe you are a wonderful husband and a good citizen."

Carlos walked up ahead of Rosie, turned and pulled Rosie to him. His warm breath whispered, "Tell me you don't love me anymore."

Rosie pushed against his chest with both of her hands, putting distance between their hearts. She couldn't think of what to say. The truth hurt too much. "I'll never be through with loving you. It doesn't work like that. I just can't live according to how you see me. It is too hard."

Carlos moved aside and started walking again. Rosie sensed the stiffening of his shoulders and body, a straightening of his head. Her words had hit the target. Maybe now he would understand, let her simply be. Rosie allowed the silence to linger while they moved closer to the caves. The sound of raindrops filled the air and gave rhythm to their strides. Their pace had quickened in response to the downpour.

Carlos was out of breath. Rosie tugged at his shirt and pulled him off the path to a dense patch of vines. The vines were so thickly interwoven that they provided a canopy of protection. Rosie tried to listen to the noises behind the rain. She motioned to Carlos to be quiet. While it was completely dark, Rosie could make out shadowy forms. Three figures were moving parallel to them. Clumsy noises of broken branches and muffled words let her know that the intruders did not suspect their presence.

Far off in the distance came the nightly booms of off-island bombing practice. Boom... boom... boom. Rosie counted three and then another set of three. Each night, like clockwork, the military practiced sending thunderous rumbles through the air. By now even the fish knew the timing. Rosie waited for the last three booms, before she spoke. Minutes passed and still she waited. Nine hits every night for years. This was the insult the island had learned to live with. Nine. Nine booms. Why were there only six?

The absence of ritual, even an insulting ritual, held significance. Rosie saw it as a warning of a larger danger. Even Carlos noticed something was amiss. He tried to whisper to Rosie, but she held her hand over his mouth, as he started to speak.

Rosie and Carlos listened as voices from the distance became animated. Rosie recognized the whining murmurs of Pedro and the unsettling taunts of Roberto and

Tomas. "That was the barge. They must have seen the barge, why else would they stop their bombing exercises?"

"Don't jump to conclusions, Pedro. We have connections with the military, nothing can go wrong with our shipments. All we have to worry about is getting rid of Carmen. She knows too much and is too greedy."

"And now your friend Carlos is too curious. I liked it better when he thought only of the business deal. He never once suspected our connection to Carmen. I don't think he knows who she is, even now."

Rosie could feel Carlos shrinking next to her. His body seemed paralyzed. Neither spoke the question. Rosie imagined Carlos systematically replaying scenes in his mind, trying to fit Carmen into his past. My poor, innocent Carlos, you are so unaware. *Tu eres tan estupido.* So clever in making deals, but so stupid when it comes to matters of the simple life. Their outward silence hung hidden amongst the vines and underbrush, waiting... as their inner ruminations screamed for some logical connection.

The voices continued as Rosie and Carlos held themselves, suspended in thought. "Carmen is good at prying out information. Her shy, innocent look always makes men believe she is harmless. No one suspects how calculating she can be. Carlos was an easy target. He loves to drink and dance on business trips. Too bad he talks a lot and remembers so little."

"It's a good thing for us that his tongue loosened. We would never have made the connection to his wife being the daughter of the Old Doctor from the jungle. Carmen traced Carlos and the plants back so easily to this island. Finally old scores can be settled.

"I want this over with. I never intended for anyone to get hurt. You said nothing about this when you first approached me. I'll still help you with the land deal, but I want no part of your scheme to get Carmen or Carlos."

"Pedro, Pedro, you still want your money, don't you? Just lead us to the caves that Pancho, from the cockfight, was so nice to tell us about."

Carlos' relationship to Carmen was clear. But the truth of the association stunned Rosie. Her suspicions were validated. All of Carlos' carefree ways became weighted with guilt. A small hiss of air escaped from Carlos' mouth. Rosie tried to force in a breath. Gasping for oxygen, she felt dizzy. Her feet folded under her and the ground came up to meet her. The pain had no source, just a prevailing presence. Neither her feet nor her arms would respond. She tried to feel them, move a finger or a toe, but a void was left where sensations should be. Rosie's heart ached. Her feet and arms felt disconnected, separate. She looked up to see Carlos' face crouched over her. He was talking to her in whispers. She closed her eyes and listened.

"They're gone now Rosie. Off to the caves. I don't know where the entrance is. Rosie, we must do something."

Rosie could barely hear Carlos' words between the dripping sound of the rain and a slow wind, rustling the leaves. An explosion sounded off towards the ocean, a boom out of sequence. All of this Rosie registered without really understanding. Once again her body had failed her. The emotional stress acted as a poison, triggering a shut down. Even her mind felt slowed. Carlos appeared frantic, but she couldn't sit up.

"Rosie, answer me. What just happened? You have to get up. We need to get out of here."

Rosie waited until Carlos had finished and then whispered, "Carlos, you will have to go alone. When my body shuts down like this it could take hours before the sensations return."

"Didn't you hear what Roberto and Tomas said to Pedro? They are planning to hurt me."

"Yes, they are trying to hurt you and Carmen, and

everything Abuelita has been working on for years. More important Carlos, there are lives to be saved inside the caves. I can't move, so you must do this on your own. There are two entrances to the caves. Don Tuto has a hidden entrance not far from here. You used to take me to the one Pancho was talking about. Pedro will lead them there, but Don Tuto will bring everyone up through his secret entrance."

Rosie closed her eyes. The strain of talking was too much. In the last few days her body had been getting progressively worse. First she had had an episode in the pigeon coup, then again when she was walking in the abandoned railroad tunnels. Her legs had slipped out from under her when she had tried to hide from Pedro and his friends, and now both her hands and legs were useless.

"Carlos, come close to me. It is already dark and the entrance is hard to find even if it were light out. So I want you to trust me and clear your mind of all thoughts. Remember when you once came to one of my faculty meetings at the University and you had no idea of where you were, or whom you were talking to. You felt out of place and lost. I told you just to watch my face and eyes and you'd know everything. By the end of the evening you knew more about the department than I did. Believe me, you will find the cave entrance and help Don Rafael and Pide. You asked me earlier if I still loved you. I am asking you to help because I believe in you, Carlos."

Carlos was ready with objections, but instead he listened to the wind. The rain was coming towards him at an angle. He looked down at Rosie and already she had closed her eyes and drifted off. He bent down underneath the woven patches of vines and leaned in towards Rosie's chest. Her breath was soft, even, reassuring.

Again he heard the wind, this time it was more of a flutter, softer, cajoling him forward. Gently he kissed Rosie's forehead and stepped back onto the path.

Walking slowly forward, Carlos smelled the air. The wind seemed to pass right beneath his nose so that the smell of guano was potent. The hidden cave entrance couldn't be that far from the stench. A faint ripple of air, almost a whisper brushed his ear. His gaze went upward. Rosie had said that Don Tuto would bring them up. Up meant that the caves were below them and that there must be a sinkhole to enter. Carlos kept a vision of Rosie in his mind. He could almost hear her sigh a sense of relief at his realization.

Rosie lay with the darkness surrounding her. Eyes held closed, curled in a ball with her knees in close to her chest, arms folded in an attempted hug. Conserving her energy, Rosie was in deep concentration. Already the much-needed oxygen was doing its work. Her mind was clear enough to see that Carlos had found the pit. He was circling around its edges, groping in the dark, for something to grip onto. If only Don Tuto had not been so careful in hiding his entrance to the cave. Rosie could see the loop of a ladder made from entwined vines. It was wrapped around the base of a banana tree. Carlos' foot was by its side. Rosie took a deep breath, exhaling as the wind pushed Carlos forward. As he stumbled, Carlos' foot caught the vine, loosening it just enough for him to notice and feel its contours.

Slowly he unraveled the ladder and let it drop over the side of the pit. Rosie could sense his fear. Carlos dropped a pebble down and waited to hear the plunk. Seconds passed with only silence, and when the pebble hit something, Carlos' heart quickened. Rosie hugged her knees closer to her own heart, slowing her breath, infusing a slower rhythm, until finally, with secure hands, Carlos gripped the rungs of the ladder and slowly descended the mud strewn walls.

Rosie felt each step downward, could smell the dampness, the stench of bats hiding in small holes bored into the walls. She also felt something hovering above her. She was between two worlds. The taste of sweat on her lips, the smell of dry clean dirt, the gentle touch of fingers brushing her cheek, lulled her to relax. Her focus slipped slightly as she felt arms lift her body and cradle her.

Downward Carlos continued, pausing with a moment's fear, then finally his feet touched the floor, slippery and wet. The water came up to his knees. Rosie knew the river meandered through a different chamber. The rise of water was alarming. Carlos would never make his way on foot. Rosie moaned her frustration.

The cave walls echoed the hollow sound and Carlos cautiously stepped forward, probing with his hands. Hidden inside a crevice was a rubber inner tube. Already wet and muddy, Carlos dropped down into the inner tube. Using his hands as paddles, he maneuvered the inner tube down the narrow corridor. The blackness was like a blanket, covering his fear and uncertainty. His hands scraped against the jumble of loosened rock protruding from the water. Numb from pain, Carlos followed the sound of water.

The rain above had ceased, but Rosie heard the forceful rush of water. Carlos was not far from where the *Rio de Los Angeles* rose to meet this tiny stream. All he had to do was find the canoes. Her strength was waning again. She could see Carlos floating. She heard the roar of the river filled with the power of the rains. In a flash she saw Monica, Miguel. She heard the calls of Don Tuto for Abuelita, the cries of a baby. The face of Carmen came to her twisted in pain and then everything went blank. She couldn't hold onto Carlos any longer. He was on his own.

TRAPPED

THEY WALKED ALONG THE CAVE SHELF, winding in and out of corridors, climbing up and over boulders, all in total darkness. Monica wrapped her fingers around her precious matches, but they were of no use. Miguel's pace was like that of a bat, ricocheting off the sides of the cave walls, moving with echoes and bumps. His pattern left her breathless and worried.

They hadn't spoken since they had left Abuelita lying on the cave floor. The roar of the river filled Monica's ears and the silence between them was born of necessity. Despite his speed and their haphazard path, Miguel was conscious of her. Occasionally he would reach behind himself, offering Monica his hand. Steady and true, Miguel kept his thoughts to himself. Monica was left with her own reflections.

Trapped in her mind were images of the women in her life, her mother, her sister and now Abuelita, Carmen and Carmela. Most of what she felt was their pain; the pain of loss and the struggle of abandonment. She had always considered her mother weak, dependent on men to make herself whole. All Monica's life she had worked at being independent, strong, so that she could fill her mother's void and not feel her own. She was always trying to protect. When she couldn't protect her sister, she fled.

As a prostitute she had an excuse not to feel. Listen and protect were her mantras. Her attraction to Carmen was to act as a guardian. Carmela and her child were another chance for Monica to fix the world, to be significant. Selfish acts. All of these were selfish. But guilt had no place in the caves. The past didn't matter, the why only offered an explanation, it couldn't change the present.

Monica forced herself to stop thinking and concentrate. She sensed that Miguel had stopped walking. Abruptly she collided with his back. He was standing completely still, listening. All Monica heard was the swelling of the river, the noise intensified by the echoes off the cave walls.

"What is it? Do you hear something other than the river?"

"Someone or something is coming. If you stand still you can feel the vibrations."

"Is this a good thing, Miguel? Should I be afraid?"

"I don't think fear has a place in this anymore. If it is a person, he or she is coming from the outside. They would be here to help us or harm us. Either way fear would only make things worse."

Miguel's words were lost as the shelf trembled. Then came the most terrifying of underground noises. A huge boulder broke loose from the ledge and the rockfall hit solid stone. The reverberations of the earth overwhelmed the roar of the river—deafening thuds as rocks splintered against the floor.

"Miguel did you hear someone shout? I think someone is hurt."

Monica got no response. Miguel was already moving forward. He had lit a torch and was scrambling over the piles of rubble. She held back. Not out of fear, but practicality. She had only the matches in her pocket and no need to confront a foe. There was a shout from Miguel and then some moans. Gradually she made her way over the debris and found Miguel with his arms wrapped around a pair of legs that were sticking up in the air.

"Quick, his head is caught under the rocks. I can only relieve the pressure, we've got to get him loose."

Monica ignored the nausea she felt at the sight. Miguel had placed his torch on a boulder to illuminate the area. Attached to the legs that Miguel held was a neck bent at a crazy angle. Frantically, Monica scratched away at the rocks and debris. Miguel straddled a shelf that had begun to split. He pushed against the wall to steady himself. His weight loosened more debris and from the ceiling, a twisted calcified formation fell by Monica's shoulder.

Too frightened to even scream, Monica concentrated on working the rocks away from the man's head. She stared at the shirt, which was pinched between the two boulders. The shirt was pulled tight around the man's neck, white, starched and expensive. For some reason she thought of Carlos and this made her dig and pull harder. Finally she tugged the shirt free. Miguel fell backwards with the weight. No sounds only blood and the crushed remains of a face. Monica heaved forward; the nausea was too much.

When she was done, Miguel was standing by her side. "Are you alright?"

Monica nodded yes and whispered, "Who was that? I didn't recognize him, but I thought it might be Carlos because of his shirt."

Miguel slowly walked around the body. He bent down and placed his hands over the man's heart, mumbled some words, and then lifted his cupped hands upwards, opening his fingers toward the sky. Monica felt a chill, pass through her.

"I think he was one of Carmen's pursuers." As he said this, Miguel rolled the body face down, so that his distorted features were hidden. Bulging from the back pocket was a handgun. Quickly, Miguel pulled the safety pin and emptied the chamber. "*Muy peligroso*, guns are very dangerous. *Gracias Adios*, thank goodness, nature has done us a favor."

"Don't you think we should have kept the gun? If you think there are others coming, we might need some protection, other than the torch."

Miguel shook his head. He was still studying the body and was looking at papers stuffed in the man's pocket. "His name is Roberto and he has pictures of your friend Carmen and Carlos. Carmen looks quite capable here."

Monica grabbed the pictures from his hand. She recognized Carlos immediately, but Carmen was dressed in an expensive party dress, one that made her look older, more sophisticated. Her eyebrows were fuller and she was heavier, voluptuous. Not the thin, petite woman she knew. The light from the torch was dimming. She handed the pictures back.

"I guess I don't know my friend very well. Carmen never approached Carlos here. Carlos didn't seem to recognize her. I thought he helped us that night in the bar because he was being nice."

"Carlos is nice, but naïve. He probably never made the connection. What he does elsewhere never impacts his life at home. We must move on now, go back the other way. I am afraid that this *salida* is closed off by the falling boulders."

Finding Carmen seemed less important to Monica. All she wanted now was to get out of the caves safely. She refused to give into her need to cry. Death made her *feel*. So much of her life she had avoided the pain of caring. Fear was easier to hide from than death. It was so final, forcing her to question, jabbing at her. She hated being vulnerable. Monica watched Miguel for a clue on how to behave. He seemed to still have his wits about him, absorbing information, not judging or feeling. Calm, aloof, functioning. Monica turned herself around and started off in the opposite direction from Roberto's body. Miguel had already put out the torchlight and was walking briskly back the way they had come.

The darkness overwhelmed her. She felt like she was in a locked closet with the lights turned out. Punished for not taking care of her family, punished for her beauty, punished for making love with no love. Her heart felt empty, weak. She was without armor for the first time in years. Tears streamed down her face, no sobs, just the wetness of regrets. The flowing river, rising from the cave floor seemed to be hers and hers alone.

She closed her eyes and listened for Miguel's steps to guide her. She stumbled, but continued on.

Out of no where, Monica heard a voice, a woman's voice. It was almost a whisper, ghostly quiet, but forceful. She stopped walking and looked. Monica saw the shadowy form of Miguel's body up ahead, but no one else was around. She scanned the cave walls above her and looked down at the river. The voice came from the water, not from the air around her. Her name was being repeated over and over, it encircled her. "Monica, Monica, *ten cuidado*, take care. Monica, Monica, don't lose heart. Monica, Monica, they are behind you."

All her senses were alive now. Monica could feel a presence. She recognized the voice to be Rosie's. Rosie was hovering around her, but was nowhere to be found. The smell of bats was stronger. Monica hurried herself to catch up with Miguel. She was breathless, but her tears of self-pity were gone. "Miguel, Rosie is here. I heard her voice. She is trying to warn us."

Miguel turned toward her. She repeated herself and then felt foolish. What if he thought she was crazy? Miguel pulled her gently toward him and stroked her face. He stared into the darkness a long while and finally whispered in her ear, "Rosie is not in the caves. She is above us, watching."

"You don't hear her, do you Miguel?"

"No, her voice is for you, not me. Rosie must have found a way into your heart for her to be able to talk to you. If Rosie were physically here, I would sense her. You are very lucky. You both are powerful women. What was her warning?"

"She said to take care, and that someone is behind us. After her voice faded, I smelled the bats more intensely."

"The bats are closer to the entrance of the cave. If there is someone coming from behind us, we have no choice but to go towards the exit used for our business. It is hidden from outsiders' view by lush ferns and mosses. Even if this opening were to be discovered, the river is a deterrent, creating a split which divides the cave into a 'v' shape. There are no bridges connecting the two sides."

"What if it is a trap? With the river flowing so strongly, can we make it out?"

Miguel looked down at the rising water and further ahead. He seemed to shrug his shoulders and started forward. Monica accepted this gesture as a choice. If it was a trap, they had themselves to rely on, and if Monica continued to be lucky she'd have the help of Rosie to guide them. Monica scanned the shelves above her. They were empty of shadows. She heard no movement of feet, only her own breath. She breathed deeply, filling her lungs with the now stale air of the caves. The air was laden with moisture, heavy with particles. As they climbed, her lungs and throat felt coated. Particles of the bat guano were airborne. Amazingly, despite the contaminated air, she felt stronger than before. She felt Rosie's spirit infused inside of her.

Monica knew before she heard and saw Miguel stop. There were people up front. She held back trying to make out the shapes and voices. Abuelita was leaning against Don Tuto, Carmela was holding her child, and there were men and women talking. They all were wearing bandanas around their mouths. The air was stifling. The stench was more than that of a few bats. She realized that it was where they made the guano into fertilizer. One by one she watched each person being lifted upward. Vines dangled from above, where there was a small hole projecting a thin stream of light, the exit.

A chilling breeze passed over her arms and Monica instinctively, looked behind. Shadows moving fast. She counted the rhythm of the steps. Some were light, some were heavy. The steps were uneven, as if someone was being dragged. Instead of becoming louder the patter was moving deeper into the caves. Echoes of curses filled her ears. She suspected the shadow people were lost in the maze of darkness; on the opposite side of the river moving away from safety, just as Miguel had predicted.

Despite Monica's stillness, Miguel had found her. He leaned in against the wall and motioned her forward. Monica shook her head and whispered, "I saw them, the people Rosie was warning us about. I think there are at least three people and one is a woman. I think they have Carmen and are dragging her."

Miguel squeezed Monica's hand and nodded.

"Everyone is being lifted out. Carlos floated in, found a canoe and started the shuttle out. How he found his way I will never know, but everyone will be safe from the rains."

"We can't leave Carmen and the others in here. Even if they have guns and are cruel bad people. Even if I misjudged my friend all these years, I can't leave them in here knowing they could drown."

Miguel said nothing in response to Monica's outburst. He took hold of his torch and lit the wick end. He waved it back and forth so that a pattern of light hit the cave walls. Across the way, where Don Tuto and Abuelita stood, came an answering motion of light. The light show went back and forth, until Miguel seemed satisfied. Finally he addressed Monica.

"You are to go with the others. I will find the intruders."

"Oh no you don't. I insist on going with you. That way I will know what is happening and I won't have to worry."

"Monica it is too dangerous now. You are to go with the others."

"No, I don't want to worry about you."

Monica's own words startled her. She hadn't expected the fervor of her feelings. When had Miguel become so important to her? His sense of balance and substance, his assured presence and wry sense of humor, Monica didn't want to let go of that. She expected an argument from Miguel, a forceful dismissal, but instead he shrugged.

"I told them you probably wouldn't go without me. They will leave a boat behind and the platform down so we can be hoisted up on our return."

For some reason this made Monica smile. Miguel seemed so sure of himself and her. She liked that. It had been a long time since anyone could second-guess her thoughts. While she was smiling Miguel had taken off. His torch was still lit, so she could see her way. Miguel stopped at the point where the river cut the cave in half. In order to follow Carmen and her captors they would have to get to the other side. The span between the two walls was over twenty feet.

Doubt settled into her mind. The impossibility of the crossing overwhelmed her. Miguel might be fearless but she could feel her feet tremble and her heart skip a few beats. And then Monica heard a whisper, the silent call of her true friend urging her to study her surroundings more intently. The river was moving fast, creating a swirl in a pool below. At the lip of the pool, water cascaded leaving deposits of calcite. The light of their torch reflected on these shimmering pebbles. Monica wondered at how many others had passed this way, seen the glow and were so overwhelmed.

No such thoughts passed through Miguel's mind. He was busy calculating distances and studying the cave walls. Monica nudged his arm and pointed to the jeweled pool. On the wall by its side, the light caught the ends of a series of vines. Miguel again squeezed her hand. It was fast becoming his way of saying thank you. Without hesitation, Miguel took a hook and some twine from his pocket. He handed the torch to Monica and then whipped the twine and hook in the air, like a lasso, and threw the line across the ravine. The hook hit its target. Carefully Miguel pulled on the vines.

The pool was a marker. The vines had been placed there to use as a makeshift bridge. Only someone extremely knowledgeable of the caves or someone who had the good fortune to hear Rosie's guiding voice would know where to find the vines. Within minutes Miguel had set the vines into the wall, looping the vines through metal eyelets embedded behind the thin stalactites that resembled soda straws.

It was obvious to Monica that they were going to cross over to the other side using these vines as a bridge. Her own strength had carried her through nights with abusive, rough clients. She was a fighter, but the power she would need for this feat was beyond her.

"Miguel, I should have gone back with the others. I can't do this."

She expected harsh words, belittling, or anger, instead Miguel studied her eyes. His own eyes seemed to bore into her, reaching deep inside of her, making her squirm and want to take flight. She could go nowhere; ensnared by the emotions Miguel elicited from her. Monica looked downward in an attempt to ward off any demands. When she looked back up, Miguel's eyes were moist, softened and questioning.

"I will show you how to cross. You won't need me once you learn the technique, but I will be here just in case."

Miguel had offered her independence, knowledge, and most important, support. The makeshift bridge dangled precariously over the river. She felt her smile come into her eyes. The challenge had already passed. Monica let her worry—and need to be in control—retreat into the background. With studied concentration she watched as Miguel demonstrated the horizontal crawl.

"We will cross together. I will cross with the left vine; you will use the vine on the right. The trick is to focus on the sliding knots. Once you start, keep moving in a rhythm; the faster you go the less tension is on any one part of the vine."

Monica swallowed twice before she gripped the vine. Mimicking Miguel, she slipped a loop around each foot and around her chest. She felt like a monkey, hanging with her bottom towards the river. By shifting her weight, Monica crawled along on the loops. The knots slid alternately, skimming across the vine. At one point her bottom began to sink and the pull made the vine wobble. Quickly she adjusted by stretching her body in close to the vine and using a powerful pull of her arms. Miguel was on the other side only seconds before her. As she neared, she felt his strong arms encircle her chest and guide her onto the cave shelf. Then the acknowledging squeeze of her hand and they were off.

The stench was stronger on this side of the cave. The path along the cave wall was narrower, but more traveled. Monica could feel the smoothness as she walked, but for some reason this wasn't reassuring. She felt a foreboding sense of doom as if she were entering the forbidden side of life, the side closer to death.

"Miguel, there is something wrong here. I feel it all around me. We should turn back, something bad is going to happen."

There was no response. Her words seemed to evaporate into the damp air. Miguel was too far ahead to hear her. The silence was weighted. She felt a pressure on her shoulders, as if two hands were holding her still. To steady herself, Monica hugged the cave wall. The pressure became a kneading of her muscles. Monica could almost feel the hands of Rosie pushing and pulling on her. All her senses told her *danger.* Rosie's insistent touch increased her fear. Miguel had said there was no place in the caves for fear. She forced herself to go forward, ignoring what she felt were warning signs. Miguel was up ahead somewhere. Danger or not, she knew the emptiness that lay behind her.

Monica moved quickly, despite the slick path. She held onto the rough knobs protruding from the walls. It was wetter in this part of the cave. The walls were seeping droplets of calcite, which fell to the floor. Bat guano, was everywhere, not confined neatly to corners or the shelves. Although she couldn't see the bats, Monica could feel their eyes, watching her progress. Rosie's presence was everywhere. Monica accepted the fear, the danger, the bats, and the heavy silence. Miguel seemed to have vanished.

Alone, once again, Monica ignored the gnawing ache. She strained to hear anything beyond the silence. She stared ahead, searching the darkness. The matches in her pocket were damp, useless. All her clothes were saturated. Monica concentrated on what she knew. Miguel was ahead of her, waiting or searching for Carmen and her companions. She could almost hear Rosie's whisper, "Patience, *mi hija,* patience my child."

Patience was hard to maintain with the fear and the loneliness creeping along her skin. Monica shivered, trying to shrug off her doubts. From the corner of her eye she spotted movement. She so wanted it to be Miguel, but there was no signal, no sign that it was safe. Cautiously she inched forward, flatting herself along the wall. The passageway was narrow and slippery. There was no room for anyone to pass. Above her head she heard flapping. The bats hung by their feet with their wings slowly waving back and forth.

Monica remembered how the bats had hovered over Carmen when they had first brought her into the caves on the stretcher. That same wave of evilness filled the cave chamber. She was sure that Carmen was near. Monica felt her presence and that of Miguel's. Her nose was useless, all smells were covered by the stench of the bat guano and it was all she could do to not gag and heave with each breath. And then it struck her. It was too silent. Carmen and the others were waiting for Miguel and her to show themselves. They were all trapped in the cave's web of corridors, stuck with righteous convictions, waiting for the prey or to be preyed upon.

Monica skimmed her hand along the wall, feeling for curves and protrusions, barometers to guide her blind walk. A spider scurried along her arm as her fingers brushed the sticky remains of the silk threads that held its spiraled nest together. Monica took the spider as a sign. The sensation was familiar, a remnant of her past when she would hole up in the closet, hiding from her mother's rampages. Whiling away the hours, she'd study how the spider caught its prey. The slightest vibration along the thin fibers signaled the spider that dinner had arrived. Ever attentive, the spider spun its prey into the web. There was no fight, no violence, just the submissive clinging to one's own end.

Pressing her ear against the wall, Monica listened for a muted echo. She felt more than heard the reverberations. The vibration was so slight she almost missed the pattern. Three waves of tapping, nothing, and then again the three taps. Taking the heel of her hand, Monica patted the cave wall three times. There was no sound, but an answering tremble. She was now sure that Miguel was just a few yards ahead of her. Carmen and her pursuers must be close at hand.

Monica kept her distance and waited. The bats became more restless, flapping and suddenly taking flight. One by one they brushed by her, and moved further into the cave. And then she heard the screams of Carmen.

"Get them away! Get the filthy bats away!"

Monica didn't wait for a signal from Miguel. She headed forward toward the screams. Four gunshots in quick succession bounced off the cave walls. Monica dropped to her knees and crawled along the slimy floor. Covered in guano, she made slow progress. The smells were overpowering and the darkness seemed charged with energy. There were no more calls for help, just the loud echoes of spent shots.

A hand came out of the darkness and pulled at Monica's leg. She could tell by the insistent touch that it was Miguel. Just as she was about to talk, he pulled her closer and covered her body. The entire cave lit up and then she heard the explosion. Stalactites dropped from the ceiling, the floor shook and cracked. And then a series of explosions continued down the corridor. Flames traveled the same path, igniting the trail.

Monica was reduced to tears. Her entire body was trembling. Miguel lifted her up and held her tight. "Guns aren't a good idea around fertilizer. This is where we dry the guano and store the fertilizer. It is a powder keg ready to ignite. Get up, we must get out of here. If the flames don't get us, the fumes will."

"I heard Carmen scream."

"We don't have a choice, the fire will consume anything in its path. We don't even have time to go by way of the bridge."

Monica covered her ears and closed her eyes. Anything to block the roar of the blaze, the echoes of screams. She began to shake uncontrollably and then stiffen into a catatonic stupor. The entire cave was lit up, hot like the sun. Miguel took a hold of her shoulders and shook her until Monica opened her eyes. His words were swallowed by the noise, but his lips said "jump".

With one arm still around her shoulder, Miguel cradled Monica. Gently he made his way toward the edge of the shelf. He pointed down to the river. The drop was at least forty feet. All Monica could do was nod in understanding. He let go of her shoulder and held her hand. She squeezed hard, held her breath and they were off the ledge. The descent was in slow motion. She could feel the heat of the fire, black wings of manic bats scrambling past and the voice of angels. They hit the water hard. It was surprisingly cool, compared to the furnace above. Immediately Miguel turned and reached for her. The river was propelling them forward. Monica lifted her arm up and signaled that she was okay. They bobbed up and down, half floating, half-swimming. Monica lavished mental praises on the miracle river that carried them away from the inferno. Two more booms, fireworks, and more screams. Half blinded by the sudden light, Monica watched in horror as three human balls of fire moved toward the ledge.

Frantically Monica called. "Carmen jump. *Jump!*" The river was too shallow and Monica found her feet thrust forward, her arms useless appendages dragging in the current. She was powerless against the thrust of water. "Miguel, she can't swim, she is afraid."

The river pushed them on, past a sharp bend, until it was once again pitch black. The bursts of fire were gone and the river opened wide into a huge lake. The impercipient stillness was solace from the truth. Carmen would never be afraid again.

Monica swam alongside of Miguel. Their strokes synchronized: slow and purposeful. The intensity of the last few days dissipated. Nothing seemed real or urgent. The lake was a mini reprieve. Once across, Miguel helped Monica climb up the cave wall. Relying on feel alone, they placed their feet in evenly spaced footholds. At the top, Miguel leaned down to hoist Monica up the last stretch. Sunlight streamed down from crevices, and Monica's face held an amber cast. The water on her skin and hair glistened. With Miguel's arms around her, she smiled as she reached his lips. Their kiss was soft, playful.

High above them they heard Rosie's voice, "I have no more patience, come on out, and join the rest of us."

SUNRISE

THE SUN WAS JUST PEEKING OUT from behind the *lomos*, tentative yet promising. Rosie felt the warmth on her face, arms, and exposed legs. Rested and relieved she smiled at the sight of Miguel and Monica.

Both carried the smell of fire and the stench of guano. Their torn and wet clothes clung to their bodies. Although they looked withered, Rosie watched their eyes. Monica's were fully alert. The challenging stare, was missing, as was the closed off look that said, 'I will let you in only so far'. There was worry and concern written on Monica's face, but her eyes were clear, open and welcoming.

Miguel's eyes were tired, drooping at the edges, but the gleam of happiness was apparent every time he glanced Monica's way. They were still holding hands as Rosie approached.

Giving them a huge bear hug, Rosie called out, *"Mis amigos, que alegro de verlos.* I am so happy to see you. I had a little trouble keeping track of where you were."

Miguel laughed. "You were right there with us, Rosie. You nearly scared Monica with your presence. We owe you our life."

Rosie smiled broadly. She hoped that Miguel hadn't spotted the tear that fell from her left eye. Neither knew how much energy it had taken from her. At one point she had blacked out. She was left in between worlds, not fully present in her body and floating blindly outside of herself. She had seen her father's face. It was stern, angry, and loving. Her mom's face was like that of a child's, innocent. *Los innocentes,* the innocent people in the world.

Rosie knew her dead father was still battling injustices. She hoped that after today, his spirit would be able to rest, and peace would come to him.

Rosie took Monica's hands and looked into her clear eyes. "I am so sorry you lost your friend Carmen. You were more than she deserved."

Monica held Rosie's gaze. So much had happened since that first night, when she and Carlos had brought Carmen to Rosie. Monica had feared and admired the power of this woman. Now she felt a deep connection both to Rosie's thoughts and heart. Surprising herself, Monica felt the wet drops along her cheeks. She could truly *feel*, without repercussions.

"Rosie, I had no choice but to care. Even if Carmen was evil and manipulative, I am not sure I would have done things differently. I thought she needed me."

"Sometimes needs get confused, but I am sure that caring is always appropriate. Come on, we need to get you dried off and comfortable. The day has only just begun and there will be other surprises. Don Tuto and Abuelita are waiting for us up at the house."

All sentimentality evaporated under the early sun's heat. Rosie walked over to Miguel, whose face had now become pensive. His thoughts came tumbling out.

"The explosions probably caused the collapse of the lower cave. I think Don Tuto got most of our people out with the flooding. We'll be shut down for a good while. I don't know if…"

Rosie put her hand up to Miguel's mouth to stop the flow of words and gave him a quick embrace. "Enough, Miguel. You've done enough. If you insist on worrying or trying to help out, then go to the island off shore. I've sent Carlos with Pide and Don Rafael to stop the barge."

Miguel stepped back to look at Rosie more closely. He closed his eyelids slightly, trying to squeeze out the truth behind what Rosie had just proposed.

"Carlos is naive. What will he be able to accomplish? The danger is too great for everyone. Politically it would be a disaster with the bombing practice. Our government would arrest him, and the barge, what do you hope to gain by stopping it?"

Rosie's eyes twinkled and mischief curled around her lips. "Carlos finally woke up and paid attention. It ate at him that his best friend, Pedro, had used him. The sale of our land for the sand and building the condominium were covers for what Pedro was really into. Somehow Pedro had uncovered that the government was using the practice bombings on the islands to conceal a large smuggling ring. The bombings were never needed for security reasons. They were signals for barges and boats to pass goods. Pedro wanted his piece of the pie, so he joined forces with the government. It wouldn't have mattered that much if Carmen hadn't found out about the *liana* vine that my father had discovered. Suddenly Pedro was caught stealing from his best friend and the island he loved. He made a choice."

Miguel looked back at the cave entrance. "Stupid deaths. What good will come of this? Carlos can't create a miracle. He can't bring back dead people or money."

To this Rosie sighed and finally let the tears fall from her eyes. "Carlos with all his diplomatic skills made some important phone calls and called in some favors, and has talked to the heads of our government. He was persuasive enough to make them see reason. Our flotilla will get back the *liana* vines that my father discovered years ago. His death won't be in vain. And as an extra bonus, the bombings will cease."

Once again Miguel looked at Rosie cross-wise. "So why am I needed out there?"

"Word has it that Jesus has miraculously recovered and he has a special favor to ask of you."

"Am I to do one of my specialties?"

"Yes, sculpt the truth."

Hours later Abuelita, Don Tuto, Monica, and Rosie were seated by Rosie's *ceiba* tree overlooking *La Finca*. They had brought a picnic of sorts; papaya slices, tiny sweet bananas, avocado, white smooth cheese, and a long crusty loaf of water bread. The sun was high in the sky, but the tall branches of the *ceiba*, shaded them from the intense heat. All evidence of the last few days and harrowing hours was erased from their faces. The only reminder of the violence was the fading stain of blood on the trees' bark. Even Nada roamed peacefully and finally settled by Rosie's feet.

Don Tuto had finished eating and was searching the skies. Overhead, one lone pigeon circled. "I think we'll know any minute now. Your pigeon is finding its home."

Don Tuto brushed off his pants and scurried down the hill to a small wooded pigeon coop. He arrived just as the spotted pigeon was landing. He put out his arm and the bird hopped on. Rosie watched from above as Don Tuto performed his pigeon greeting. He bobbed his head forward and back a few times mimicking the bird. He then cupped the bird in both hands, patted its head, and finally removed the note from the metal capsule tied to its leg.

Before Abuelita could even stand, Don Tuto had run back up the hill. Waving the note, he read, *"Liana* Vines Intact."

Rosie and Abuelita clung to one another. Laughter filled the air. "Rosie, it is almost over with. I am finally free, *mi hija*. I have paid my debt."

Rosie caressed Abuelita's face. "It has been a long time in coming. You have honored my father's wishes and passions for all the years I have been here and those before I ever came. He would never have wanted you to sacrifice more of your life."

"And I won't waste any more of my time on it. Don Tuto and I have a plan."

Rosie shook her head. "Oh no you don't. You two aren't going to live in the caves. I forbid it. No more recreating the past."

Don Tuto smiled. "No, the caves will always be my refuge, but Abuelita has this idea for a restaurant. Thought we might use Monica to run the place, and we'd be silent partners."

Monica put her hands up to the sky and twirled herself around in circles. Above, the deep blue expanse held lines of white clouds. The strands were entwined one behind the other, mingling her thoughts and emotions. Below her was the ocean, deeper and bluer. She had never felt so rich. "*Tu sabes,* you know, that is something I think I'd be good at."

Rosie winked. "Be careful, Monica. I have never known them to be silent."

"As long as they aren't hiding any more secrets, I'll be fine. I could use my education—and all the social graces I have accumulated throughout the years—in a more acceptable way. Who knows, maybe I'll even be able to bring my sister down to…"

Abuelita's face erupted into a stream of creases leading to smiles around the eyes and lips. "*Mi hija*, slow down. *Cojelo suave*. We'll have lots of time to plan. You are still tired from all the events of this past week. We should go back to town and let you rest."

Nada looked up, ears alert, and nose sniffing. Rosie's attention followed Nada's movements. Her senses were stirred by a familiar smell, an electrical charge in the air. She could no longer sit. As Nada started walking down the knoll, Rosie followed. She looked back at Abuelita who acknowledged her intuition by nodding. Already her heart was racing. She was afraid to speak for fear all her hopes of seeing Jesus would vanish.

The island lines of communication had spread the word that Jesus was back, but Rosie's faith was now faltering. Her emotional need for his presence was overwhelming. Throughout all that had happened she never once let herself believe that Jesus was dead. Shadows and small signs of his presence had been everywhere. At her darkest moments she had felt his arms around her, but that was only a memory. And perhaps it was a dream.

Nada was running and barking in circles and then taking off. Rosie was out of breath trying to keep up. First she ran down to the landing dock and then through the coconut farm. Rosie slowed her pace and quieted her heart. Nada seemed to be following the spirit of Jesus. Jesus was everywhere. Rosie looked up the trunk of each coconut tree. She could imagine his quick agile ascent. But no one had scaled these trees in days. The ground was bare.

Tired and disappointed, Rosie unbuckled her sandals and let her feet feel the hot sand. The refined grains sifted through her toes as she meandered along the perimeter of her property. She knew Carlos would halt the condominium project, and maybe with time she could restore the trees and land. Slowly she walked along the beach until she could climb the hillside where her failed rice paddies struggled along. The sun was sliding slowly behind the hill, so the heat had left the air. She settled down among the rows of tiny green stalks and weeds.

The soil felt cool to her feet compared to the hot sand. Every sensation she felt was a celebration. She had hoped that the *liana* vines could offer a remedy to her condition, but she truly needed more sophisticated studies to find an answer. She pondered going back to the University and whether she could legitimize hers and Abuelita's work to get a grant. She burrowed her toes into the dirt, making small tunnels, not wanting to think past the coolness, the richness of the earth.

Even though there was no hope of salvaging the rice, Rosie began to weed. Weeding had always been thera-peutic, a way of sorting out her thoughts.

Unconsciously, Rosie began to state her thoughts out loud. "Without Jesus I will have to hire helpers. Carmela and the others, who worked in the caves, might want a change of pace. I will be okay as long as I keep focused."

The sun seemed to disappear quickly as a long shadow fell over her. She turned to see Nada jump up and then she heard a familiar voice. "If you focus too much you will miss what is right in front of you."

Words caught in Rosie's throat. She struggled to unfold her legs, but she couldn't stand up quickly enough, when she felt the strong hands of Jesus lift her off the ground. Their eyes locked and then she felt the warmth of his arms wrap around her. It wasn't a dream, but the real thing. Rosie touched his cheeks, eyes and lips.

"I was so afraid, you were really dead. I was forcing myself to go on. Abuelita and I were sure that you used the extract of the vine to slow your heart rate, but I feared that it had stopped it completely."

Jesus let her down softly to the ground. He pointed to the tunnel she had dug with her toes. Slowly a worm poked its head out. "I too have more than one heart."

ASK AND YOU SHALL RECEIVE

"*CUIDATE*, BE CAREFUL, WATCH OUT, STAND BACK." Monica smiled listening to Pide direct the people around the remodeling site. Don Tuto was up on the roof, fitting in a large skylight between tiles. The remains of chiseled stucco had been swept into huge mounds and were being shoveled into buckets and then passed on to pickup trucks. Monica recognized a few of the women from inside the caves as part of the brigade and others, who were filling in the newly formed gaps in the wall, with glass blocks.

Monica was tired. She had been working at a furious pace for months. The transformation of the bar into a restaurant had been on the brink of failure many times. One of the hardest hurdles had been a permit for the cave women to work. Rosie had been a godsend, creating a nursery at *La Finca,* for the babies and young ones, so their young mothers could leave them safely; but many of the women had no paperwork and didn't exist in the eyes of the administration. "*Oye,* Carmela, could you tell Rosie when you see her at noon, that all will be ready for her meeting this late afternoon. My phone system has not made an appearance yet and I am too lazy to send a courier pigeon."

"Don't worry, I will go quicker that a pigeon, I have my *bebe* waiting for my sweet milk."

"*Gracias.* I won't see you for a few days, so rest, but remember to study as you are a little behind on your math lessons."

Carmela shook her head and let her words mix with laughter, "Monica, you are so strict. At this pace my dreams will come true before I wake."

Don Rafael pulled up along side of Monica in *La Fatinga.* "*Buenos Dias,* Monica. You are looking fit for work."

Monica looked down at her coveralls and white powdered legs. "It is so nice of you to notice. Don't worry, I'll change before we open today. I just had to come down and make sure everything was ready. I have been cooking and setting up the tables. This physical work is nothing compared to all I have had to do. Government officials need all kinds of persuasion."

Don Rafael surveyed the work site. "Not much is left. I'll return if Don Tuto needs me to help with the new entrance way, otherwise I'll be off to my *colmado.* Make sure you keep your customers happy or they might decide to hang out at my store."

Monica batted her eyelashes and swayed closer towards *La Fatinga* and yelled as Don Rafael pull away, "Not if I can help it."

Rosie stood half-naked in front of her small closet. It had taken longer than she expected to get ready. Her fingers had held the green stain of weeds and her nails had been dark with embedded dirt. She rubbed moisturizing lotion into the reddened cuticles as she surveyed her clothes. Rifling through the meager selection, she thought of Carlos and the dresses he liked. Today she needed to make an impression. Everything depended on the outcome of this meeting. For just a moment her hands wavered, until they fell upon a new outfit that Carmela had sewed for her.

The green reminded her of the fields that lay across her land. Lush and variegated with hues of yellow and blue, mixed so that the eye could almost tell what was planted by the richness of green. There was no pattern on the cloth, just the merging of greens, yellows and blues.

Carmela had fashioned the cloth into a combination skirt and pants outfit. The legs flowed wide but could be pulled tightly, by lacing, to hug the ankles. Rosie slipped into the pant legs and zipped up the skirted front. The material was cool and silky, fitting tightly around her waist and then billowing out over her thighs and finally closing snuggly by her feet. She chose a yellow sleeveless shirt with a scalloped neckline. Upon the advice of Carmela, she had cut her long black hair and was left with short curls that framed her eyes. Rosie topped the outfit off with a flowered scarf, which she wore across her forehead and flowing over her shoulder.

When she stepped out of her small cabin, Carmela was standing out in front of the greenhouse, holding Dominique on her hip. "Rosie, you are going to have to hurry. Your meeting is in less than an hour."

Rosie ran over to Carmela and gave her a hug and planted a kiss on Dominique's nose. "Aren't you the bossy one. You just couldn't wait to see what I'd wear."

"Spin around for me once. I have to make sure you pass."

"Nope, I am off. I have my deliveries to make and I know I am just perfect, thanks to you."

Rosie mounted her bike and headed into town with her load of orchids.

The road was dust free from an early afternoon shower and despite the pressure of her upcoming meeting, Rosie found herself humming. Today's load of orchids was light. She had only one stop to make before she headed down to the restaurant. It was to an old, dilapidated farm that her neighbor, Pancho, had recently sold to the most recent winner of *Boleta*. Pancho could finally retire and go to the United States where his grandchildren lived, and the lucky gambler could try his hand at an old dream.

As she approached the farm, she noticed months' worth of changes. Gone was the one-room wooden and tin-roofed house. Gone were the coops for fighting cocks and animal pens for pigs. In their places were various shaded outbuildings containing vegetable starts and one larger structure raised on *zocos*. Instead of the more expensive cement homes, the new owner constructed a house modeled after all the *jibaros* from the country. The scraps of wood were replaced by mahogany, which resisted pesky termites and their love of decomposing wood. Built up on stilts, the house had a façade that opened on all four sides. The windows were wooden slats without screens or metal bars. The house was painted a pale peppermint green with peach trim.

Rosie selected one of older orchids from her basket. It was a hybrid of the 'Bee Orchid' and had survived the destruction of her greenhouse. She climbed the wooden ladder up to the porch and placed the orchid alongside a sign at the entrance way. The sign had recently been painted and was not completely dry. The name was most fitting *Casa de Suenos,* House of Dreams.

Although Rosie was sure that no one was home, she called out with just a small hope of seeing the new owner. "*Hola*, anyone home. It's me, Rosie." With no answer, she mounted her bike and headed back down towards the pueblo.

She was barely down the road, when an old sugarcane truck screeched to a halt. Jesus stepped out and came along side of her. "I just delivered fresh vegetables to Monica. I thought I'd see you at the restaurant. Do you need a ride down."

"No thanks. I still have plenty of time before my meeting. I was just bringing you a house-warming present."

"You saw my new sign?"

Rosie chuckled, hearing the enthusiasm of a child just given a jar full of jellybeans. "Yes, I saw your beautiful sign and all the work you have done. Maybe we can meet later tonight, after my meeting. I have to get these orchids down to Monica. *Adios*."

She could still hear his voice echoing throughout the hills, "*Suerte, suerte, suerte,*" as she rounded the corner to town.

Pide was busy sweeping the new sidewalk in front of the restaurant. His new job was unofficial, but Monica had presented him the broom as a gift, on the day the restaurant had opened. At least ten times daily patrons would witness his meticulous strokes, brushing a clean path for their entrance. He only charged a *peseta*, and most of clients were responsive to his services. The sidewalk was Carlos' idea, a way of beautifying the *pueblo*, and keeping pedestrians safe from cars hopping onto the pavement. From the upstairs balcony hung the traditional baskets of flowers, but along the entry way a small path was designated for diners. Poinsettias lined the path on either side with conch shells propped up on bamboo poles to hold candles for evening patrons.

"Doña Rosie, I can take your bike. I'll guard it with my life. If you'd like I'll take the orchids inside. Your friends are already inside."

"Pide, I was wondering what you have been up to. I miss you up at the farm. When you have some free time, I'd like you to see all the new greenhouses and the pigeon coop."

"There is nothing I'd like more, but as you can see I am so busy."

Rosie nodded, knowing exactly what Pide was saying. He had to watch out for Monica, and when he felt she was safe he'd be up to visit. She gave Pide the requisite *peseta*, took a deep breath and entered knowing she was already late."

The sun followed her inside the restaurant. Light streamed down from the skylights above. The walls, with their open slats, let the breeze flow through. The removal of rebar from the windows was a bold act. Monica was making a statement without saying a word. On the walls local artists had painted scenes from the town—rows of coconut trees lined the beaches, sugarcane trucks, tipsy with cargo, teetered on dirt roads. The mural showed the present and with a sense of cleverness, created the future. All the stores were shown with sidewalks, and widened streets. The school was larger than life and women were pictured driving trucks and working. Above the counter was a framed *Boleta* ticket. Underneath it a sign read, "Ask and you may receive. Luck and prayers help, but hard work and friends made this restaurant happen."

Rosie smiled as she walked to her table. She recognized the officials from the Planning Department, the Health Department, and the University. Pide with his wry sense of humor had not followed her instructions. Instead of placing an orchid on each table, he had made a huge centerpiece of twenty orchids centered behind Miguel's latest sculpture. Rosie spied Pide peering in from outside. His look was a taunt, just the push Rosie needed.

"Hola, mis amigos. I won't apologize for my tardiness, as I can tell you are all enjoying yourself. Thank you for coming to talk to me about the plant studies I wish to conduct." As she seated herself, she picked up Miguel's sculpture.

"I am no longer afraid to talk frankly with all of you. I left the University for many reasons, one of which was my health and the other was to pursue studies about this plant." Rosie pointed to the *liana* vine, which was wrapped around a *flotilla*. The vine appeared to be holding the boat together and at the same time strangling those aboard.

"This vine has remarkable healing qualities, which I and Doña Teresa have been working on for many years.

Not only can the vine slow the heartbeat, act as an anesthetic, mollify nerve spasms, it can also kill. We wrongly hid our studies for fear that the drug cartels would find us. Our own fears brought them to us. I am asking all of you to support me with a grant. I am asking you all to help me find a cure for what ails me."

Rosie continued talking for more than half an hour. She answered questions and outlined where and how she wanted the study conducted. Courses of meals had come and gone, when she finally shook the last of her guests' hands. Her throat was sore and her voice was almost absent, but she felt heartened. Hopefully she'd hear the verdict on her proposal within a week. She had no illusions. As the only woman at the table, the men would make the decision to help her, only if they too could ride on success. That was okay with her.

On her way out of the restaurant Rosie spotted Carlos at a corner table. He was dressed in a crisp blue *guabera*, which highlighted his eyes and tan. The Mayor, a few bankers, the owners of the local cement factory, and a group of farmers surrounded him. The rumors that Carlos would be running for Mayor in the next election were true. Monica moved in and around the table, making sure that the food and drinks were adequate. Rosie heard her full laugh, her appeasing answers. As the new owner, Monica could match wits with the best of them. She looked stunning in her emerald wrap-around dress. Making sure she was the perfect hostess, nothing of her bare skin showed. Monica left everything to others' imagination.

Rosie headed home on her bike. She knew she was the odd lady of the town, loved by everyone, understood by few. Her eyes filled with tears and as she tried to blink them away, the sun created a series of colorful bows of light. There was much to do.